SNOOK

Amarquis Publications, LLC
amarquispublications@gmail.com

This is a work of fiction. Unless otherwise indicated, all the names, characters, businesses, places, events and incidents in this book are either the product of the author's imagination or used in a fictitious manner. Any resemblance to actual persons, living or dead, or actual events is entirely coincidental.

Library of Congress Control Number: 2020918096
ISBN: 978-0-578-79567-6
First Amarquis Publications Paperback Edition December 2020

Cover art & interior designed by Indie Designz
Printed in the United States

Acknowledgements

As always, I first give thanks to God for all of His many blessings. Without Him, I wouldn't be able to do what I love. God is always right on time. Thanks to my family and friends for all of your support. You definitely make this ride smoother. When I get an idea for a storyline or opinions on cover art, I turn to those closest to me. Thank you to everyone. I do not want to leave anyone out. You know who you are. Thank you! I can't forget my home team, the Smiths. They contributed greatly to this project as well. Thank you for your continued support, encouragement, and contributions during the publication process.

A special thanks to my editors: Carla Dean, Khloe Cain, and Joseph Editorial Services for their work on this project. A special thanks to my graphic designer, Dafeenah (Indie Designz) for all of your hard work throughout the years. Thank you for being consistent, patient, and creative.

Thank you to my readers for asking when the next book was coming. Your anticipation kept me writing. This book definitely took a while to write, but you hung in there with me.

I have managed to push through yet another book. Some people assume that writing a book is easy. It's not. My goal was to give my readers something special, showing growth in my writing. I feel that I have accomplished that. Although it has been years between books, I hope you find this book a worthy read. Enjoy!

Much love,
Snook

DEDICATION

THIS BOOK IS DEDICATED TO
ROGER DAVIS, SR.
A KING.

Chapter 1

Thick smoke flowed out Koshie's mouth, slowly and steadily moving into Jayda's. Jayda inhaled, closed her eyes, and then sat back in the chair—her eyes red and small. Koshie rested her head beside Jayda, and the two watched as Shay and Yolanda danced. The friends were at a party hosted by a popular kid from their high school named Jay. For the past four years, Jay was hailed as the school's best basketball player, and many top colleges were fighting to recruit him to their school's team.

Shay worked her hips, grinding them into Jay's pelvis, while Yolanda, who'd had too many drinks, was dropping it like it was hot for no one in particular.

"Look at your friend. You better go out there and get her off that floor," Koshie said.

Jayda shook her head and laughed.

"That's *our* friends out there being nasty and shit. I'm too fucked up to move," Jayda replied.

When Koshie didn't respond, Jayda looked over and noticed Koshie fumbling with something in her hands. Despite her head feeling heavy, she managed to slowly lift it enough to see Koshie trying to open a small baggie that contained four pills.

"What are you doing?" Jayda asked.

"I'm about to pop these little babies right here," Koshie answered.

"What's that?" Jayda inquired.

"The shit that's going to set my night off right. I paid good money for these."

"Molly?"

"Yes. Haven't you had one before?" Koshie queried.

"No."

"Do you want one?" she offered.

"No, I'm good with the smoke and this drink," Jayda said, holding up a red cup and taking a sip.

Koshie shrugged before popping a pill in her mouth. Then she took the cup from Jayda's hand and took a gulp.

"You better slow down. You know you have to drive us home," Jayda reminded her.

"Relax," Koshie told her. "We're not leaving for a couple more hours. I'll sober up by then."

Jayda turned her attention back to Shay and Yolanda, who were now dancing with each other. They ran over to Koshie and Jayda, pulling them to the dance floor.

Jayda reluctantly joined in with her friends, and they danced and laughed while having fun together. Their bond was undeniable, although the four did not become friends all at the same time. First, Yolanda and Jayda met in middle school. Then the two of them met Shay in high school. Koshie was the last to join their friend circle, and she carried herself differently from the others. She was what they called a "bad girl." She had a juvenile record, used drugs, and loved to fight. Koshie even introduced the others to drugs and alcohol, which they only did to impress her. Yolanda managed to keep her system clean the longest before folding to the peer pressure.

"I'm trying to get with Jay, but she's been following him around all night," Shay said.

They all stopped and looked towards the kitchen where Jay and Melanie seemed to be engrossed in conversation. Melanie was a popular girl and a great basketball player who maintained a balance of beauty, femininity, and skills both on and off the court.

"From the looks of it, he's been following her around all night," Jayda commented.

"Stop hating, fat ass! I know he doesn't want her because he told me," Shay stated matter-of-factly.

Having been reminded she was the biggest out of the four friends, Jayda shrunk into herself.

"You know I was joking, right?" Shay asked, noticing the hurt on Jayda's face. "Don't take me so serious all of the time. I'm only teasing you, but if you don't like it, I won't call you that again."

"You know she doesn't like it," Yolanda interjected. "Hell, it makes me uncomfortable too," she added.

"If you call me fat again, I'll fatten those red lips across your face," Jayda responded.

"Come on, girls! Not tonight. This could be the last party we all have together before we graduate," Koshie slurred. "I'll be stuck here working for the man, while you girls go off to college and make something of yourselves."

"Okay, Koshie. Let's sit down over here," Shay said, pulling Koshie to a chair and pushing her down to sit.

"I don't feel so good," Koshie warned, beads of sweat forming on her forehead.

Yolanda rushed off to the kitchen for water.

"See if you can get a cold cloth from the bathroom. She's burning up," Shay said.

Jayda walked down the hall to the bathroom. The door was closed, so she knocked. There wasn't an answer. She twisted the door handle, but the door was locked. She knocked harder.

"Are you done in there? I have an emergency out here!" Jayda shouted through the door.

The door only opened a crack when someone's head appeared.

"I'm kinda busy in here. Give me five minutes," Jay said.

"Koshie is sick. I need a cold cloth," Jayda told him.

"I'll be out in a minute," he replied.

He tried to close the door, but Jayda pushed against it, stopping him.

"Give me a cold cloth, or I'll tell everybody that you and him are in the bathroom together for the second time tonight," Jayda threatened.

Jay's mouth hit the floor.

"Pick up your face and hurry up!" Jayda shouted.

She could hear the other person running water in the sink. Seconds later, she was handed a cold cloth through the cracked door.

"Thank you!" she said, then turned and walked away.

"You better not open up your fat mouth about this?" Jay yelled after her.

Jayda laughed to herself.

When she returned, Koshie had almost finished gulping a bottle of water. Jayda gently placed the cool cloth on Koshie's forehead.

"Hey, Shay. Jay was in the bathroom. If you want to talk to him, I think you should go back there and wait for him to come out," Jayda suggested.

"You think so? Wouldn't that be weird?" Shay questioned.

"Not if you want to talk to him before we leave," Jayda responded.

"Keep an eye on her. Don't let her out of your sight," Shay said, referring to Koshie, who still had the cloth applied to her forehead.

"I got her," Jayda said, waving off Shay. Then she sat back and watched to see what was going to happen next.

Shay headed down the hallway and stood outside of the bathroom. Two minutes later, Jayda saw a young man coming from the bathroom's direction and walking down the hall alone. Next came Jay and Shay walking and talking. Not the sight she expected to see. Jayda looked confused. As Shay walked by, she winked at her friends.

"I need another drink," Jayda said.

"Get me one too," Yolanda requested.

"You're the only other one who has a license to drive. Koshie is tore up," Jayda reminded her.

"Bring me a damn drink," Yolanda demanded.

They stayed a couple of hours longer waiting for Yolanda and Koshie to sober up. Shay spent the remainder of her night dancing with Jay. Jayda had to keep an eye on everyone. After the party, the four of them headed to Koshie's car. Koshie was still out of it, so they had to carry her to the car.

"Who's driving?" Jayda asked.

"Koshie's ass sure can't. If she is, I'm walking home," Shay said.

"I'll drive," Yolanda volunteered.

"Are you sure you're okay to drive?" Shay wanted to know.

"Neither of you can drive. I'm good, trust me," Yolanda assured them.

Yolanda sat in the driver's seat, Shay in the passenger seat, and Jayda was in the backseat with Koshie, who was passed out. On the way home, they recounted the night.

"Shay, what was up with you and Jay tonight?" Jayda asked.

"Girl, you're not going to believe this," Shay told her.

"Try me," Jayda replied.

"Jay is going to take me out next weekend. Once I lock him down and have a kid or two, I'll be set. You know he's going to go pro, right?" Shay had it all planned out.

Jayda sucked her teeth and rolled her eyes.

"I wasn't going to bring this up, but I saw a boy in the bathroom with Jay tonight," Jayda shared.

"He said you were going to say that. They were in there getting high. They weren't doing what you think they were doing," Shay told her.

"Did you smell any weed, because I didn't?" Jayda said. "It looked like the boy was on his knees."

"Shut the fuck up!" Shay shouted. "You're just jealous. I know he wasn't doing anything like that."

"Suit yourself. It won't be the first time you hook up with a lowlife. Jay's playing you. He has so many girls that I can't even keep up. Everyone knows it but you."

Turning around in her seat, Shay tried to hit Jayda, and the two girls started swinging at each other.

"Stop it! Stop fighting!" Yolanda yelled.

Taking her eyes off the road, Yolanda attempted to pull Shay off Jayda while keeping the other hand on the steering wheel. Suddenly, bright headlights illuminated the inside of the car, blinding Yolanda. Startled, she jerked the steering wheel, causing the vehicle to veer to the left. The force flung them around the car. Horns blared, and tires screeched as Yolanda tried to gain control of the vehicle, but the impact was unavoidable. The girls screamed as the car collided with another car, sending the other car into a ditch.

Yolanda slammed on the brakes, and the screams ceased. Dust and darkness were all around them.

"Is everyone okay?" Yolanda managed to ask as she coughed to clear her lungs of the white powder from the front airbags that had deployed.

Shay stared out the window in shock. Breathing heavily, Jayda clutched the seatbelt while one of her arms protectively remained over Koshie, who was still out even though her body had shifted from the crash.

"Answer me!" Yolanda shouted.

"Yes, I think so," Shay finally replied, then asked Jayda. "Are you okay?"

"Yeah, but I think I hit my head," Jayda told her before trying to wake her friend.

"Koshie! Koshie!" she called out, shaking her.

"Check to see if she's breathing," Yolanda suggested.

Placing her index finger under Koshie's nose, Jayda felt the warm air. She nodded to let them know Koshie was breathing, then gave her one final shove. Koshie moaned, shooed them off, and shifted in the seat.

"We hit somebody," Shay said, stating the obvious.

"I know," Yolanda replied, still shaking from her adrenaline.

"Well, somebody needs to get out and check on them," Jayda urged.

"I'll do it," Yolanda said.

"I'll come with you," Jayda told her, unlocking the door.

"Me too," Shay said.

The three exited the vehicle and walked to the rear of the car, leaving Koshie still asleep in the backseat.

"Damn! My back hurts," Shay commented, reaching for the area paining her.

Lifting her friend's shirt slightly, Jayda examined her back. "It's red, but it's not bleeding. You might've pulled a muscle."

When Shay turned around to face her, she noticed blood dripping from a gash near Jayda's hairline. "Your head!"

Jayda immediately lifted her hand to touch the wound.

"Ouch!" she yelped. "Where did that come from?"

"You said you hit your head. Let me see." Shay leaned in closer to examine Jayda's injury. "You're going to need stitches for sure."

"I can't believe this!" Yolanda cried. "I fucked up everything! My parents are going to kill me!"

Shay and Jayda rushed over to help Yolanda as she slid down the back panel of the car.

"Everything is going to be okay," Jayda tried to assure her. "It was an accident."

"Look at her," Shay said.

Yolanda had cuts all over her face and blood on her hands; shards of glass were still in some of the cuts.

"No! Don't do that!" Jayda shouted when Shay tried to remove a piece of the glass. "She'll bleed more."

Ignoring her friend's warning, Yolanda yanked it out.

"Who cares?" Yolanda screamed through her tears. "My life is over anyway."

The girls suddenly remembered someone else had been involved in the accident, when the red glow of brake lights and cries for help grabbed their attention. Skid marks on the road led them to the disabled vehicle.

"They're hurt!" Jayda exclaimed, then took off running towards the car with Yolanda and Shay following behind her.

Smoke was coming from the engine, and the smell of gasoline filled the air.

"Help!" a voice cried from inside the vehicle.

Without hesitating, Shay jumped down into the ditch and yanked open the driver's side door.

"Oh my God!" Shay said, stepping back.

Inside the vehicle, an elderly man was holding his arm and bleeding profusely from his head; the blood covered most of his face. Shay looked up at Jayda and Yolanda with fear in her eyes.

"We have to get him out of the car," she said. "Help me."

After getting the seatbelt unfastened, the three girls pulled the man from the car and sat him on the side of the road, making sure they were a safe distance from the vehicle in case it exploded.

"Wait here," Yolanda told the man. "We're going to call for help."

"Hold on. We have to stop the bleeding," Jayda responded, pointing to the man's injury.

"Come on," Yolanda said, urging Shay and Jayda to follow her.

They ran back to the car.

"I'm going to jail. I'm drunk, and I almost killed a man. What am I going to do?" Yolanda cried.

"It was an accident," Shay said.

"Yes but look at me. I'm not going to pass a sobriety test, and that's the first thing the police are going to do when they arrive," Yolanda said. "My life is over. I'm not going to college. Hell, I ruined everything. My life is over!"

"Everything's going to be okay. We just have to explain that it was an accident, that's all," Shay said.

"I can't go to jail! I can't do this! If the two of you weren't in there fighting, none of this would've happened!" Yolanda yelled, placing blame. "My life is going to be ruined, not yours!"

"We have to call for help. Now! That man is not okay," Jayda voiced.

"We have to get our story straight first," Yolanda said.

"We are not going to lie about what happened. What could we possibly say?" Shay asked as she opened the door and searched for her cell phone, which she found on the car's floor.

"I have an idea," Yolanda said, looking at Koshie through the window. "This is Koshie's car, and she was supposed to drive us, right? Why not put her behind the wheel? She's been passed out this entire time. She doesn't even know what happened."

Jayda and Shay looked at each other.

"We can't do that to her," Jayda said, shaking her head.

"But we can let Yolanda go down for this?" Shay asked.

"That's not what I'm saying," Jayda told them.

Yolanda raised an eyebrow. "Then what are you saying? Look," she continued before Jayda could respond. "Koshie has had her run-in with the law. She can wear this one."

Sirens could be heard in the distance.

"This is fucked up," Jayda expressed.

"Did you call for help?" Yolanda asked, her question directed to Shay.

"No. I just found my phone," Shay replied, holding her phone in the air. "We don't have much time though. What are you going to do?"

"Help me move her to the front," Yolanda instructed.

"I can't believe you are going to do this. It was an accident," Jayda countered.

"Choose a side, Jayda. You know where loyalty lies; it's between the three of us. Koshie was just an extra in this. You know that. She's fun, and she's risky. But that's it. We are true friends, and friends have each other's back," Yolanda reminded her.

After some contemplation, Jayda decided to side with the majority. "Okay, let's do it. We have to get our story straight though."

"That's my girl," Yolanda beamed.

"Just to be clear, this is some fucked-up shit. But I'm going to do this for you," Shay said.

Yolanda and Shay pulled Koshie out of the backseat and placed her in the driver's seat, resting her head on the steering wheel. Shay then put Koshie's hand on the steering wheel to make sure her prints were left behind before allowing them to fall to her sides.

"See, that's what I'm talking about!" Yolanda was impressed with the way Shay was handling things.

Jayda rolled her eyes.

A fire truck could be heard quickly approaching.

"We got this, girls," Yolanda said. "Thank you! I love you, guys."

"After this is over, I don't ever want to speak of this again," Jayda snapped.

"Okay," Shay said, then added. "Same script, different characters. Don't forget."

"I got this," Yolanda assured them. "My life depends on this. I'll stay with her. You two go and help the old man."

Three months later, Shay, Jayda, and Yolanda sat alongside Koshie's family as Koshie pled guilty to involuntary manslaughter. Since she was of legal age, she was charged as an adult. No way did the three of them think the elderly man would later die from his injuries. The worst they thought would happen was Koshie would get a DUI. She had done time before as a juvenile. They thought if anyone could handle it, she could. But now, with prison coming into play, they weren't so sure.

When they left the courthouse, they left behind Koshie. No visits, no letters, and, most of all, no mentions.

Chapter 2

It was a bloody weekend in the city, and the emergency room was busy with traffic. Three shootings had occurred in one day. The following day, there were another two shootings; they were believed to be in retaliation of the previous day's shootings. This all happened within a twenty-four hour period, sending the medical staff into a frenzy as they tried to care for the patients. In addition to the families, friends, wives, girlfriends, and side chicks that filled the hospital's waiting area, it was also flu season, which resulted in a long wait for those who wanted to be seen by a doctor.

Jayda, a registered nurse, tended to two of the victims who had sustained minor injuries. They were being treated and would most likely be discharged. Unfortunately, one shooting victim was dead on arrival. Another victim was in surgery, and the other was in ICU. Jayda's patient suffered shots to the hand and shoulder. As she showed her patient, Alonzo, how to change his bandages, his phone rang during her instructions. He didn't hesitate to answer.

Jayda rolled her eyes.

"Hello?" Alonzo answered.

He took a brief pause to listen as the caller spoke.

"I can't talk right now, but you know what to do. The streets are gonna feel this one!"

Jayda held on to the bandages so Alonzo's movements wouldn't unravel them. She was sure the dose of morphine she had given him had kicked in because he didn't flinch from the pain. When he began to nod, there was no doubt the medicine was starting to work.

"You should probably call them back," Jayda suggested.

"I'm gonna hit you up when I get out of here," Alonzo told the caller.

Jayda shook her head. She had overheard several conversations similar to Alonzo's and heard things she knew she should not have. She even heard someone put out a hit on the person who shot them or someone they knew, and sure enough, that very person would be a victim.

She was tired, and her shift was coming to an end. So, she wrapped his wounds and gave him the short version of how to care for them since she would be providing the same information in writing. Alonzo listened but was beginning to nod off again.

"Hey, I need some more of that medicine. My arm is hurting," he told her.

"I'll check with the doctor and see what else you can have for the pain."

Before Jayda could step out from behind the white curtain, she heard a small commotion by the nurse's station and rolled her eyes.

"Can somebody show me where bed twelve is? They told me out there that my fiancé is in bed twelve!" a woman shouted.

"Hold up. Hold up. That sounds like my lady. Go get her for me," Alonzo said.

Jayda curled her lip and shot Alonzo a sharp look.

"Shit, she'll find you," slipped from out of Jayda's mouth.

"Damn," he said.

Jayda instantly knew her response to his request was unprofessional. "I'm sorry."

"You good. I knew your ass was hood. My boy only fucks with real bitches."

"Who's your boy?" she asked.

"I know your man, Khalil. I recognized you from the big ass portrait you have of yourself in your house."

She wasn't surprised at all. It wasn't the first time a random person she had never laid eyes on labeled her as Khalil's woman. She would normally grin while neither denying nor confirming their claim.

"You've been in my house?" she asked.

"Yeah, once or twice," he replied, then his face lit up. "You're the one who helped him get those prescriptions that time. For real, you're the one that put him on. Can you hook a brother up? I'm good for it."

Jayda looked out the curtain to see if anyone was standing within earshot.

"Hell no, I can't *hook you up*. I don't know what he told you, but I've never done anything like that for him, or anyone else for that matter. So, don't come in here talking that shit to me," Jayda said in a hushed tone. "I'm a nurse, and I take my job seriously. Whatever Khalil told you is a lie. He was probably talking about one of his other bitches because it wasn't me."

"I ain't trying to come at you like that. My bad," he apologized.

Jayda hoped she had convinced Alonzo that she had never done anything illegal or abused her job to help Khalil sell prescription drugs on the streets. Truth is, she did, but of course, she would never admit it. There were a few times that she risked her job and freedom to give Khalil what he wanted. She was surprised he had told someone, and she would make sure she addressed it once she got home.

The curtains to the treatment area were ripped back, and a tall woman with wavy, waist-length hair dived on top of Alonzo in tears.

"Baby! Oh my God! Are you alright? I came as soon as I heard," she cried.

Alonzo yelped. "Get off my arm!"

The woman quickly jumped up.

"I'm sorry, baby. Look at you. What happened?"

"I got shot," he answered sarcastically.

"I know. Did it have anything to do with the robbery?" she inquired.

"Bitch, shut the fuck up!" he snapped.

With that, Jayda left to tend to her other patients. When her shift ended, she headed home. Jayda had a full night planned as she did every year on that very date.

Once home, she showered and dressed in a short, slinky, comfortable black dress. Then she lit candles all around her living room and poured herself a tall glass of wine. After sitting down on a chaise lounge to relax, she carefully unfolded a faded piece of wrinkled paper that was almost falling apart. She felt a lump form in her throat.

"Happy birthday to me!" she said, holding the glass of wine in the air before taking a huge gulp.

"I wish I could've met you. I love you, Mom!" she repeated her actions, taking the remainder of the wine to the head. She then read the letter aloud.

Dear Jayda,

I gave you this name because I've always loved that name. I said if I ever had a daughter, I would name her Jayda. I'm writing this letter to tell you how much I love you and how much I wanted you. When I found out I was carrying you, it was the happiest day of my life. I knew pregnancy was something I was warned against. My heart couldn't handle the both of us. No matter what you've been told and by whom, I did this for you. I sacrificed my life for you. I knew you were given to me for a purpose and that God was in control. His will be done. The time we had together was the best nine months of my life. We had a connection and communicated with each other. You know me, but you may not remember me. You felt me and heard my voice. Most of all, you felt my love. I want you to go through life with purpose. Move through life with purpose. Think and act with purpose. You were not the death of me. Don't you ever believe that. You gave me LIFE! I gave you LIFE! Remember, you are special, and God will reveal his purpose. When He does, fulfill it. Remember me in your heart. I will be with you as you are a part of me. Take care of your father. I know he will be a great father. That is why I chose him. I love you, Jayda. You are the best thing that ever happened to me.

Love,
Your mother, Tina

By the end of the letter, Jayda was sobbing and heaving. She believed and felt every word. She felt the love of her mother, but she also felt guilty about her mother's death. She was the reason her mother died while giving birth to her. She was conflicted in her heart. She strived for perfection as a daughter, a friend, and a nurse. With everything she did, she attempted to live up to her mother's expectations. While doing so, she discovered just how imperfect she was.

The mother Jayda knew growing up was actually her stepmother, Cheryl. Up until the age of twelve, Jayda didn't know that Cheryl wasn't her biological mother. She loved Jayda as her own and was good to her. One day, her father, Quentin, and stepmother, Cheryl, sat her down to tell her that her birth mother was in heaven and that Cheryl wasn't her biological mother. He explained that her mother passed away shortly after she was born and was now watching over her. He also explained that Cheryl was still her mother and loved her very much. Cheryl confirmed that she loved her as her own daughter and would always be there for her. They felt she was old enough to know the truth.

Jayda responded with tears after receiving the information that shattered everything she thought to be true. She sat in silence as her twelve-year-old brain tried to comprehend what she had been told. Despite learning that she once had another mother, she still felt Cheryl was her mother. Jayda believed it in her heart. After all, Cheryl was the only mother she knew.

She let the warm tears fall down her chubby cheeks, not bothering to wipe them away. Her father took her into his arms and held her close as she sobbed into his chest. Without saying a word, Cheryl leaned in and rubbed Jayda's back.

Cheryl had married Quentin when Jayda was only six months old. Cheryl was a blessing to Quentin. She loved them both and took good care of them. She didn't have children of her own, so she gave Jayda all the love she had. She taught her how to be a lady, cook, and clean. Jayda admired Cheryl for being the woman that she was and always showed her appreciation for all she had done for her.

Her mother and father separated while she was away at college. During her second semester, she noticed that whenever she called home to speak to her parents, her father was never around. Cheryl would tell her that he wasn't there without offering any other explanation. Knowing her father, she knew it was unlikely that he would be out after nine o'clock. He usually turned in early because he worked the morning shift. When she came home unexpectedly one weekend, she found that her mother was living in their family home alone. Her father had moved out to a one-bedroom apartment.

She was upset at the fact that they tried to hide it from her. After getting their two-sided story, she learned they grew apart after she left for college. Without Jayda, they found themselves unhappy with each other. According to her mother, she felt her father had taken her for granted. According to her father, he felt her mother nagged too much, and he just couldn't take it any longer. Jayda felt like they got what they wanted and were done. Her mother was able to raise a child, and her father got someone to help raise his daughter. Jayda was the missing link, resulting in their unhappiness. When the job was done, so were they.

Despite Jayda begging and pleading with her parents to try to work things out, they didn't. Her mother moved back to South Carolina with her family, and her father moved back into their family home. Although her parents weren't together, they didn't get a divorce. Her mother was still very present in her life. Jayda visited her and spoke to her often.

It was her birthday and the day her mother died giving birth to her. From the day she left the hospital, her father had raised her. She wasn't aware of why her mother died until she was given a letter that her mother wanted her to have on her eighteenth birthday. Her mother died from complications of childbirth due to a heart condition that led to heart failure. On each of her birthdays since then, she had the same ritual.

She carefully folded the letter and placed it back in the keepsake box where she kept pictures of her mother and a few pieces of her mother's jewelry. Then she blew out the candles and headed for bed. She expected her boyfriend, Khalil, to join her later.

Before she could lay down, her cell phone rang.

"Happy birthday, friend!" Yolanda and Shay both screamed into the phone.

"Thank you, ladies!" Jayda said, blowing her nose.

"Why do you sound like you've been crying? What did he do now?" Shay asked.

"Calm down. I'm just blowing my nose. I'm waiting on Khalil now. He's supposed to be bringing home one of those ice cream cakes," Jayda shared.

"Are you going to treat yourself to a piece?" Yolanda asked.

"Of course she's not. She's too scared to gain an ounce. I told her that she has to treat herself to something bad sometimes. Once a year wouldn't hurt her. Tell her, YoYo," Shay said.

"Yes, have a piece of cake," Yolanda said, agreeing with Shay. "You exercise and eat right year round. One slice of cake isn't going to hurt you."

"I know. I might try a piece," Jayda told them.

"What were you doing when we called?" Yolanda asked. "You sound funny."

"Nothing, just thinking about my mom. My birthday is the same day she died, so it's hard to be happy on such a sad day. That's why I don't celebrate on my actual birthday. It's too hard," Jayda explained.

"We know how you feel on your birthday. That's why we always try to show you a good time. A birthday is a blessing and a time to celebrate. I understand that you're mourning your mother, but you should celebrate life as well," Shay advised.

"Thanks for calling, ladies. I had a rough night at work, so I'm trying to unwind before Khalil gets here," Jayda replied.

"Yeah, whatever," Shay said.

"Enjoy your night," Yolanda told her.

Jayda ended the call with her friends and laid back on the bed. Hearing their voices had lifted her spirits, but not enough to truly enjoy the blessing of being on Earth another year.

Chapter 3

A single mother of two; Shay had a six-year-old daughter named Tyra and a four-year-old son named Tyler Jr. She worked as an account manager, putting her accounting degree to work. She was fresh out of a relationship with Tyler Sr. With her ex-boyfriend, and their combined income, she had been able to live in a good neighborhood with top-rated schools. Their relationship came to an end when he was laid off and could no longer support them. Shay waited all but four months before she called it quits. Jayda and Yolanda didn't agree with Shay's hasty decision to end a good relationship due to financial hardship.

Shay was all about the money though. The rule was if she had to work, then her partner needed to do his part too. That was when the rules changed. If her partner were well off enough that she could be a stay-at-home mom, then she would. Her fifty percent was cooking, cleaning, and taking care of the family. In her book, taking care of a man was a no-no.

After ending the relationship with Tyler's father, she and the children relocated to an area that she could afford. They moved into a home in a rough part of town. Shay didn't have a problem with the environment because she grew up in a low-income neighborhood. She just never imagined having to go back.

"Come on, it's time for bed," Shay called out to her children.

They ran to their mother, showing their teeth.

"Mom, are my teeth clean now?" Tyra asked.

Shay inspected both Tyra and Tyler's teeth.

"Yes, they are perfect," she said, then grabbed their small hands and led them to the bedroom that they shared.

"Climb in," she told Tyler while pulling back the sports-themed sheets for him to get into bed.

"Mommy, I'm not sleepy." The fact that he was rubbing his eyes told her differently.

"It's bedtime, son," she said, kissing him on the forehead.

Shay turned around to find Tyra already in bed, with her princess theme comforter over her head. She walked over and pulled down the comforter. She sat on the edge of her bed and kissed her daughter on the forehead too. Tyra didn't give her a hard time going to bed like Tyler, who opposed bedtime.

Knowing her son, he wouldn't fall asleep for at least an hour. He would fight his sleep for as long as he could. Usually, she let him fall asleep on his own, but tonight, she was expecting company.

"I'll be right back, you two," Shay said, leaving the room.

She returned with medicine in hand.

"I don't want that," Tyler objected.

"I know you don't like taking medicine, but you have allergies. This is going to help you feel better," she coaxed.

"But I'm not sick," Tyler replied.

While Tyler whined, she proceeded to give him the medicine, administering the recommended dosage. Tyler frowned while hesitantly accepting the medication. Shay felt guilty about medicating her son, but she didn't want to upset her guest.

"Good job!" Shay praised.

"Nasty," Tyler complained.

"Okay, to bed you go," she said.

Tyler laid down and closed his eyes tightly. She looked over at Tyra, who had fallen asleep.

"Do you want me to read to you?" Shay asked.

Tyler nodded his head with his eyes still closed tightly.

"I'm going to read you this book, and then you have to go to sleep," she told him.

"Okay," he said.

Shay picked up the book from the nightstand. She read only five pages before Tyler was fast asleep. She kissed him, and after checking to be sure Tyra was still asleep, she kissed her again. She took one last look at her sleeping kids before closing the door behind her.

Shay showered and slipped into a red negligée that complemented her pale skin complexion. Then she moisturized her skin and sprayed his favorite perfume on her neck, chest, and between her thighs. As she waited for her guest, she relaxed with a glass of wine and a blunt.

There was a heavy knock on the front door.

"Who is it?" she called out in a sexy tone.

"Open the door. You know who it is," a male's voice responded.

Shay swung open the door and said, "Well, damn. Of course, I know who it is. What happened to being romantic?" she asked.

"Are you going to let me in or what?" he said.

Shay looked Rob up and down. As much as she wanted to curse him out for being rude, she didn't. He was looking fine in his team hoodie, torn jeans that fit him just right, and a pair of boots. His diamond necklace hung from his neck, and the bling from his diamond earring caught the light just right.

Shay stepped back so he could come inside. He walked past her without a hug or kiss. Shay looked back at him and rolled her eyes as she closed and locked the door behind him. She followed him straight to her bedroom. Rob sat down on the bed and took off his hoodie, leaving on a shirt that displayed his chiseled muscles.

Shay stood in front of him with her hands on her hips. Then she stuck her leg out and did a full turn to get Rob's attention. Acting as if she weren't in the room, he continued to remove his jewelry and boots.

"Hello?" she said.

"What?" he asked.

"What? Do you see this right here? How can you ignore all of this?" she questioned.

"I see you. You always look good to me. I don't have to tell you that every time," Rob said as he began taking off his shirt.

"Oh no, you don't. You know the rules up in here. Until you get her name off of your chest, I don't want to see it. So, keep that shirt on," she told him.

"Come on. Do you know how hot it gets in here when I'm getting busy?"

"Getting busy?" Shay chuckled. "Who says that? Oh, I forgot you young folks use those types of terms."

"Getting busy, fucking, making love. It doesn't matter. I'm not leaving on this shirt," he said, taking it off.

"See, I knew you were going to do this," Shay said, rolling her eyes.

She cringed when she thought back to the first time they had sex. Everything was going well until he climbed on top of her and removed his shirt. Right across his chest, in bold letters, was a female's name—the same name as his child's mother. She was face to face with the tattoo. Needless to say, things went south for her. She was no longer turned on but turned entirely off.

She walked over to the dresser, opened the top drawer, and threw a tank top at him.

"Put this on. If you want to go shirtless, get the tattoo removed like you said you were going to do."

Rob put on the tank but didn't try to hide his frustration.

"Are you happy now?" he asked.

Shay smiled and said, "Not until you get your baby momma's name off your chest. Then I will be happy, and you can get naked for a change."

"I didn't come over here for all that mouth. Wait. Oh yeah, I did come here for your mouth," he laughed.

"I'm sure you did," she said, licking her lips.

Shay began lighting the candles that she had strategically placed around her bedroom. Then she walked over to the bed and stood in front of Rob, whose expression had suddenly changed from glaring to one of lust. Grabbing two handfuls of Shay's ass cheeks, he spread them apart and kneaded them with his large hands. She pulled out both of her breasts, and he began to suck her nipples, being sure to share. She threw her head back in pleasure.

Rob laid back on the bed, and as Shay straddled him, she felt the bulge in his jeans. Rob had the kind of dick that you just had to put in your mouth. It was beautiful—long, wide, brown, and smooth. While she grinded her hips into him, Rob unbuckled his pants, slid them off, and unleashed the beast. He used his dick to tap her on the ass. It always turned her on how he could make that dick jump. Shay lifted up, placed her hot bottom directly on top of him, and began sliding her juices up and down the length of his dick. She felt him grow even harder. Just when she was ready to slide his dick inside of her, he jumped up.

"What are you doing?" she asked, looking puzzled by his interruption.

"Hold up."

He reached into his jeans pocket and pulled out a condom. Shay watched in disappointment as he pulled on the condom. He laid back down. She sighed, twisted her lips, and unenthusiastically climbed back on top of him.

"What's wrong?" he asked.

"Nothing," she said, irritated.

He took his massive dick and tapped her clit. She slid down on him slowly, his girth taking her breath away. They both let out a moan. She leaned down to kiss him and began to ride him. Once he reached his end, he erupted.

Afterwards, he was sure to flush the used condom down the toilet. He was always careful to dispose of his sperm. Shay was upset that things once again didn't go her way.

Shay had been trying to get pregnant by Rob, but it was hard to get him to have unprotected sex with her. Each time, she attempted to turn him on so much that he would either forget to put on a condom or wouldn't care. That day had yet to happen. A football player, Rob was her ticket to eighteen years of hefty child support payments. He had liquid gold, and she wanted it. She and Rob met while he was in town for training camp. To get what she wanted, she knew she had to come up with another plan to get the liquid gold.

Chapter 4

Applause filled the room as a line of women walked in front of the small audience. Koshie smiled while shaking hands with the director, Ronald, as he handed her a certificate of completion. As she looked out into the audience, there weren't any family members—just clients and staff. She thought about her mother and imagined her cheering her on from the front row. She could imagine her mother smiling in her famous chocolate lipstick and brown liner.

This is for you, Mom.

After the celebratory dinner of spaghetti, salad, and garlic bread, the women were given instructions on how they were to integrate back into society. Koshie listened, but she had her own plan. After being incarcerated for so many years, she had some unfinished business to handle. Being housed almost three hours away from home had limited the number of visits she received. Even then, that was more visits than some other women received. She was still grateful for the times her mother and older cousin, Sage, made the trip to visit her. Since the passing of her mother three years ago, Sage stepped up.

Koshie was now a woman. She wasn't the tall, skinny, smooth chocolate-skinned young girl that she was when she first went to prison. She had aged from the hard living inside, but a much worse evil consumed her. The thought of a man losing his life because of her tugged at her every day. There was no memory of the night after the party. She remembered partying hard that night, indulging heavily in drugs and alcohol, but she had no recollection of what happened following the party. She didn't recall the drive home, but since Jayda, Yolanda, and Shay said she was the driver, she believed them.

Koshie shifted on her feet as she waited for an answer on the other end of the phone. She could hear Ronald in the background going over the morning report. Ronald was the director of the inpatient drug program where Koshie lived since being released from incarceration. She had completed the program and was now able to live on her own. She had a week to move out before her bed was assigned to the next person.

The call went to voicemail.

"Fuck!" Koshie said.

From the other room, Ronald shouted. "No profanity!"

Rolling her eyes, Koshie replied. "Sorry, Ronald."

Koshie redialed the number. This time, someone answered.

"Hey! It's me," Koshie said with a smile.

"Sorry I missed your call. I was seeing a friend out," Sage explained.

"I'm so glad you answered. I'm getting out!" Koshie said.

"That's great! When should I pick you up? I've been planning your return for a long time. Your room is all fixed up for you," Sage rambled on. "You were a child when you left here, but you have a grown-woman bedroom now."

"You didn't have to do that. I would've been fine with what I had," Koshie told her, although grateful.

"No, things are different now. Your mother made sure you would be taken care of when you came home. She planned very well for this day. I've maintained everything and honored all of her wishes. Trust me; you're straight."

Koshie swallowed hard as she thought about her mother.

"Well, thanks. Can you pick me up Thursday?"

"I'll be there. I can't wait for you to come home."

"Are you sure about that? I know how you like to have company, and I don't want to be in your way."

"This is your mother's house. I've pretty much been house sitting for you. The question is, will I be in your way? I was hoping I could stay a while longer—"

"Say no more," Koshie said, interrupting her. "You are welcome to stay as long as you want."

"Thanks, cousin. I promise to be out of your hair soon. I have something in the works. I've been trying to clean up my credit so I can buy a house."

"You can do it. You've always gotten what you wanted. If buying a house is your goal, I have no doubt you will do it."

"Thanks for the encouragement. I really need it."

"Did you get that information I asked you about?" Koshie asked. "I want to catch up with my girls when I get home."

"Oh, yeah. I found your friends online. They seem to be doing well for themselves. The crew is still together and living their best life," Sage informed her. "Did you want me to reach out and let them know you're coming home?"

"No! Don't make contact with them yet. I want to surprise them. I'll get with them when I get home."

"Oh, okay. When was the last time you spoke to any of the girls?" Sage inquired.

"It's been a while, but they know I'm coming home soon."

"You're going to need all the support you can get when you do. Catching up with old friends can be good for you as long as they aren't a bad influence. From what I can see on their social media, they don't seem like they will be bad people to be around. I don't want you getting caught up with the wrong crowd."

"You don't have to worry about that," Koshie replied. "After everything that I've been through, I don't ever want to see another courtroom again. I'm coming home to stay."

"I hear you. Just make sure you remember that before you do anything that can send you back inside."

"Of course. I can't wait to come home."

"We can't wait to have you. I'll see you Thursday," her cousin said before ending the call.

Chapter 5

I t's my birthday!" Jayda shouted over the music, then threw back a shot of tequila and sucked a lime wedge.

She threw it back with so much force that she had to adjust the birthday tiara on her head. The pink sash adorning her chest read "Birthday Girl" and she had added her name to the back in rhinestones.

"Happy birthday, bitch!" Shay said, licking the salt from the back of her hand and taking a shot in celebration of her friend's special day.

"Happy birthday! May this year be as good to you as it was to me," Yolanda said before taking a sip of Diet Coke through a straw.

"I hope it's not too good because you got knocked up," Jayda commented.

"What are you talking about? This is prime time for making babies," Yolanda said.

"That's right. Get them out the way early so you can enjoy your thirties," Shay added.

Jayda and Yolanda both shook their heads at Shay.

"What?" Shay asked nonchalantly.

"This place is great! And these wings are good," Yolanda said, sucking her fingers.

"I've been here a couple of times with a few nurses from the hospital. They love this place," Jayda told them.

"Oh, my! She must not like these wings. I knew I shouldn't have gotten them so spicy," Yolanda said, rubbing her pregnant belly. "Shay, do you remember the day we were initiated into this bond we have?"

Shay rolled her eyes and responded "Of course, YoYo, but do we have to talk about this? I still think it was weird."

"Yes, we do. It's part of her birthday," Yolanda said.

"It was all Yolanda's crazy idea. After Jayda's sweet sixteen birthday party, we spent the night at her house. You stole a bottle of gin from your dad," Shay said, pointing at Yolanda. "After a few drinks, you came up with the idea that we should become blood sisters. You got that idea from watching too much television. Long story short, we were too scared to cut ourselves. So, we each pricked our fingers. Yolanda placed her bloody finger on a piece of paper, drawing a circle in her blood. Each of us traced the circle in our own blood one at a time, bonding us together forever," Shay stated sarcastically.

Yolanda laughed. "It worked, didn't it? Look at us now. After that night, I swore I felt a strong energy and bond form between us. You two said the same thing," Yolanda said. "Oh, don't forget the chant."

"Friends forever, friends forever, friends forever," the three women said in unison.

"Tonight, we aren't just celebrating a queen. We're celebrating the bond of true friendship," Shay said.

"I'll drink to that." Jayda raised her glass.

"I love you guys," Yolanda expressed through tears.

"Oh, no. Here she goes with those hormones. Always crying about something," Shay said. "You could ruin a wet-ass dream."

"Shay, you're lucky you're even our girl," Yolanda said, quickly gaining control of her emotions. "If you weren't in that bathroom trying to fuck Kenny back in school, we probably wouldn't have been friends."

"Do you remember how we met?" Jayda asked Shay.

"Of course, I do," she responded.

Jayda and Yolanda had been friends since middle school. In high school, they remained close friends. One day, Jayda rushed into the restroom between classes, having to use it with urgency. She had sat through English holding her bladder because that teacher didn't allow bathroom breaks. She rushed into the stall, not noticing there wasn't any toilet paper. She contemplated on racing to the next stall or waiting for someone to come in the bathroom. She was risking being late for class or getting caught with her ass out.

"Fuck!" Jayda said to herself.

She got herself ready to jump up and race to the next stall, when she heard high heels clicking against the floor. She relaxed and was about to ask for help until she heard the person pushing open each stall door until they got to her stall.

"Damn it. Someone is in here!" Shay said.

"So what?" a boy replied.

"I'm not fucking you with someone in here already. We're going to have to wait," Shay told him.

"Come on, man. You said we were going to do it," the boy said.

"I know, but we just have to wait," Shay pleaded.

"I'll holla at you later," the boy replied, clearly frustrated as he left out the restroom.

Jayda knew it was now or never. She had to say something.

"Excuse me. Can you please hand me some toilet paper?" Jayda said.

"It depends on who's asking. Who's in there?" Shay asked, walking to the stall and standing there.

Jayda frowned and said, "Jayda."

"Fat Jayda or skinny Jayda?" Shay questioned.

"Who are you?"

"I'm Shay. Now which Jayda are you? Fat or skinny?"

"I'm curvy, bitch," Jayda said.

"Oh, good. Because if you were that skinny bitch, I wasn't going to help you out."

Jayda sighed and waited for Shay to hand her the toilet paper. As she waited, she tried to think about who Shay was. She didn't know anyone named Shay at the school. A few seconds later, a hand and a face appeared under the stall door.

"Here you go," Shay said, handing Jayda a roll of toilet paper.

"Thanks, girl," Jayda said.

"You're welcome, cockblocker."

The girls laughed.

Jayda exited the stall and went to the sink to wash her hands. Shay stood by watching.

"You're YoYo's friend, right?" Shay asked.

"Yeah, we're best friends," Jayda replied, then asked, "Who was in here with you?"

"Girl, I was trying to see what Kenny was working with. You know the quarterback Kenny, right?"

"Kenny? Girl, don't waste your time with such small things. You feel me?"

"Is it really?"

"Yes. Small and uncircumcised," Jayda shared.

Shay frowned. "Ewwww. I hate those. How do you know?"

"Everyone knows," Jayda told her. "Where have you been?"

"I'm new. I just transferred here a month ago."

"Damn, you move fast."

Shay shrugged her shoulders.

"So, how do you know YoYo?" Jayda asked.

"She's in my science class. She's about the only one who speaks to me in class. She seems like a nice person."

"She is," Jayda confirmed. "That's why she's my bestie."

"You're cool too."

"Thanks. You are too."

"You know. You're really a pretty girl," Shay told her. "Don't let people get to you about your weight. Look at you. You're fly as shit."

Jayda looked at Shay and rolled her eyes.

"Girl, get out of my face with all of that. I'm so tired of always hearing that shit. I don't want to hear it from you too. I know who I am, and what people think of me doesn't matter to me."

"Okay, okay," Shay said, holding her hands up in mock, surrendering. "I wasn't trying to offend you or anything."

"But you did by saying stupid shit out your mouth like that. Look, I'm already late for class. Thank you, but I got to go."

"Well, bye."

"You should be taking your ass to class too. Instead of in here trying to fuck on a little ass dick," Jayda said, laughing.

"Tragic," Shay responded.

That was how Shay became friends with Jayda and Yolanda. After they finished reminiscing about their past, the women shared a laugh and more hugs. They were so grateful for having each other.

"Hello, ladies," a man said, approaching the women.

"Hello," Shay was the first to say.

"May I buy you ladies a drink? I see it's someone's birthday," the man acknowledged.

"Yes you can," Shay said.

The man was fit, bald with a beard, and dressed in a well-fitted shirt and fitted jeans. Jayda made sure to check out his shoes. She noticed he was wearing high-end men's footwear. She wouldn't typically be attracted to a man with a bald head, but it suited him perfectly.

He smiled at Shay and then turned to Jayda.

"Happy birthday, beautiful," the man said, then lifted Jayda's hand to his lips and kissed it softly.

She immediately noticed the expensive watch on his wrist. Jayda began to blush. He looked her in her eyes, and her heart skipped a beat. She was caught in his gaze. She experienced something she had never experienced before; she saw flashes of a future with the stranger who stood before her.

"Say thank you, Jayda," Yolanda said.

"Thank you," Jayda said.

The man waved over the waitress, and the young woman quickly came over to the table.

"What can I get you?" she asked.

"Please give these ladies a round on me," he told her.

"Sure. What can I get you, ladies?"

The women placed their drink orders. Shay ordered an extra drink since Yolanda couldn't partake.

"Thank you for the drinks," Jayda said.

"You're more than welcome," the man replied with a smile. "You ladies enjoy your night. And you have a very happy birthday."

He turned to walk away, leaving the women in awe.

"Excuse me, sir," Shay called out to him. "You didn't give us your name."

"What are you doing?" Jayda whispered.

"I know you're not going to let that fine man just walk away like that," Shay responded.

The man walked back over, reached in his pocket, and handed Jayda a business card.

Then he looked at Shay and said, "My name is Jamison."

"My name is Shay. This is Yolanda, and the birthday girl is Jayda. It's nice to meet you, Jamison. Isn't it, Jayda?" Shay asked.

"Nice to meet you," Yolanda said.

Yolanda kicked Jayda under the table, snapping her out of her gaze.

"Jamison, thank you again. It was nice meeting you tonight," Jayda expressed.

"I hope you give me a call," Jamison said.

"She will," Shay responded for Jayda.

Jayda watched him walk back to the bar, where he took a seat beside a few men who were already seated. She had this very same thing happen on a few occasions. This one was a bit different though. The man was different; his approach was different. She waited for the men to high-five at the bar, but it didn't happen. Jamison joined his group of friends and jumped back into the conversation. He didn't look back, and neither did his friends.

"Jamison sure is fine. Let me see that card."

Shay tried to grab for the business card, but Jayda moved it out of her reach.

"No. He gave it to me. If he wanted you to see it, he would've given it to you."

Yolanda grunted.

"Well, just tell me what it says. Is he a doctor or something? He looks so distinguished," Shay commented.

Jayda read his business card. "He's an attorney."

Yolanda grunted again.

"I see you're holding on tight to that business card. What about Khalil?" Shay asked.

"What about him? I love Khalil. I can hold on to this just in case I need an attorney to defend me one day," Jayda said.

"Yeah, right." Shay chuckled. "I ain't mad at you. That will be more than an upgrade from Khalil. That would be the greatest come up yet, other than Yolanda and Ryan."

Yolanda shrieked.

"What's wrong?" Jayda asked.

Shay jumped up from the table and went to Yolanda's side. Jayda stood to her feet.

"I think the baby is coming!" Yolanda said.

The women jumped into action, Shay more so than Jayda. Shay gave Jayda instructions to call Ryan and tell him to meet them at the hospital. Jayda managed to call him on the way out of the bar. Shay held up Yolanda, who was panicking and in pain. Jayda drove them to the hospital while Shay coached Yolanda in the backseat on breathing techniques and tried to keep her calm.

That night, Jayda celebrated her birthday, met a man who made her heart skip a beat, and her friend was about to have her baby. It would be a night they all would remember. No one knew it would set off a chain of events that would change their lives forever.

Chapter 6

Jayda left the hospital after watching her goddaughter come into the world. She didn't have children, but she wanted to have a family of her own someday. Watching Ryan support Yolanda during her pregnancy made her long for a man who was as supportive as him. She was happy that Yolanda found love and married. She also envied the relationship they had. Although Jayda was in a new relationship, there were things the relationship lacked and left to be desired. Instead of counting Khalil out, she wanted to work on their relationship in hopes of having something that mirrored Yolanda's marriage. Shay and Yolanda accused her of trying to fix him, but Jayda didn't agree with them.

Jayda met Khalil at the hospital where she worked. Khalil had come in with his son, Brock, and the boy's mother. The boy had fallen off his bike and needed a few stitches to close a cut on his leg. Khalil openly flirted with her in front of his son's mother. It seemed odd at first, but she was also flattered. She had lost over one hundred pounds in the last year and a half from weight loss surgery. So, the attention he gave her was a boost to her confidence. She tried ignoring him, but he kept complimenting her on how well she was doing her job.

At some point, Brock's mother said, "I see he's trying to charm you out your pants. But, trust me, he's not worth the trouble."

"She's just mad that I've moved on from her. I'm a single man now," he retorted.

"I don't want you. She can have you!"

The two of them proceeded to get into a shouting match right in the emergency room. Jayda looked at Brock and saw the expression of hurt on his little face. She was sure he was used to his parents fighting, but she wasn't.

"Look, I'm just trying to do my job, that's all," Jayda said.

She looked directly at Khalil and noticed how handsome he was. She had been so busy working with the patient that she didn't get a good look at him until then. He was tall, dark-skinned, and medium build with a neat afro.

"Umm, let me see if his discharge papers are ready." Jayda looked down at Brock and said, "You are such a tough guy."

Brock smiled. "Thank you."

As they were leaving the emergency room, Khalil found Jayda and handed her a piece of paper with his number written on it. She looked around to see if anyone saw them, but no one was paying them any attention. Smiling, she slipped the paper in her pocket and then gave him her number, also. He wasted no time calling her. After that, she found herself in a relationship with a convicted felon who brought her more pain than joy.

Arriving home, she dragged herself to the front door. The sun beat her home hours ago. She dreaded the encounter she would face once she saw Khalil. It didn't matter why she came home the next day; it would be a problem. He was that type of person. It was nothing for him to miss a night at home though. He would have all kinds of excuses as to why he didn't make it home. He would come back the next day and act as if it was nothing. Running on no sleep, she didn't have the energy to argue with him. She planned to go into the house, take a shower, and get some sleep.

She fumbled around, trying to find her house key. As she went to insert the key into the lock, the door opened from the other side. Startled, she dropped the keys on the porch. At the front door stood Khalil in a pair of gray sweatpants, a white t-shirt, socks, and slides. If looks could kill, she would have imploded.

"Where the fuck have you been?" he asked.

"I called you. I left a voicemail when you didn't answer," Jayda replied.

She tried to walk into the house, but he blocked her path with his body, leaving her pinned between the doorway and his body.

"Where were you?" he questioned.

"Yolanda went into labor. I was with her at the hospital," she told him before pushing past him into the house. "If you would've answered your phone, you would've known where I was."

"You know I don't check my voicemail. You could've texted me or something," he said.

"I did text you. I even called the house phone. Were you even here last night?"

"Don't try to question me about where I was? You're the one who went out partying and didn't come back home."

"And how many times have you gone missing?" Jayda shot back. "You've missed many nights from my bed."

"There you go with that 'my' shit. I live here now too. What's yours is mine."

He followed Jayda to their bedroom, close on her heels. She dropped her things and began to undress. Khalil stood beside her, watching her closely.

"What is your problem?" she asked in frustration.

"So, you think you're just going to stay out all night and come back in here like shits sweet? Who were you with?"

Jayda sighed. "You know I went out with Shay and Yolanda for my birthday. And like I told you, Yolanda went into labor before the night was over."

She finished undressing and walked towards the bathroom to take a shower. Before she could open the bathroom door, Khalil yanked her by her hair and twisted it in his fist. She screamed as she felt her hair being ripped from her scalp. A burning sensation ran through her scalp.

"Stop! Let go!" she screamed, grabbing his hands in a failed attempt to get him to release her.

"You think you can disrespect me like that? You know better than that. Whoever you picked up and stayed the night with better be worth this ass whooping you're about to get. I told you about thinking you can do what you want to do. I'm your man, and you're going to respect me," he spat.

Jayda began to cry as her scalp burned, and her hair snapped in his hands.

Khalil took a hard yank and pushed her towards the bathroom, banging her body against the closed door. She let go of his hands and tried to stop the impact of her face slamming into the bathroom door, but she didn't move quickly enough. Jayda screeched in pain as her face banged directly into the door. Her teeth embedded themselves into her lip, and her nose pained, causing her head to hurt more. More tears poured from her eyes.

Khalil opened the door and pushed her into the bathroom so forcibly that she slid across the floor, hitting the bathtub. Her naked body bucked from the cold tile and bathroom tub. He closed the door behind him and stood over her.

"Now get in there and wash your ass before you get in *my* bed!" he shouted.

"I'm telling you the truth. I was with the girls all night. You can call them. They will tell you," she begged.

She held up her hands to protect herself. Warm blood oozed out of her nose and over her lip. As a reflex, she licked it and tasted blood. She grabbed her nose, and blood poured into her hands.

"Oh, my God! Look what you did to me," she said.

She crawled onto her knees so she could grab a towel for her bloodied nose. Reaching for a towel, she yanked it off its bar.

Khalil kicked her in the ribs. She buckled over in pain.

"I bet you won't try that shit again!" he yelled.

He turned and walked out of the bathroom.

"I didn't do anything!" she shouted.

Crawling on her hands and knees, she went to the door and slammed it closed behind him. Then she sat on the floor and leaned her back against the door. She cried into the towel. She listened as Khalil slammed drawers and cursed. She knew he would be leaving the house soon, so she waited. She looked up at the ceiling as if the answers to her problems were written there.

She stopped fighting back once she realized that fighting back only caused him to hurt her more. She was tired of the abuse. She didn't seem to know the way out of the relationship. Just when she thought she had the strength to leave, her flesh would win. It wasn't the fact that she needed him financially or because she feared being alone. That wasn't the problem. She fell victim to her flesh sexually. She and Khalil had a chemistry that was unmatched by any man she had ever been with. Sex with Khalil always left her spinning. One time, he made love to her so good that she felt like she was in heaven.

She listened for the front door to close. Once she heard him leave, she stood to her feet and walked out into her bedroom. It was still and quiet. She could hear Khalil backing out of the driveway. She peeked out of her bedroom window to confirm that he had left. Once he was gone, she breathed a sigh of relief.

Her tired and battered body was in pain. She stood in front of her mirror and looked at her naked body. Her eyes were puffy, and her lips and nose swollen and bloody. She touched her nose, which was spread across her face, and winced at the pain. She turned to her side. She had two dark bruises. She faced forward and stared at herself in the mirror. She didn't recognize the person that she had become. The person that she knew herself to be was strong and confident. That person would never allow a man to treat her the way she was being treated. In the mirror, a weak and fearful woman stared back at her.

She wanted to look away from her image, but she forced herself not to. She screamed at her reflection. She felt lighter. She screamed again, and that scream felt even better. So, she looked in the mirror and screamed until she released the heaviness in her heart.

"No more!" she screamed. "I am better than this. I do not deserve to be treated like this."

She had to hide from everyone for a few days until her bruises and swelling went down. Avoiding Shay and Yolanda was going to be a challenge, especially since Yolanda just had her baby.

Jayda's house phone rang. She let it ring while she went to start her shower. She was hurt and exhausted. Then her cell phone rang when she didn't answer the house phone. She decided to answer when she saw it was Shay.

"Hey, I was just about to jump in the shower. Are you home?" Jayda asked.

"Yeah, I just got in. I told you to let me know when you got home. Did Khalil act a fool when you got there?" Shay asked.

Jayda didn't immediately answer. She wanted to tell her how he slammed her face into the door and pulled out her hair, but she was too embarrassed to tell her the whole truth. So, she went with the half-truth.

"Yeah, we argued, and he left. You know how jealous he gets. He accused me of being with another man," she said.

"The nerve of him. He's mad at you for missing a night at home when he does it all the time. I hope you told him about himself."

There was a pause.

"Are you okay?" Shay asked.

"Yeah, I'm okay," Jayda replied.

"Did he hit you?"

Jayda didn't answer.

"Did he put his hands on you again?" Shay pressed.

"Look, I'm tired," Jayda responded.

"So, he's still hitting you. My best friend, who has all the answers to everyone else's problems and has enough strength to carry other people's burdens, can't find it in herself to leave a man who is busting her upside her head. Is that what you're telling me?"

"No, it isn't like that," Jayda said.

"Oh, it's like that. Do I need to come over there?"

"No!"

"Jayda, it's not okay that he's over there beating your ass. Do you think we don't know what's going on over there? We see you, remember?"

"I'm going to handle it. But on my time," Jayda told her.

"We love you and don't want anything to ever happen to you. Domestic violence sometimes leads to someone being seriously hurt or ending up dead. I don't want that to happen to you."

"It's not like it happens all the time. You saw us fight one time, and now you think it happens all the time when it doesn't. Stop judging me, Shay."

"You know what, we both need some sleep. I didn't call you to fight with you. I'm sure you've done enough of that with him. I love you, and I'll talk to you later."

Jayda hung up the phone without saying another word. She went to get in the shower finally. She was angry with Shay. She didn't like the fact that she spoke the truth. She wasn't comfortable in her role as the victim or as the friend who needed to be rescued. She was supposed to be the friend who did the rescuing. She wanted to get back to who she knew she was.

After showering, she moisturized her aching body and tended to her bruises. Her night routine for her face was not going to happen because it was painfully swollen. She put on a long nightgown and wrapped her hair in a towel. In the shower, she had watched as long strands of hair washed down the drain. She didn't want to comb it or manipulate her hair any more than what she already had. After the way he pulled her hair, she was sure he had left there with a handful of her hair in his hand.

She gave herself a once-over in the mirror and decided an ice bath for her face was just what she needed. So, she prepared a large bowl with ice cubes and some water. She sat at the kitchen table with a white towel. Jayda then took in a deep breath and placed her face into the ice bath. She fought the urge to remove her face as the cold cubes touched her aching face. The coldness numbed the pain but was still a shock to her system. She forced herself to hold her face in the ice bath as long as she could. After about five minutes of soaking her face, she was finally ready to go to bed.

When Khalil returned home, he did exactly what she knew he would. He climbed ever so gently into bed and aroused her with his tender touches and soft kisses. She didn't open her eyes, but she was awake. Butterflies fluttered in her stomach as he turned her over and lifted her gown to her waist. He kissed her belly up to her breasts. She began to breathe heavily. He worked his way back down and kissed her passionately down below. Her back arched, and they both moaned. He made love to her and apologized with each stroke, pleasing her.

Chapter 7

Yolanda and Ryan had finally settled into their new life as a family of three with their daughter, Ryanna, named after her father. Yolanda was enjoying the time off from work and the time she had to bond with her daughter. Their parents were over for a visit; Yolanda and Ryan welcomed the company. It was all hands-on deck and gave them a chance to rest.

Ryanna's complexion was very light. Her eyes were gray, and her head was almost bald except for a thin, sandy brown patch of hair on top. With Ryan being white and Yolanda being black, her appearance represented that fact. For Yolanda, her daughter's looks were a small concern. She knew her daughter might face some form of adversity and possibly have to pick a side, black or white. She secretly hoped her daughter would be darker and take more after her than her father.

Yolanda was back on her feet. She favored her recliner, where she felt most comfortable while sitting. She was still exhausted after grabbing a few hours of sleep. As she sat in the recliner, she yawned and looked out of the window. She listened to Ryan and her family talk over each other, but she didn't say much. She didn't feel the same excitement that everyone else was feeling. She felt dread. She dreaded the fact that she was responsible for a baby.

All Yolanda had ever wanted was a family with Ryan. They tried so hard to get pregnant. They started trying to get pregnant on their wedding night. Since they had both completed their education and were in their careers, they didn't feel a need to wait to have children. However, after a year, she still wasn't pregnant. Yolanda had tried most of the tricks, including standing on her head after sex. She and Ryan didn't have any known medical reasons as to why they couldn't conceive. Ryan suggested they change their diets to a healthier diet and exercise more. Her doctor agreed with Ryan and gave a few more suggestions. Within six months of taking supplements, dieting, and exercising, she conceived. When she found out she was pregnant, she cried tears of joy.

Yolanda looked at Ryan as he held Ryanna in his arms. He held her so close to him. While talking with the others, he didn't take his eyes off his daughter. She watched him steal glances at the person he was talking to but soon turn his attention back to his bundle of joy. She smiled at him.

"Are you okay, honey?" her mother asked, walking over to Yolanda.

"Yes. I'm just tired. I had no clue it was going to be this hard," she confessed.

Her mother placed a hand on her shoulder and squeezed lightly.

"You did a great job. You did a better job than I did. At least you weren't standing on the bed and screaming, *get it out*!" she said.

They shared a laugh.

"Yeah, baby. Your mom scared the doctor so much he had to call for backup," her father chimed in. "I was so embarrassed by the way she acted. But, once she had you, she turned into the sweetest, loving mother. I couldn't have asked for anything better."

He walked over to them and kissed both her and her mother on their cheek. She loved to see her mother and father dote on each other. It reminded her that not all married couples fail. Her parents had made it through some tough situations; they managed to make it through together.

"Are you ready? I was going out with John to warm up the cars," he asked his wife.

"Yes. We should give them some time alone with the baby. I'll be out in a second," her mother told him.

"Walk out with Carolyn," her father said, then looked at Yolanda. "If you need anything, and I mean anything, be sure to give us a call."

He kissed her and left out of the house with Ryan's father, John.

As her mother began to walk away, Yolanda grabbed her hand.

Her mother turned to her and asked, "What's the matter?"

"Mom, I don't think I can do this. Just the thought of being alone with her scares me sometimes," she whispered.

"What do you mean, it scares you? Your motherly instincts will kick in. You will know just what to do to care for your baby. You've had years of practice with your dolls," her mother said with a chuckle. "When the baby cries, you soothe them. When they are hungry, you feed them. When they need to be changed, you change them."

"I know that. I just don't feel right," Yolanda expressed. "I want to be happy. I mean, I am happy. Then I feel different inside. I just can't explain it."

"Look, don't think about it," her mother said. "You're doing too much thinking. This is a natural process. Trust me."

"But something just doesn't feel right. What if I have postpartum depression?"

"That isn't real. It's just an excuse some women use when they can't cope with motherhood. You might feel a little off, but you have to give your hormones time to level out. It's just the first month. Get you some rest and take care of my granddaughter," her mother advised.

Her mother slid her hand away and proceeded to gather her things to depart, leaving Yolanda feeling alone in her feelings.

"Carolyn, are you ready?" her mother asked.

They said their goodbyes and left. As soon as the door closed behind the grandmothers, Yolanda had an overwhelming feeling to cry. She put her hands to her mouth and began to sob. She didn't know why she was crying. Ryan jumped up and rushed over to her.

"Why are you crying?" he asked, holding Ryanna in his arms.

"I don't know," she sobbed.

"What do you need me to do?" he asked.

"I don't know."

"Honey, please stop crying. Are you hurting? Do I need to call the doctor?"

Ryan reached down with one hand but then realized he couldn't help her with the baby still in his arms. He seemed to weigh the decision to part with his daughter to help his wife.

"Put the baby down for a second, please," she said.

"Right. Just let me put her back," he told her.

Ryan spun in circles, trying to figure out how to lay the baby down. He couldn't seem to figure out how to release her from his arms.

"She won't break. Support her head and lay her down on her back," she instructed.

Yolanda laughed as Ryan placed his daughter carefully down in the bassinet.

All of a sudden, she didn't feel sad anymore. Ryan helped her out of the recliner and on to the sofa. Then he sat down beside her and stroked her hair.

"Now what was all of that about?" he asked. "And don't tell me that you don't know."

"I'm feeling strange. I think I have postpartum depression," she said.

"It's possible. We can call your doctor tomorrow. I just want you to be okay.

We knew this could be a possibility. I did read about it in that book you asked me to read."

"So, you read the book? I didn't see you read it."

Ryan smiled and replied, "Yes, I read the book. I wanted to know what to expect. This is my first time too."

She was surprised to find that he had taken the time to read the book. She blushed.

"I love you so much," she told him.

"Yeah, I know."

He pointed to his cheek, and she kissed him.

They were interrupted by a knock at the door.

"Come in," Yolanda called out.

"It's me…Shay."

In came Shay with a flower bouquet and a smile that immediately lifted Yolanda's spirit.

"Hey, girl. I wanted to come over while I was out. Sorry I didn't call you first," Shay said.

"You're fine. Our parents just left. I thought you weren't coming?"

"I wasn't, but I wanted to see you and my goddaughter," Shay said.

She gave Ryan and Yolanda a hug, then placed the flowers on the table.

"Thanks for the flowers. They're beautiful," Yolanda said.

"You can sit here if you like," Ryan offered. "I have to cook. Are you staying for dinner?"

"No, thank you," Shay answered.

Shay took a seat beside Yolanda after taking a look at Ryanna.

"She's starting to look just like her daddy. She's so cute," Shay said.

"She's beautiful just like her momma," Yolanda corrected.

"I guess she looks a little like you too," Shay stated sarcastically with a roll of her eyes and then asked, "Have you spoken with Jayda today?"

"No. Why? What's going on?" Yolanda inquired.

"She had a fight with Khalil. As usual, she's trying to cover for him. He must've beat her ass because she's in hiding. When I asked her to meet me here, she gave me all kinds of excuses," Shay shared.

"Did you ask her what happened?" Yolanda asked.

"She tried to sugarcoat it as usual."

"I don't know why she tries to hide the truth about Khalil. He's abusive towards her. She tries to lie about what happens when they fight, but when she goes missing, I know she is hiding something. We need to talk to her," Yolanda said.

"Somebody needs to because she won't listen to me. I get that she loves Khalil, but a man who hits you doesn't love you. As smart as she is, she still puts up with it. She seems to be the one who always has the answers, but she needs to listen to her own advice," Shay voiced.

Ryanna began to cry. Yolanda felt a sunken feeling. She looked towards the kitchen where Ryan had gone, then looked towards Ryanna. She could feel Shay watching her.

"Do you need me to get her for you?" Shay finally asked.

"Yes, please hand her to me. She's probably ready to eat," Yolanda said.

Shay stood and walked towards the baby.

"Wash your hands first. You know you can't touch babies without washing your hands first," Yolanda said.

"Girl, that's a myth," Shay told her.

"Myth or not, you better wash your hands before touching my baby."

After Shay washed her hands and showed Yolanda, she picked up Ryanna and handed her to Yolanda. As Yolanda held her daughter in her arms, she felt such joy in her heart, pushing away the sunken feeling. She held her daughter close while breastfeeding her and cried tears of joy for being blessed with such a precious gift. Even though her emotions were all over the place, the feeling of love she had for her child overshadowed the negative feelings.

After Shay's visit, Yolanda turned on the news. The day went well with visitors, which was more exhausting than she thought it would be. She didn't have the energy to keep up, but she managed.

"It's so sad what's happening in the world right now. I know it's nothing new. Stuff like this has been going on, but thanks to social media, cell phone cameras, and all this new technology, everybody is being exposed. They can no longer hide their evil. They're shooting down black males like it's hunting season," Yolanda said.

"What happened now?" Ryan asked from the kitchen.

She held Ryanna closer to her as she breastfed her. Watching the news always sent her into a frenzy after listening to one news report after another. It made her fear the world in which her child would grow up.

"Your people done killed another black man," she answered.

"Who?" Ryan asked.

"What?"

"Who?" Ryan shouted from the other room.

"Stop yelling and come in here. The baby's trying to go to sleep," Yolanda told him.

Ryan came into the living room where Yolanda was nursing Ryanna on the sofa. His hands were dripping wet as he stood in the middle of the floor, looking at the television.

"You want to eat, right?" he asked her.

"Wipe your hands," she said, ignoring his comment.

Yolanda pointed the remote towards the television and rewound the news report to the officer related shooting. Ryan listened as he dried his hands on the apron he wore.

"They're my people now?" Ryan asked.

"I was joking with you," Yolanda said.

"That's not funny. It's like they have a license to kill or something with their badges."

"Exactly! Then there are no convictions, and they're just walking around like an injustice hasn't occurred. Sadly, this is nothing new. It's been happening."

"By the way, I didn't like your joke about them being my folk," Ryan told her in all seriousness. "You're constantly making inappropriate comments about me being white. If I didn't know you, I would think you are a little racist."

"Me? Racist? I married you, didn't I?"

"But what do you always say? I'm the blackest white boy you ever met."

"I know that's right." She winked.

"I don't know what to do with you sometimes."

"Oh, yes, you do."

Ryan shook his head at her comment and said, "And you're the whitest black girl I ever met."

"Now you know that ain't true."

Yolanda placed Ryanna, who was done nursing, on her shoulder and began patting her on the back as she slept. She took in her fresh baby scent and kissed her softly several times.

"Let me get some of that love," Ryan said.

He kissed both Ryanna and Yolanda before returning to the kitchen to finish cooking. Still sore from the delivery, Yolanda stood to her feet slowly and went in the nursery to place her daughter in her crib. Then she returned to the living room to wait for dinner. As she finished watching the news, her phone rang.

"Hey, Shay," she answered.

"Hey, girl. I just wanted to let you know I'm home. What is the baby doing?" Shay asked.

"You just left five minutes ago. She's sleeping," Yolanda said, laughing.

"I just love her so much," Shay said. "So, how are you?"

"I'm just fine."

"I mean, how are you adjusting to everything? I know how it is. I had two babies, and it ain't easy."

"I'm adjusting," Yolanda replied, then added, "I'm thankful I have Ryan to lean on."

"Me too. Not everyone is blessed to have the baby's father there to help."

"Speaking of Ryan… Thanks for checking on me. I'll talk to you tomorrow," Yolanda said, trying to rush her friend off the phone.

"I know you and Ryan are not trying to do the nasty already. Your ass is going to end up pregnant again. Do you know how fertile a woman is after childbirth?"

"No more kids for me. We made sure of that. One and done."

"Yeah, you say that now and will end up with one on your hip and one in the belly."

"No, I won't be looking like you. I tied my tubes."

"You what?" Shay nearly shouted, surprised by the news.

"Yes, I tied my tubes. We only wanted one healthy child to spoil and give them the world if we can. Do you know how hard it was for me to conceive? Girl, please. We're good over here with the one we have."

"I can't believe you made a decision like that without talking to your girls first. I know you're married and all, but we could've given you some advice. I would've told you not to do it just yet. There's no telling how you're going to feel months or even years from now. You could've had the surgery later. There are many other birth control options out there. I know Jayda would agree with me on this."

"Jayda already agreed with me. After Ryan and I talked about it, I talked to her. If she would've thought I was making the wrong decision, she would've told me. I don't regret what I did at all. I have my daughter. She's here, she's beautiful, and she's healthy. What more can a woman ask for?"

"I'm surprised you talked to her and not me first. I have children. She doesn't."

"There you go with the shade. I know you have children, but I had already decided on what I was going to do."

"Yeah, but I know Jayda's opinion mattered. You know what, let me mind my business. It's your life," Shay stated with a hint of attitude.

"Yes, it's my life, and it's a good one."

"On that note, I'll let you go."

After ending the call, Yolanda retrieved the bottle of pain killers that her doctor hesitantly refilled. She complained of having pain that wasn't being helped with the medication she was taking and insisted she needed something stronger. The truth is, she wasn't in the kind of pain that couldn't be resolved with over-the-counter medication. She wanted the drug because it made her feel good. She liked the feeling of being high. She hid the fact that she was still taking medication from Ryan because she knew he wouldn't like it. He didn't care for her taking such strong medication that made her loopy and sleepy while caring for their daughter. He feared for her safety as well as the safety of their child.

Chapter 8

Hey, cousins!" Koshie screamed, delighted at seeing her cousins Sage and Sam.

Koshie leaped into the arms of her cousin, Sam, who spun her around.

"It's been a long time. Let me look at you!" Sam said.

"Sage! Oh, my God! I missed you!" Koshie said, hugging her.

As Sam looked her over, Koshie put her head down. Using his forefinger, Sam placed it under her chin and lifted her head.

"I'm nothing much to look at right now. I'm just ready to go home," Koshie told him.

"You're still beautiful, and you're still my favorite little cousin."

"Look at you! You're big! I see you've been working out. Your arms are huge." Koshie squeezed Sam's biceps.

"Koshie, we are so happy you are finally home. It's been too long," Sage said.

They began walking towards the car as they talked.

"Yeah, I'm not little Sam anymore. I'm working out now and eating right. I can show you how to do this. I'm a personal trainer now."

"I can stand to lose a few pounds," Koshie admitted. "You would think I would've lost weight with all of that crap they feed you."

"Is the food as bad as they say it is?" Sage asked.

"All crap. Sometimes uneatable. You have to make do with the things you have access to," Koshie told her.

"No, that's those Sutton genes. Thick in all the wrong places," Sam said.

Koshie laughed.

"I haven't laughed like that in a very long time," Koshie said as she followed Sam and Sage.

She scanned the area with her eyes, searching for the car she knew him to have last. She quickly reminded herself that too much time had passed for him to have the same vehicle.

"What are you driving now?" Koshie asked.

"This is me right here!" Sam said with a huge smile.

"This is a big truck. It's like a monster truck!"

"Get in!"

Sam and Sage caught her up with all of the updates in the family on the ride home. There were new cousins and other additions to the family. There were also a couple of deaths that she didn't know about. To her, the only loss she suffered was her mother. All of the information was a bit overwhelming and a lot to take in on the first day out. She listened as she rode quietly. She rolled down her window to breathe in the fresh air that blew into the car. She paid attention to everything she saw that they passed along the way. She people watched as she got closer to home, searching the streets for familiar faces.

"We are almost there. Are you ready?" Sage asked.

Sam turned onto the street that led to her neighborhood. Koshie noticed he had finally stopped babbling.

"Yeah, I've been waiting to come home for a long time. I just wish my mom was here," Koshie sorrowfully said.

"I know. She did set you up real nice. She made sure you were taken care of before she died," Sage told her.

"I know. I just can't wait to take a bath and lay in my own bed," Koshie replied.

Koshie's stomach rose when they approached her house. It was a mixture of nervousness and anxiety. To her surprise, the house looked exactly as it did the day she left. Her mother was a stickler for curb appeal. The outside of the home was well kept along with the front yard. She could imagine her mother looking out the window, anticipating her arrival as they had talked about often.

"We're here," Sam announced as he parked in front of the house.

Koshie didn't respond. Instead, she anxiously got out of the car and walked towards the house. Sam and Sage followed behind her. When she reached the front door, she looked back at them.

"Well, I don't have the keys. Open the door," she said.

At that moment, the door opened from the inside, and a sea of faces greeted her. "Welcome home, Koshie!"

"Oh, my God!" Koshie screamed.

She staggered back a few steps from all of the excitement. Sage pushed her inside. Immediately, Koshie recognized her aunts, uncles, and cousins. There were some others she didn't know.

"Come on in here," her aunt said, grabbing her by the hand and leading her to the kitchen.

Moved by all of the love and support she received from her family, Koshie began to cry. She looked back to find Sage but was swallowed up by the crowd of people surrounding her. There were so many people hugging and kissing her that she didn't know who they were coming from.

"Thank you so much," Koshie said to no one in particular.

"We pretty much fixed a little bit of everything. We want you to relax and enjoy a home-cooked meal with family. Would you like that?" her aunt asked.

"I would love that," Koshie answered.

It looked like Thanksgiving. From what she could see, there was turkey, ham, fried chicken, fish, macaroni and cheese, collard greens, and more. Her mouth began to water from all of the delicious aromas.

Her aunt kissed her on the cheek and gave her a tight hug.

"First, I want to get out of these clothes and take a bath so I can get more comfortable," Koshie said.

"Of course, take your time," her aunt told her.

Koshie tried to turn to leave the kitchen but was bombarded by her cousins, all asking her questions simultaneously.

"Give the girl a minute to breathe. Let her out so she can get ready to eat with us," her aunt said, and just like that, they parted like the Red Sea.

Koshie walked out of the kitchen and made her way to the bedroom.

"Koshie?" Sam called after her. "Are you alright?"

"Yes. I need a bath and to get out of these clothes. Did you see all of that food? Man, I can't wait to eat."

"We'll be waiting, and don't take too damn long because I'm starving," Sam said.

"I see that hasn't changed," Koshie joked.

Sam gave Koshie the finger. In return, she stuck her tongue out at him. Koshie then closed the door behind her. Her room was different. She turned up her nose at the new furniture and bedding. It wasn't what she would've picked. Her mother told her that she was redecorating her room, but she never gave Koshie any options. It was her mother's style, not hers. She shrugged it off as she decided to accept her mother's gift.

Needing something to wear, she went to her drawers. In her drawers was everything she needed for someone who had nothing. She didn't care about the style; she just appreciated that they were the right sizes. She wasn't skinny anymore. She now had curves and breasts. That, her mom got right. She checked her closet. There were new jeans, skirts, blouses, shirts, and sweaters. There were only three shoe boxes, which contained a pair of tennis shoes, black pumps, and boots. It was evident that her mother didn't know when she was going to come home. She overly prepared by buying for all the seasons. She even had a winter coat.

Koshie sat on her bed and smiled. A tear fell from her eye as she thought about how much her mother loved her, even after all of the hell Koshie had put her mother through as a teenager. She acted out by getting into trouble with the law, running away, and sometimes disrespecting her. Through it all, her mother loved her, and when needed, she gave her tough love. She regretted taking her mother through so much stress as her only beloved child. She made her mother a lot of promises since then, and she was going to try and keep those promises.

Her stomach growled, reminding her that she had a feast waiting on her.

Chapter 9

Jayda stood in the line at the pharmacy behind one of her neighbors, Mrs. Fitzgerald. It was the first of the month, and like her, she was refilling her father's prescription for the month. She waited impatiently as the single pharmacist filled one prescription after the other. Usually, she would use this time to get her father out for some fresh air, but he was too weak to leave the house that day. She also had to meet Yolanda and Shay. They would get together twice a month for a girls' night out. They would meet at one of each other's homes and the next time out on the town.

"How is your father?" Mrs. Fitzgerald asked.

"He's doing fine. He still works out in the garden sometimes. You should come over and see what he's done so far," Jayda told her.

Mrs. Fitzgerald was next in line. The pharmacist greeted her by name before going to retrieve her medication. Jayda rolled her eyes and looked down at her watch.

"Are you in a hurry, Ms. Jayda? I'm sure your dad is just fine. We're not as dependent on you all as you think. We do enjoy our alone time, you know?" Mrs. Fitzgerald said.

"I'm meeting my friends, and I don't want to be late. My dad has made it very clear that he doesn't want me waiting on him all of the time," Jayda shared.

Mrs. Fitzgerald paid for her prescriptions and moved out of the line so Jayda could step up to the counter.

"It was nice seeing you. Tell your father we will be by to see him as soon as William feels up to it," Mrs. Fitzgerald said.

Jayda remembered that Mr. Fitzgerald had Alzheimer's disease. He and her father had golfed and played chess together for years until he became ill. Then the two of them began to see less and less of each other.

"He'll love that. Mrs. Fitzgerald, if you need anything, please call me. I'm right next door most days," Jayda said.

"Oh, baby, thank you. I know I could count on you," Mrs. Fitzgerald replied with a wink.

Jayda hugged her, then watched the once tall and elegant woman stroll away. She looked as if she had shrunk a foot. Ramona, Mrs. Fitzgerald's daughter, waved and went to meet her mother halfway down the aisle.

"How can I help you?" the pharmacist asked.

"You know why I'm here. I'm here to pick up my father's medication," Jayda said.

"Of course. We have three prescriptions ready for Mr. James," the pharmacist said before walking away.

Jayda's phone rang. She pulled it out of her handbag and saw that it was Yolanda calling. Instead of answering it, she placed the phone back in her bag. The pharmacist returned to the counter and checked her out.

As Jayda proceeded to leave the store, her phone rang again, and once again, it was Yolanda. Jayda was pretty sure she was only calling to make sure she was going to be on time. Whenever it was Yolanda's turn to host girls' night, she would be anal about everyone being on time. However, when she called a third time before she could get out of the door, something told her to answer.

"I'm on the way! Stop calling me like a crazy lady, YoYo!" Jayda yelled.

"Jayda! Where are you?" Yolanda frantically screamed through the phone.

"I'm at the store. What's wrong?" Jayda asked.

The fear in Yolanda's voice froze her. She had never heard her sound like that before.

"I need you to get over here right now!" Yolanda said.

"Where is Ryan? What's wrong?"

"He's not here. I already called for help, but I need you."

"What happened? Are you hurt? Is the baby hurt?"

"Jayda, just get here!"

Jayda could feel her heart pounding in her chest as her mind raced. She began to panic. She grabbed her chest and was stuck where she stood.

"I'm on the way!"

Yolanda hung up. Jayda didn't know what was wrong. All she knew was that she needed to get to her friend, so she raced out of the store.

Jayda laid on her horn. The horn blared, forcing cars to clear the way for her

SUV. She swerved in and out of lanes as tears clouded her vision. She didn't care about being stopped by the police. She secretly wanted the police to follow her because she didn't know what she was about to walk in on.

Jayda arrived at Yolanda's subdivision expecting to be greeted by first responders since Yolanda said she had already called for help. There wasn't a fire truck, police car, or ambulance in sight. She slowed down as she approached the house. An uneasy feeling came over her as she pulled into the graveled driveway of Yolanda and Ryan's home. It rained the night before, and the gravel had settled into the mud. Every time she visited Yolanda, she thought, *Why did they build such a beautiful house and fail to pave the driveway?*

Jayda stepped out of the car into the muddy graveled driveway in her heels. She shook her head. She was ruining a pair of her favorite heels. She looked down to see how she could try to maneuver her way to the sidewalk. Then she glanced up to see Yolanda standing on the porch, talking on the phone. She appeared unharmed, but her face read of pain.

Jayda rushed down the sidewalk towards Yolanda. Yolanda's eyes were red and puffy. She was crying.

"What happened? I thought you said you called for help," Jayda said.

She grabbed Yolanda and hugged her for a moment before letting her go. Holding her by the hands, she examined her closely.

"Are you hurt?" Jayda asked.

"No, I'm not!" Yolanda said through tears.

"Where is Ryanna?" Jayda inquired.

Yolanda began to cry harder. Sobbing, she fell into Jayda's chest.

"I'm sorry," Yolanda whispered.

"Sorry for what?" Jayda asked.

The look on Yolanda's face sent chills down Jayda's spine. Yolanda began to back away from her.

Jayda rushed past Yolanda and opened the door to the house. She stepped in and was taken aback by a dark, eerie feeling that almost forced her back out of the door. She knew something terrible had happened in the house, but she had to find her goddaughter Ryanna. Pushing through her fear, she raced towards the nursery.

"Ryanna!" Jayda called out.

She didn't expect the infant to answer, but she felt that calling out to her would lead her to the baby.

The closer she got to the nursery, the heavier the dark feeling settled over her. The door to the nursery was slightly open. She pushed the door open further, and a cool breeze rushed past her. She looked over at the crib and walked slowly towards it.

"Ryanna?" she said quietly.

When she reached the crib, she saw Ryanna lying on her back. She looked more closely and noticed that she didn't appear to be breathing. She began to rub the baby softly at first and then more roughly. She felt for a pulse and didn't find one. So, she began to perform CPR.

"I tried that! It didn't work," Yolanda said from the doorway.

"Call 9-1-1!" Jayda screamed.

"I did!" Yolanda cried.

Jayda continued to perform CPR as Yolanda rambled on in the background. When she realized it wasn't working, Jayda stopped and held the baby close to her heart.

"God, no! Not her!" Jayda cried.

She kissed the baby and rocked her in her arms. Yolanda hugged both Jayda and Ryanna while sobbing.

Yolanda whispered in her ear as tears poured from her eyes. Jayda tried to keep her composure but found it hard. She turned and hugged her friend.

"Why did you move her in here?" Jayda asked.

"I didn't know what to do. I was scared. I panicked," Yolanda explained.

"I'm so sorry this happened to you. You're not going to go through this alone. I got you,"

Jayda told her.

"They're going to think I hurt my baby. I can't go away for this. I didn't mean to. I would never hurt her!" Yolanda cried.

"I know you would never hurt this baby. We just have to convince everyone else," Jada told her. "We are going to fix this, I promise you."

Footsteps rushed towards them. Once EMS entered the room, Jayda handed baby Ryanna to them. Then she stepped out of the room to let them work on her, but she already knew what they didn't. Ryanna was gone.

"Yolanda! Where are you?" Ryan called out.

More bodies filled the house—police, firemen, and EMS.

Yolanda began to run to Ryan, but Jayda pulled her back.

"Let me talk to him first. I don't want you saying the wrong thing to him. Let me explain to him what happened," Jayda explained. "You aren't the first mother to find her baby unresponsive. Do you understand?"

Yolanda stared at Jayda but didn't respond. Jayda left her friend and went to

Ryan. He was trying to fight his way into the house but was being held back by the police. Jayda, the fixer and problem solver that she was, went into action. She spoke calmly to the police and explained to them who Ryan was and why they needed to let him in. It worked. She then informed Ryan of what had happened and reunited him with his grieving wife. Jayda took charge and lifted some of the burden off of Yolanda.

Jayda's role had always been the calm one and the thinker. She could think her way through almost anything. Her friends came to her for help with everything, and she would give them the best advice. Most of the time, things worked out, or she gave them peace of mind. There was no question as to how far she would go for her two best friends. Now she was preparing herself to plan her first funeral—the funeral of her goddaughter.

Chapter 10

Hours had passed since the death of Yolanda's daughter, Ryanna. She was transported to the hospital but was pronounced dead on arrival. Yolanda and Ryan went to the hospital. Jayda and Shay stayed at the house as family and friends began to arrive once the tragic news spread. Family, friends, and neighbors descended upon the family's home, bringing dishes of food, cards of condolences, and flowers.

When Ryan and Yolanda returned home, they were surrounded by those who loved them. Ryan seemed to be the strong one as he greeted each of their guests and spoke for both he and Yolanda. Yolanda sat down on the nearest sofa. Shay and Jayda quickly joined her. Yolanda watched Ryan's every move as Jayda and Shay sat on each side of her. She didn't move, and she didn't speak. You had to know her in order to read her eyes and know what she needed. She looked at Shay. Shay rubbed her hand, gave her a small smile, and then left to get her some water. When Shay returned, Yolanda took the bottle of water from her hand and stood to her feet. The room fell silent. All eyes were on her. Jayda stood up beside her and placed a hand on her shoulder.

"Thanks, everyone, for coming here to support us. I don't want to be rude, but I need some time to process all of this. I prayed and asked God for a daughter. He blessed us with Ryanna. She came to us just when we were ready to give up on having children. Now, she's gone, and it's because of me," Yolanda said.

Her voice was almost unrecognizable; it sounded like someone else was talking. Both Shay and Jayda looked at each other strangely.

"This isn't your fault. You didn't do anything wrong," Jayda interjected.

"But I…" Yolanda began.

"What happened today was a tragedy," Jayda explained, then addressed the others who were looking on. "Please pray for both Yolanda and Ryan. They will need all the prayers and support they can get."

"Please excuse us," Shay said, then led the way out of the crowded room towards the bedroom as Jayda and Yolanda walked closely behind.

When they approached the long hallway leading to the bedrooms, Yolanda burst into tears.

"My baby! She's gone!" she wept.

They quickly ushered Yolanda past the nursery. When Shay opened Yolanda and Ryan's bedroom door, somebody was already in there. Jayda and Yolanda froze, shocked to see someone in the bedroom.

"What are you doing in here?" Yolanda asked, not sounding a bit pleased.

She shook her arms loose from Jayda and Shay. She seemed strong all of a sudden.

Nicole, Yolanda's older sister, was placing pillows on the bed. She didn't immediately respond to Yolanda's question. They all watched her meticulously smooth out the purple blanket on the bed. She looked up at the three women who had entered the room.

"What are you doing in here?" Yolanda repeated.

"I knew you would need to rest, so I took it upon myself to make sure you had a clean bed. It's too much too soon—all of these strangers in the house. You need to be around family right now," she said, glaring at Jayda and Shay.

Shay lunged forward, ready to give Nicole a tongue lashing, but Yolanda stepped in front of her.

"I am with my family," Yolanda replied. "Shay and Jayda are more of a sister to me than you've ever been. This is your…second time in my home since we've moved in here. How many times have you seen your niece since she's been born? She's your only niece. She *was* your only niece. Get out of my house!" Yolanda shouted, pointing to the door.

"Now is not the time to push family away. I'm here for you. That's what matters right now. I know you're angry and hurt, but don't push those that love you away," Nicole said.

"You heard her. I think you should go," Shay spoke up.

"Sure, I'll give her some space, but I'm not leaving my sister at a time like this," Nicole retorted.

She turned and walked to get her clutch from the dresser. Jayda could only imagine how much that clutch must've cost. It was green and matched her blazer and heels perfectly.

"Oh, I found this under your sheets. I wasn't sure why you had it there," Nicole said, holding out a pink receiving blanket.

"I put it there. I thought it would make her feel closer to Ryanna," Jayda said.

"Hmmm, okay. But it was under the sheets." Nicole placed the blanket on the bed.

Yolanda grabbed her mouth, rushed over to pick it up, and let out an ear-piercing scream. As she smelled the blanket, she let her tears fall upon it. This brought the room to tears. No one intervened; they let her be. The tension among the women didn't exist. The hatred that the two sisters had for each other didn't exist. Four women grieved for a child that passed too soon.

"Why? God, why my daughter!" Yolanda screamed.

She fell onto her bed and held the blanket up to her face, crying into it. She raised her knees to her chest and curled into a fetal position. She mumbled to herself. The words she was speaking were hard to hear because she was talking so low. Jayda rushed over to her first.

"It's going to be okay. We got you. You're not going to go through this alone," Jayda said, trying to console her.

"How will he ever forgive me for what I did?" Yolanda sobbed.

Jayda looked to Shay and Nicole to see if they heard what she said. From the confused expressions on their faces, she knew they did.

"Nicole, can you go and check on Ryan and the guests, please?" Jayda asked.

"I'm not leaving her like this. I'm her sister. I should be here with her," Nicole replied.

"It will only take you a few minutes to do that. Ryan needs help too. Just come back when you're done," Jayda said, giving a fake smile.

Nicole finally agreed to go. "I'll be right back, Yolanda. I'm going to check on Ryan."

Yolanda, who was still mumbling, didn't respond.

Nicole left the room, closing the door behind her.

"Shay, please run her a hot bath. I think it would calm her," Jayda said.

Shay was torn to pieces, her light skin the shade of apple red from crying. A tough girl, Shay wasn't the type to be easily moved to tears, but she couldn't stop her tears from falling.

"I'm so sorry this happened to you. I just can't believe all of this. I don't want to question God, but why did this have to happen to you?" Shay sniffled and walked in the master bathroom.

Once Shay was out of sight, Jayda quickly turned to Yolanda and whispered.

"What the hell are you doing? Are you trying to sabotage things?"

"It's my fault. I shouldn't have fallen asleep with her in my bed. I normally would put her in the crib, but I didn't. I laid her beside me in my bed. I didn't know that was going to happen. She was under me. I tried to revive her. I did. I tried to save my baby. I didn't mean to hurt her," Yolanda babbled.

"You didn't intentionally hurt her. Everyone knows how much you loved your daughter. Telling Ryan and everybody what really happened isn't going to bring her back. Remember, you set this story in motion. You placed her in the crib and told everyone that was where you found her," Jayda reminded her.

"I just want to tell the truth now. I was scared and didn't know what to—"

"Look," Jayda said, interrupting her. "You should've called for help right away and told the truth the first time. Now we are in the thick of it. You can't recant your story now. You are going to draw suspicion. Even though it was an accident, who knows what's going to happen now," Jayda said.

"You're right," Yolanda said.

"The best advice I have for you is that if you decide to change your story, make sure you get a lawyer. Talk to your husband before you do anything," Jayda said.

Yolanda sat up on the bed and used the pink blanket to dry her tears. She then folded the blanket into a square and placed it neatly under a pillow.

"What would I do without you? I can see in your eyes that you are disappointed in me. Yet, you are standing here with me. Thank you."

Jayda hugged Yolanda.

"Come on so you can try to relax a little. The next few days are going to be rough, but I'll be right here with you," Jayda said.

Shay reappeared in the bedroom; her face not pained any longer. She scowled at Jayda and Yolanda.

"Really? You were going to keep the truth from me too?" Shay said.

"No, Shay. You don't understand," Jayda said.

"Shut up, Jayda! I would expect this from you, but not you, Yolanda. You didn't trust me enough to tell me what really happened? That's fucked up. How could you lie about something like that? I would never lie about my child's death! If it was an accident, you should've told the truth," Shay said.

"Calm down before someone hears you!" Jayda said.

Yolanda crumbled into a crying mess again. "I'm sorry. I didn't know how to tell you."

"But you could tell Jayda? She doesn't even have kids. How could you relate to her more than me?" Shay questioned.

"My daughter just died because of me! Now you know. I'm going to talk to Ryan and tell him what happened. Then I'm going to let the police know what happened. I can't go on with this lie. Whatever happens, happens," Yolanda said.

"If that is what you want to do, I support you. But if you are going to do this, you need to do it sooner rather than later," Jayda suggested.

"Let her tell her husband on her terms. Stop trying to fix her," Shay said.

Jayda looked up at Shay. "What's your fucking problem?"

"You're my fucking problem. How could you let our friend lie about something like this? She could be in serious trouble now. What kind of friend are you?" Shay said.

"The same kind of friend who sat in your shit with you, in your right and wrong. Don't get on your high horse with me. And if you keep coming for me about not being a mother, we're going to have a problem," Jayda warned her. "Yeah, I caught all of that."

"Stop it! This is not the time for you two to start fighting. I have to take responsibility for my actions, even if it was an accident. I just need my sisters to be by my side," Yolanda told them.

"We got you," Shay said.

"You know we got you," Jayda said.

Yolanda relaxed in the bath while Shay politely asked everyone to leave on Yolanda's behalf. Ryan seemed to have run out of charge. He was pale white and seemed to have zoned out. Jayda, Nicole, and Shay cleaned up after everyone left.

"Thank you for everything," Ryan said.

"No problem. That's what family is for," Nicole said.

"Right. That's why I'm so grateful she has friends like the two of you. I don't know how we are going to get through this, but I know she will be alright as long as she has the two of you to help her deal with it," Ryan said to Shay and Yolanda.

Shay smirked at Nicole, who rolled her eyes and headed for the door.

"You need to go to your wife. You two will need to be there for each other more than ever. Keep a close eye on her tonight. If you need anything, please call me or Shay. We will be here," Jayda said.

"Ryan, come here, please," Yolanda called out.

"We can let ourselves out. Go to your wife," Shay told him.

Nicole swung open the front door and slammed it shut behind her while Ryan was hugging Shay and Jayda. He then went to be with Yolanda. Shay and Jayda let themselves out and prayed that things went well for Yolanda. The legal implications of suffocating a child could land even a grieving mother behind bars.

Jayda wanted to help her friend. She was at a loss. She didn't want to see Yolanda go to prison for a tragic mistake. She had a thought. She wondered if the lawyer, Jamison, could help. She ripped through her wallet, looking for the business card that he had given her. She found it behind her driver's license, where it was hidden. She dialed the number and prayed he would be willing to represent Yolanda.

Chapter 11

I t's about time. I'm starving," Koshie said as she sat down at the table and kicked off her shoes.

"We have only been waiting fifteen minutes. That's not long for a place like this. I've had to wait up to an hour to get a table here before," Sage said.

"At least I had time to look over the menu while we waited. I know exactly what I want to order," Koshie said.

"Me too," Sage said.

"All that shopping got me tired, and my feet are killing me. It's been too long. I haven't shopped like that since stealing clothes and selling them around the way," Koshie said.

"Doesn't it feel good to be able to pay for your purchases now? Look at you. Most people like you come home to less," Sage said.

"I know. I'm grateful for everything my mom did for me," Koshie said.

The waiter came over to the table and took their orders.

"Don't forget to thank me. If it weren't for me, you wouldn't have a job. I can't believe how hard it is for a felon to find employment. After putting in all of those applications, you didn't get but two interviews. How are you supposed to take care of yourself? I see why people end up back inside. It's hard out here," Sage expressed.

"I know. It's my life," Koshie said.

"Sorry. I hope I didn't offend you," Sage said.

"Of course not. Thank you for helping me get a job," Koshie said.

"You're welcome, cousin. I had to beg my manager to give you a chance. Once he saw you, that sealed the deal. Just don't let him get too close. I think he has a thing for you now," Sage said.

"He has been really nice to me. It's just a hotel job, but he said I could work my way up. I don't plan to be there long though. I want to have my own business one day. I just need this job to keep them folks off my ass," Koshie said.

A notification sounded. Koshie reached inside her handbag and pulled out the new cell phone she had purchased.

"I have a new friend request," Koshie said.

"Did you find your friends on there?" Sage inquired. "I know you're ready to catch up with them."

"I did," Koshie told her.

"And?" Sage asked.

"They haven't responded yet. Not everyone sits on social media all day, every day like you. I did find some old friends from school. It's been cool reconnecting with them," Koshie said.

"I'll be right back," Sage said, then left to go to the restroom.

While her cousin was gone, Koshie scrolled through her social media and noticed many posts had *#tbt*. Thanks to Sage, she found out that meant *Throwback Thursday*. Seeing she was tagged in some photos, Koshie scrolled through the pictures. Many were photos of her and her friends from back in high school. They were also tagged in the pictures, and the comments underneath were welcoming her home.

The photos posted brought back so many good memories. Koshie smiled and laughed as she continued to scroll through them. When she got to the pictures that looked like they were taken the night of the party that changed her life, her smile faded. One picture caught her eye, and she zoomed in on the photo.

There was a picture of a group of guys making goofy faces. In the background, Koshie was being carried by Jayda, Shay, and Yolanda to her car. She apparently couldn't hold herself up without help. So, there was no way she was the driver that night. There was only one person who could've driven, and that was Yolanda because Jayda nor Shay had a license.

"I'm going to kill them bitches," Koshie said, slamming down her phone.

Sage rushed over to her. "What's wrong?"

"I can't believe this! I knew it," Koshie said.

"What happened?" Sage asked.

Koshie showed the pictures to Sage, who studied them. After a few moments, she saw it and took the phone from Koshie.

"Oh, my God!" Sage said. "It wasn't you. You didn't do it."

Still holding the phone, Sage clicked on each picture posted.

"Oh, my God!" Sage said. "Look!"

Sage passed the phone back to Koshie. Koshie's eyes filled with tears.

"I knew it. I was fucked up that night. I was too fucked up to drive. Someone else did this. All this time, it wasn't me," Koshie said.

"We can leave if you want. We can get something on the way home," Sage said, standing to gather their shopping bags.

"No, I want to stay. I'm not going to let them steal anything else from me. I'll take care of them." Koshie used her napkin to wipe away her tears.

"Are you sure?" Sage asked.

"Sit down. Let's eat," Koshie said.

Sage put down the bags and took her seat.

"You know what? I knew deep down inside they were lying, but I couldn't prove it. So, for my peace of mind, I accepted that I was the one to blame for the accident. There were times while locked up that I thought about the what-ifs. I would think about all of the horrible things I would do to them bitches if they had lied on me. Then I would shake off the thoughts. I had to accept my situation because I wouldn't allow myself to think my friends would do something like that to me," Koshie said.

"You know what? I think it all makes sense now. That's why they haven't reached out to you all these years. Now they are ignoring you, knowing you are home. They must be shitting their pants right now. They don't know what you know. If they were okay with sending you away, they are capable of anything. Just be careful," Sage said.

"They better be careful because I have nothing to lose," Koshie said.

"You have everything to lose. Don't mess up your life trying to seek revenge. Karma pays us all a visit," Sage said.

"I have some visiting to do for myself," Koshie said.

Sage sat back in her seat and shook her head.

"What?" Koshie asked.

"I see that look in your eyes," Sage said.

"Good," Koshie told her.

Chapter 12

The days following the funeral, it rained for four days straight. Each night following Ryanna's death, Jayda stayed with Yolanda. During that time, Khalil was very understanding of Jayda's need to be there for her friend. She would come home after her shift at the hospital to shower and change. They would see each other briefly, and then she would head out the door to be with Yolanda. Khalil expressed his condolences and showed his support by going over there one night with dinner.

Jayda scrolled through Khalil's cell phone. She only had about fifteen minutes to collect what information she happened to find. Khalil was in the shower. He had left his phone on the bed, pretty confident that it was locked and secured. Unbeknownst to him, Jayda had the passcode. He was drunk one night and slowly tapped out his four-digit code while she watched and memorized it.

Khalil had been behaving strange and secretive. The sex was different, and he seemed distant. She knew there was someone else. The last time he acted that way, he was seeing his son's mother behind her back. That's when they first started dating. He said sex with her didn't mean anything to him and that he only did it so she would keep him off child support. Jayda broke up with him but got right back with him after he promised never to do it again. His son's mother put him back on child support after that.

Jayda typed the four-digit passcode into Khalil's phone, unlocking it. His screensaver was a picture of him and Brock. She found that odd. The last time she saw his screensaver, it was a picture of him and her. She immediately became angry. She first scrolled through his photos but didn't see anything unusual. He had about ten pictures in his gallery. Nothing raised her suspicions. She then proceeded to his phone log and came across a few names and numbers she didn't recognize. One phone number was listed repeatedly in his log and with long talk times. Using her phone's camera, she took pictures of the phone numbers.

She then inhaled a deep breath and checked his text messages. The latest text messages were from her and Brock. She didn't feel the need to read anything from Brock until she saw another familiar name—Ashley. He had introduced Ashley to her as his best friend. She had never met her in person but spoke to her on the phone. She clicked on the text messages from Ashley. Immediately, nude pictures filled the screen. She scrolled down and read their numerous texts. It was clear they were in some sort of relationship.

"Bitch," she said.

She sent a text message from his phone.

This is Khalil's girlfriend. Why are you sending pics of your ass to my man?

She waited for a response. She was pretty sure the woman wouldn't respond, but to her surprise, there was an immediate reply.

I have more pics, not just of my ass. I have the kind of pics that will break your heart. So, let it go.

Jayda began to burn with anger.

Break my heart? she responded. *Never. Side chicks never win. Leave my man alone or else…*

Jayda held the phone tightly as she anxiously waited to see what Ashley would say next.

Okay, since you're forcing my hand. Ask him where he was last month on the ninth. He wasn't home with you, that's for sure. He was with me when I gave birth to our daughter. Here are the pics that will break your heart. Seek and you shall find… Enjoy!

"Lies. At least they better be," Jayda said through clenched teeth. Her stomach turned.

The phone vibrated several times. Jayda took another deep breath and looked at the text.

There was picture after picture of a beautiful baby girl. Then there was the picture of Khalil holding the baby. The last photo was of Khalil, Ashley, and the baby. He looked like a happy father of a newborn baby girl. There were pictures of him holding the baby and pictures of the three of them at the hospital when she was born. He was smiling like she had never seen before other than with Brock. Tears fell from her eyes. Khalil had a baby with Ashley.

When she heard the shower turn off, she quickly forwarded as many messages to her phone as possible.

"That shower was all I needed," Khalil said, stepping into the bedroom.

He had a towel wrapped around his waist. She couldn't help but stare at his well-defined body as he walked over to the bed and picked up his phone. Jayda waited for him to notice her tears. When he didn't, she spoke.

"So, you have a baby girl?" she asked over the lump forming in her throat.

"What the hell are you talking about now? What baby?" he asked.

"Certainly not the baby you made me abort a couple of months ago. Certainly not that one. It makes sense now. You had another woman pregnant at the same time. I knew it."

"I don't have a baby. Where are you getting this from? Are you still listening to your jealous friends? And you know why we had that abortion. I don't want any kids right now. You knew that."

"I saw the picture of you and Ashley's baby."

"You've been in my phone?"

"Yes, I've been in your phone! I even talked to Ashley. I want you out of my house. I'm done with you," she said.

"Well, fuck you! I told you to stay out of my damn phone!"

"No, fuck you! You need me! I don't need you!"

Khalil raised his hand. The smack to her face echoed across the room, causing her to stumble backwards. She grabbed her face in shock, then charged towards him. Grabbing her, he made a fist and punched her in the face, knocking her to the floor. He climbed on top of her and hit her a second time. She became dizzy. He grabbed her throat, choking her with both hands. She clawed at his hands, trying to get him to release her. She gasped for air as she fought to get his hands from around her neck. She was becoming weak; her arms grew limp and dropped down. Just when she thought she was about to pass out, he let go of her neck.

She gasped for air while grabbing her throat. Her nose was full of blood, preventing her from breathing through her nostrils. She looked around the room for Khalil. She sat up and then stood to her feet.

She didn't see Khalil until he grabbed her from behind and spun her around. She began to swing wildly at him while screaming at the top of her lungs. She thought he was going to kill her this time.

"Get off of me!" she screamed.

Khalil grabbed her arms, preventing her from striking him further.

"Stop acting like this! You're fucking everything up! We were good until you went looking for something you didn't want to know. You did this to yourself."

Releasing his grip on her, Khalil turned his back to her and started pounding his head.

"You're insane," she said.

"I'm insanely in love with you. I didn't mean to hurt you," he said.

"I hate you! I want you out of my house!"

"Come on, baby! I made a mistake. She doesn't mean anything to me. I was going to tell you, but I didn't know how."

He reached for her.

"Don't touch me! It's not just about her. It's about this!" she said, pointing to her face.

"I love you, Jayda! I fucked up!"

"You had a baby while we were together, and you made me kill my baby! I could never forgive you for that. I won't, not this time!"

"We can have a baby if you want. We can do it right now. I'll do whatever you want me to do."

"Die, bitch! Can you do that for me?"

"See, you're just hurt and mad right now."

Khalil dropped his towel, revealing his chiseled stomach. He stroked himself as Jayda watched. She hated him at that moment but loved what she was seeing. His tatted chest and arms were calling out to her, and his penis was fully erect.

"Sex won't fix this, Khalil. You hurt me for the last time. I swear to you this is over," she said, wiping at her tears.

"Baby, I know what you need. You need me. Let me show you how much I love you. Just give me a chance."

Jayda laughed. "I swear you are the dumbest man I've ever been with. You can't show me like this. You showed me by what you did. Love don't hurt like this."

Khalil pressed his body against hers. She pushed against him, raising her fist to strike him. He caught her by the wrist and forced his tongue into her mouth. She pulled back from him and turned her head away. His kiss was hot and sweet, just the way she liked it. He tasted so good. She glared at him as he held her tightly. He looked as if he was going to cry.

"I'm so sorry, baby," he said, then a tear fell.

He tried to kiss her again. This time, she let him. She cried through his long, deep kiss. She felt weak in his hands as she let out her cries. Her hands unfolded, and he let her wrist go. She placed both hands by her side, helpless to how he was making her feel. Her mind was telling her not to do it, but her body was craving him.

Her heart was too broken to feel anything. She let him lay her on the bed, and the cycle repeated itself. He hurt her and then pleased her, just as he always did. He made love to her so good that she almost forgot what he had done. However, revenge was lurking in the corners of her mind and heart. She wasn't going to let him get away with humiliating her in that way. Cheating on him wouldn't be enough. Breaking it off still wasn't enough. She had to make him feel the pain of killing her unborn child for his selfish reasons. She took the blame too for being so naïve.

When they finished, she rolled onto her side and said, "I want you gone. This is over."

He rolled onto his back and stared at her. She looked back at him boldly. She felt strong. Strong enough to take whatever he was going to say or do.

"If that's the way you want it, fine. I'm out. I'm not begging your ass to let me stay here," he said.

"Take what you have here with you. The locks will be changed. I don't want any excuses for you coming back around here," she said calmly.

He jumped out of bed, tossing the sheets in her direction. She jerked back, not knowing what to expect. He looked at her in pity and laughed.

"Look at you," he said.

He roughly threw on his clothes and shoes. She watched as he cursed her and angrily tossed his clothes and belongings into a suitcase—the very one he showed up with one day. She had to laugh at that.

"Where is that ring? The one I bought you for your birthday," he asked.

He was already rummaging through her jewelry box.

"It's in the box on the right," she said.

He looked surprised.

"You had this planned?" he asked.

"No, but that's where I keep my ring. Take it. I don't need it," she said.

He grabbed the ring box and stuffed it into his pocket.

"Don't come calling me tomorrow, begging me to come back," he said.

"I won't," she replied nonchalantly.

After he walked out of the bedroom, she listened in anticipation for him to leave. It seemed to take longer than needed, and she began to get nervous. She sat up in her bed, expecting him to return for a fight. A few seconds later, she heard the front door open and then close. She waited a few seconds before running to the window to see if he had really left.

Out the window, she saw him walk slowly to his car and throw his things into the trunk. He looked back at the house for a few seconds and then got into his car, pulled out of the driveway, and drove away.

She breathed a sigh of relief.

At that moment, her fear turned into anger. She was sick and tired of being used and abused. She needed to ensure herself that she would leave him once and for all. So, she decided to do something she had never done before. She was going to call Yolanda and Shay to tell them the truth. She was going to confess everything to them so she could be held accountable if she was to take him back. Knowing her friends, they were going to hold her feet to the fire on this one, and that was just what she needed. She called Shay first.

"Hey, girl," Shay answered.

"I have to get YoYo on the line. Hold on," Jayda said.

"Oh, shit. Now what?" she said.

Jayda added Yolanda to the call.

"Hey, what's going on?" Yolanda asked.

"It's a cold world, ladies," Jayda began. "Talk me down off the edge. I'm going to hurt him."

"What happened?" Shay asked.

"What did he do now?" Yolanda inquired.

There was a deafening silence on the line.

"He has a baby," Jayda revealed.

The phone went silent.

"Oh, no. I can't believe it. Of all the things that man has taken you through, he had the nerve to have a baby on you!" Shay said.

"I'm so sorry that happened to you. I know how much you love him," Yolanda said, listening as Jayda sobbed.

"I've wasted a year of my life on his ass! He's going to pay for this. Trust me!" Jayda said.

"Don't do anything stupid. He's not worth it. He's showing you who he is," Yolanda told her.

"Fuck that. Get his ass! That's the problem. We let them get away with too much. When my ex cheated on me, I went up to his job, flattened all the tires on his car, and busted that front windshield. Then I tried to do him bodily harm when he came outside," Shay recounted.

"We know," Yolanda interjected. "Let's not give her any ideas. Jayda, do you need me to come over?"

"No. I couldn't ask you to do that. You're going through enough yourself. I don't want you to worry about me," Jayda said.

The phone went silent again.

"Well, I can't come over because I'm having company tonight, and I don't have a sitter," Shay explained.

"Don't worry about me. I'll be alright. I just can't believe he thought he could hide a baby from me," Jayda said.

"Who is she?" Shay asked.

"Do you remember me telling you about his best friend Ashley? The one who I've never met, but they were supposed to be like brother and sister. Well, she's been upgraded to a baby momma. The baby is about a month old," Jayda said.

"Oh, no he didn't play you like that! And he made you have an abortion. I know you regret that now," Shay said.

"Hold up. Wait a minute. You had an abortion? Tell me you didn't," Yolanda said.

"Thanks, big mouth," Jayda snapped.

"Oh, sorry. You didn't tell her yet. My bad, girl," Shay said.

"I was pregnant. He wasn't ready. So, I had an abortion," Jayda said.

"When was this?" Yolanda asked.

"A few months ago. You were pregnant, and I didn't feel comfortable talking to you about having an abortion. That wouldn't have been right," Jayda expressed.

"Really? And, Shay, you kept a secret that long? I don't know who either of you are anymore," Yolanda said. "Lies and secrets. That's what I'm going to start calling you two."

"Well, I agreed with her. I didn't think it was right talking to a pregnant woman about abortions," Shay said.

"I bet you did agree with her," Yolanda said, then asked Jayda, "What do you want to do?"

"He's done. But I will have the last laugh this time," Jayda said.

"Don't do nothing I wouldn't do," Shay blurted out.

"Think about your job and your father. Who is going to take care of him if you end up behind bars? No man is worth losing everything for, and you have a lot to lose. Sorry, but not sorry," Yolanda said.

"See, that's why we never tell your level-headed ass anything! You're always on that 'do the right thing' shit!" Shay said. "Let her do what she's going to do. I got her back and hope you do too."

"Of course, I do. Just like when I had your back that time you found yourself in trouble behind a man. I bailed you out of jail. I did that for you. Now was he worth it?" Yolanda asked.

"Okay, I made a mistake. You just won't let me live!" Shay said. "Look, jail is for animals. It was the worst experience. If you're going to end it with Khalil, just let him go and move on. That's what Yolanda would like for me to say to you," Shay said sarcastically.

"Well, ladies, thanks for being there as usual. I'm just so exhausted right now. I'll talk to you later. I'm done with his ass," Jayda said.

"I love you. Please don't do anything stupid," Yolanda said.

"I can't make any promises that I'm not sure I can keep," Jayda responded.

"Good night, ladies. I have to put the kids to bed," Shay said.

Jayda rushed to get dressed so she could call a locksmith to change her locks again. As she passed the mirror, she saw her face. It was swollen and bruised. She was more determined than ever to let that be the last time he or anyone else abused her. She had to make the call to the police to put an end to the abuse and the relationship.

Chapter 13

Yolanda stood in front of the full-length mirror that hung on the back of her bedroom door. She looked at her reflection, staring at her shoulder-length hair that she wished was at least six inches longer. She had been struggling with her weight after giving birth to her daughter. Her nose was wide, but it fit her round face. She wished her nose was smaller. She smiled and moved closer to the mirror. She stuck her tongue in the gap between her two front teeth. She hated her gap. Whenever she caught herself smiling, she became self-conscious and covered her smile with her hand.

"A smile speaks of confidence, so you should never hide it," her father would tell her.

She stood to the side and pulled her hair into a ponytail. Then she took in a deep breath, sucked in her stomach, and smoothed her shirt down with her free hand. In the mirror, she immediately appeared to be somewhat thinner. The roll of fat that bulged over her jeans was pulled in and smoothed out. That reminded her of what she once had. When she could no longer hold her breath, she released the air along with her stomach, sending it back over her jeans.

"I'll definitely need my Spanx tonight," Yolanda said.

"Honey, you look beautiful," Ryan said.

Standing behind her, he straightened his tie in the mirror.

"You're my husband. That's what you're supposed to say," she said.

She pouted her lips. Ryan pulled her to him, and she turned to kiss him.

"You have to get ready. We're going to be late," he said.

"I'm not going. I don't have a dress that I can fit right now. I'm too fat. Look at me."

"Stop talking about yourself like that. You're gorgeous. Stop being so hard on yourself."

He turned her around to face him.

"This pudge reminds me of her," she told him. "As much as I want to get rid of it, I want it to stay to remind me of my Ryanna."

"I miss her too. We have to cherish the time that we were allowed to spend with her."

"Yeah, sure. Everyone thinks they know the right things to say to me. Words can never ease my pain." She sighed as she turned back around to face the mirror.

Still standing behind her, Ryan watched her staring at her reflection. She was expressionless, appearing to look past the images in the mirror.

"Let's change the subject. I don't want to upset you."

He waited for a response from her but didn't get one.

"You are still the most beautiful woman in the world to me," he continued. "So, what you aren't as small as you were before. Some men like their woman with a little meat on their bones," he said.

She laughed. "Yes, *some* meat, not this much. I'm only one meal away from being as big as Jayda was before she had surgery. I think that's what I'm going to do."

"You're nowhere near as big as Jayda was, and you're not having surgery."

Ryan walked away, leaving Yolanda standing there, and disappeared into his walk-in closet. He came out with a garment bag.

"What is that?" she asked.

"Open it."

She slowly zipped down the garment bag to find a black dress. She pulled the dress out of the bag and examined it.

"Do you like it?" he asked.

She checked the dress size, then placed it against her body and looked in the mirror.

"Yes. How did you know my size?"

"I looked at the sizes of your other dresses in your closet. So, I guessed you would need one size larger."

"It's beautiful. Thank you."

"You're going to be the most beautiful woman in the building. Nice and thick, just the way I like it."

"Really, Ryan? That's what all you white boys say."

"I'm just trying to make you laugh. You know I'm not your typical white boy, am I?"

He gyrated his hips.

"You're so nasty. I'll choose you every time, baby."

She leaned in for a kiss, but he moved back.

"You know I don't like those white boy comments, right?" Ryan asked, looking serious.

"Relax. Don't take everything so seriously all of the time," Yolanda responded.

Without saying another word, Ryan walked out of the bedroom. Yolanda knew he was upset. Instead of running behind him, she decided to get dressed. Their interaction with each other was becoming more and more awkward. They continuously danced around the subject of Ryanna. Yolanda would often shut down whenever the two of them had a conversation about her death. She suffered from depression and guilt. She also required medication to function.

They were advised during therapy that it was best to discuss what happened rather than avoid it. Yolanda and Ryan both attended grief counseling and had taken advantage of receiving spiritual guidance from their pastor. Most of the advice they received worked, and other times, it didn't.

When Yolanda and Ryan arrived at the hotel, the deejay was playing songs from the oldies but goodies list—her mother and father's generation of music. It was the first family or social event she had attended since the funeral. The special occasion was her father's retirement. Yolanda immediately looked for Shay and Jayda. As she scanned the room, she saw Nicole standing with their mother. Her mother held a glass in her hand that Yolanda was sure she hadn't taken one sip from. She wanted to speak to her mother, but she decided to wait until Nicole no longer guarded her.

"Is that my baby girl?" Bernard asked.

He walked over to Yolanda and Ryan, surprising them both.

"Hey, daddy," she said.

She hugged her father and nestled into his chest. He held on to her.

"How are you doing, son?" he asked Ryan.

"I'm hanging in there," Ryan replied.

Bernard offered Ryan his hand while he still had Yolanda in his arms. Ryan shook his hand. Yolanda let go of her father, and he took a good look at her.

"You sure look beautiful. Ryan, you are one lucky guy," he said.

"Yes, I am," Ryan said.

Bernard twirled Yolanda around. She laughed and smiled.

"Are your friends coming tonight?" Bernard asked.

"Yes, they're supposed to be here. I was just looking for them," she told him.

Just then, Yolanda's mother, Lauren, walked over to them. She hugged both Ryan and Yolanda.

"Hello. I'm so glad to see the two of you. How are you doing?" she asked, giving Yolanda a sympathetic look.

"As good as I could be, but I'm here to celebrate my father's retirement. He worked hard for so many years for us. Thanks, mom and dad, for everything," Yolanda said.

"We just did our jobs as parents," Lauren said.

"Well, you two enjoy yourselves tonight. I have a whole room to entertain," Bernard said, then grabbed Lauren's hand and moonwalked to the dance floor.

They both laughed.

"Do you want a drink?" Ryan asked.

"Yes, please. I'll find us a table," Yolanda said.

Ryan kissed Yolanda and went to the bar. Yolanda spoke to a few people she passed on her way to an empty table. She took off her coat and placed it on the back of the chair. After taking a seat, she searched the room again for her friends.

"Glad to see you could make it," someone said from behind her.

Yolanda rolled her eyes but didn't turn around.

Nicole walked around the table to where she could face Yolanda.

"You look nice," Nicole commented.

"Thanks," Yolanda replied dryly, still not making eye contact with her.

"This thing between us has to end one day, especially with all that has happened with…" she started.

"Don't you dare speak her name. You didn't even know her. You only saw her twice. Some aunt you were," Yolanda said.

"So, you're still holding grudges. I've apologized for not being there, but you know why I didn't come around. It's about you and me. You've been upset with me for years now. When are you going to get over it?"

"Get over it? How can you just get over the fact that your only sister had you kicked out of your parents' house at the age of seventeen? Who does such evil?" Yolanda said.

"You brought drugs into mom and dad's house. You knew better. I only suggested they put you out because we all could've gone to jail."

"Are you serious? It was one joint, and it wasn't even mine."

"Yeah, it was your drug-dealing boyfriend's drugs, right?"

"Get out of my face."

"No. We are going to deal with this once and for all."

"You heard her. Get out of her face," Shay said, taking off her coat and placing it on the table. "Don't make me act a fool up in here."

"You don't scare me. This is my sister, and we're talking about something personal. If anyone is going to leave, it's you," Nicole said.

"Nicole, we don't have anything to talk about. Nothing has changed between us," Yolanda said.

"Fine, I'll leave you alone for now," Nicole said, then walked away.

They watched her walk over to Bernard and start dancing with him.

"Hey, what's going on over here?" Ryan asked.

He handed Shay and Yolanda glasses of champagne.

"It looked like you and Nicole were having a heated conversation," Ryan said as he rubbed Yolanda's shoulders.

"Is that why you took an hour to get a glass of champagne?" Yolanda said sarcastically.

"Hey, I'm not getting in the middle of a catfight. I'll wait until the dust clears, and then I'll sweep in to rescue you," Ryan said jokingly.

Shay and Yolanda rolled their eyes at him. Ryan shrugged his shoulders and laughed.

"Oh, look. There's Jayda," Ryan said.

He waved his hand in the air to get her attention. Spotting them, Jayda sashayed over to their table wearing a huge smile.

"Nice that you can join us. Where's your Boaz?" Shay asked sarcastically.

"I'm single tonight, ladies and gents," Jayda said.

"Do you want some champagne?" Ryan asked her.

"Sure, if your wife doesn't mind," Jayda said.

"I see you're on one tonight. I don't want to see you bailing out on us as soon as Khalil calls. You're talking like a big girl now, but let's see how long that lasts," Yolanda said.

"And on that note, I'll be right back, ladies," Ryan said.

"Khalil? Who's that?" Jayda said, feigning ignorance.

"What's going on? You came prancing in here with that fake smile you have when you're stressed. I see through you and that makeup. Did you take him back?" Yolanda asked.

"No! Of course not," Jayda responded.

"You're lying. I knew you were going back to him, but I didn't want to be the one to say anything," Shay said, finishing her champagne.

"Ladies, he is the least of my problems right now. I pressed charges against him. He crossed me for the last time," Jayda said.

"You finally called the police on him for knocking you upside your head?" Shay asked.

Shay and Yolanda waited for Jayda's response.

"Well?" Shay said.

Jayda leaned in closer towards her friends, who, in turn, leaned in towards her.

Jayda glanced around quickly and said, "I put him on ice. It's over. They have a warrant for his arrest. I guess his momma tipped him off when the police came looking for him. I changed my locks and blocked him from calling or texting me."

"No, you didn't. I give it two days before he's back in your bed," Shay said.

"He played me for a fool for the last time. He had a baby on me. You would go against the grain on this," Jayda snarled. "You could at least support me."

"It's not that. I just know how much you love him. He's done some horrible things to you, but I know this baby is a different kind of hurt. I'll support you, friend," Shay said.

Jayda smiled. "Thanks, Shay."

"But I still put money on it that he's back in your bed in two days," Shay said jokingly.

"Shut up! You don't make the best decisions either," Jayda said.

"Good for you. You need to move on from Khalil. One day, he's going to kill you," Yolanda said, taking a swallow from her drink.

"Right! That's what I was saying. But she's not going to get mad at you for saying it," Shay stated.

"How could you say something like that? We fight sometimes, but no one is going to get killed. The both of you are really tripping," Jayda said.

"I know you are the fixer in this triangle, but even you have your issues. You accept that Khalil cheats on you, abuses you, and in light of current events, he had a baby on you," Yolanda said.

"Let's be clear; we all have issues. All I wanted was support from my girls, and this is what I get?" Jayda asked.

"Pipe it down. We all need a little truth sometimes. You never seem to hold back when you give us the truth. So, sit in it, like you tell us," Shay said.

"Ain't that the truth. Jayda will read your ass from here to hell. Won't she?" Yolanda said.

"Yes, you will. That's why I love you," Shay said, putting her arm around Jayda.

"That's why I love y'all because y'all don't hold back on me either," Jayda said.

Yolanda laughed and said, "The secrets we hold."

Yolanda tapped her glass with a fork, attracting more attention than intended. She rolled her eyes at the onlookers.

"Tonight, I wanted to share the good news with you. I am no longer under investigation, thanks to Jamison. Ryanna's death has been ruled an accident; a tragic accident. They are not going to press charges against me. They said I suffered enough with the loss of my daughter. They are so right," Yolanda said.

"Thank God that is over," Jayda said.

"Yeah, now you can move on," Shay said.

There was something in Shay's voice that made Yolanda feel uncomfortable. She wasn't sure if she was being sarcastic or if she meant what she was saying. Either way, she noticed.

"There's something else we need to discuss. I couldn't talk to you about this over the phone. Let's go to the ladies' room," Yolanda said.

Shay and Jayda looked at each other strangely before all three ladies stood up and walked to the bathroom. Once inside, Yolanda checked the stalls to be sure no one was inside.

Almost in a whisper, Yolanda asked, "Have either of you seen or talked to Koshie yet?"

Shay placed a hand on her stomach, and Jayda started to pace.

"Well, have you?" Yolanda asked.

"We swore to never speak of her. Why are you bringing this up now?" Shay asked.

"She's home. She didn't get life in prison, Shay. You knew she was coming home one day," Yolanda said.

"No, I haven't seen or talked to her, but she sent me a friend request," Shay said.

"Me too," Jayda said.

"Neither of you thought to say anything?" Yolanda said.

"I dreaded this day," Jayda said.

"Do you think she knows what we did?" Yolanda asked.

"Who knows?" Shay responded.

"I don't think so. If she did, she would have made it known by now," Jayda said.

"If I could go back and change what happened that night, I would," Yolanda expressed.

"We all would. That was fucked up," Jayda said.

"We haven't talked about this in years, and I don't want to talk about it now. She was locked up all those years for something she didn't do. That wasn't right," Shay said.

There was a brief silence.

"If any of you run into her, just be careful. I think she knows something. I can just feel it," Yolanda said.

"If that was the case, don't you think she would've exposed you by now?" Jayda asked.

"No, not if she wants revenge," Yolanda said.

"Knowing Koshie, she would've struck by now. I'm still here, and so are you two. We are still standing. She would've killed Yolanda if she knew she was the one driving that night. Period," Shay said.

"That's what I'm saying. We've been acting like she's a plague," Jayda said.

"She is the plague. She is my hell and yours too. You both had a hand in what we did," Yolanda reminded them.

Shay and Jayda looked at Yolanda strangely.

"Don't look at me like that. What do you think would happen if we were exposed? I'm going to make sure that never happens. If anyone sees or speaks to Koshie, tell me. The game has changed since she's home. If she shows up, just act normal. Don't act all nervous and shit like you have something to hide," Yolanda told them.

"Okay, let's not talk about this again. Just keep each other informed on current events involving Koshie. Just thinking about the past makes me sick," Shay said.

Chapter 14

Yes, honey! Get it, Shay!" Yolanda shouted.

Shay was in the soul train line, breaking down the robot. The guests clapped and danced as she made her way through the line. When she finished, the next person came down doing the wop.

"I think your girl has had five too many drinks," Shay whispered into Jayda's ear.

"I know. I tried to take that last glass from her, and she damn near took my arm off," Jayda said.

"We need to keep an eye on that one. I think she is spiraling out of control and trying to hide it," Shay said.

Yolanda was talking with a woman who she seemed to wish that she wasn't. She smiled and looked away from her.

"Yeah, I agree. We got her," Jayda said.

It was Yolanda's turn for the soul train line. She got separated from her friends because in her drunkenness, she found it necessary to carry on long conversations with those around her. Just as Yolanda stepped out, the song changed to *Flashlight*. She began to clap her hands and stomp her feet offbeat.

"Oh, yeah! Flashlight!" she began to sing.

She started gyrating and jerking her arms, head, and upper body in unrecognizable moves. The horror on everyone's face and lack of cheering made it clear that someone needed to step in and save her. Shay danced over to her, grabbed her hands, and danced with her to the end of the line. Once there, they joined the others in cheering on the next person.

"Hello, Jayda," a deep voice said from behind her.

She was in mid-stroke with Shay as they were doing *the butt*. Jayda didn't let that stop her from executing the perfect rendition of the dance. She slowly turned around, not missing a beat as she wound her hips and arched her back. She turned to find a dapper Jamison dressed in a black tuxedo and looking more handsome than the last time she had seen him. She stood up straight and fixed her dress.

"Oh, hello, Jamison. I didn't expect to see you here," Jayda said.

"I was invited by Yolanda and her parents. I thought she would've told you that I was coming. If you would've returned my calls, I could've told you myself," Jamison said.

"I've been really busy lately. I didn't get around to returning your call. I'm sorry about that."

"I understand. I know you're also in a relationship. I probably shouldn't have expected so much." He looked around the room. "Is he here with you? I don't want to get you in trouble or anything."

Jayda smiled and replied, "No, I'm single. I'm not here with anyone."

"Are you single just for tonight? I've heard about you and your man."

"I'm available. What about you? Where is your date?" she asked, looking around the room.

"I'm with her right now. Honestly, I came here to see you."

"Is that right?"

"Yes, Jayda. I was hoping to take you out. Yolanda filled me in on your situation, and if it's not too much right now, I'd like to get to know you better."

"What can I say? Yolanda has told you my entire life story. If there is anything else you need to know, I can fill you in," she said sarcastically.

"Come on. A guy has to do his homework, right?"

"I guess I need to do my homework too."

Walking closer to her, Jamison took her hand as the music changed. An old school slow jam played through the speakers. They stepped closer, embraced each other, and stared into each other's eyes. The sounds of the horns and piano led their bodies as they moved as one. Jayda laid her head on his chest, closed her eyes, and took in his scent. Jamison rested his face in the crease of her neck and held her close. She enjoyed the dance, having never experienced one like that before. It was almost magical. She didn't know Jamison well, but she felt their souls communicate with each other.

She told him how she didn't want to be hurt again; he told her that he would never hurt her. For the first time in a very long time, she felt safe in a man's arms other than her father's. Part of her wanted to pull back and retreat to what she knew, but she knew she had to take a chance. She promised herself that when the dance was over, she would give Jamison a chance.

When the song was over, she didn't want the dance to end. It was perfect. She slowly opened her eyes and lifted her head. Their eyes met as she wiped away a tear.

"Wow," she said.

"Yeah, that was amazing. Did you feel that?" he asked.

"I did."

They stared deeply into each other's eyes. Right when he moved in for a kiss, Yolanda rudely interrupted them.

"That's my girl! You better get your man!" Yolanda screamed over the music.

Ryan was right behind her. He apologized and tried to get Yolanda to go with him. She resisted by yanking away from him.

"Oh, my God. She's drunk," Jayda said.

She walked towards Ryan and Yolanda. Jamison followed her. When she reached Yolanda, Ryan walked away.

"Surprise! Now, this is a man. This is the kind of man that you should be with, not Khalil," Yolanda said.

"Thank you, but I need you to come over here with me," Jayda told her.

Yolanda still resisted.

"See, Jamison. I told you she's smart," Yolanda said.

"Yes, she is. So, maybe you should listen to her," Jamison said.

Jayda took Yolanda by the hand and led her back to their table, where Ryan sat looking disgusted. She forcibly sat Yolanda down in her seat and stood over her. Yolanda reached for a glass on the table that held a small amount of wine.

"No more for you," Ryan said, moving the glass out of her reach.

"What's wrong with you?" Yolanda asked.

"I think you had enough to drink tonight," he said.

"Who are you, my father? My father is over there," she said, pointing towards the dance floor.

"Calm down. Drink this," Shay said, handing Yolanda a bottled water.

"I don't want this! Give me a real drink!" Yolanda shouted.

She threw the bottled water across the table, knocking over and breaking a glass on a plate. The chaos got the attention of Nicole.

Scowling at them, she rushed over to the table and said, "What's going on over here?"

"We're about to leave," Ryan said, standing to his feet.

He reached for Yolanda's hand that remained on the table.

"It's time for all of us to leave. Sorry about that, Nicole," Jayda said.

Yolanda stood to her feet but was wobbly. Ryan held her up. She placed her head on his chest and began to cry. As they left the ballroom, Shay grabbed their things and followed them.

"What's going on with her? She's losing it," Nicole commented.

"She's not losing it. She's still grieving, just handling it badly. We got her, don't you worry," Jayda said, then turned to walk away.

Nicole grabbed her by the arm. Jayda yanked away.

"That's what I'm worried about. You and that sack-chasing friend of yours could've gotten my sister arrested. You think you two are all she has. Don't forget she has real family. Real family that loves her and is here for her. We will always have her best interest at heart," Nicole said.

"You're right about one thing. She does have a loving mother and father. As for you, if she doesn't even acknowledge you, why should I?" Jayda shot back.

"Blood is thicker than whatever you think you have with my sister. In the end, family will always be there. You wish you could be me, but you will never be connected like we are. So, you and that other one keep on playing fake sister with her. It's kind of cute," Nicole said.

Jayda wanted to smack the smug look off Nicole's face. She dropped her clutch on the floor, but before she could raise her hand, Shay grabbed it.

"Time to go. This bitch ain't worth it," Shay said as she kneeled and picked up Jayda's clutch from the floor.

"One day, bitch," Jayda said, trying to pry her hand loose.

"But not today. Now get the hell out of here," Nicole said.

"Ladies, I think we should call it a night," Jamison said.

He took Jayda by the hand and guided Shay towards the door.

Shay looked back and said, "I just saved your ass from a good ole ass whooping."

Once Jayda, Shay, and Jamison were outside of the hotel, Jayda screamed out of frustration. Ryan and Yolanda came out of the hotel shortly after them. Yolanda was crying and clinging to Ryan.

"Honey, what's wrong?" Shay asked.

"I'm sorry. I just miss her so much," Yolanda sobbed.

"Watch her while I get the car," Ryan said as he crossed the street to the parking lot.

Shay hugged her. Jayda was so mad that she didn't want to console her friend after ruining her perfect night, but she did. She joined them in a group hug.

"It's going to get better, but not like this. You've upset Ryan," Shay told Yolanda.

"I know. He hates me anyway. I can tell. He can't hide it," she said.

Shay and Jayda looked at each other in surprise. They had never heard her say anything like that before.

"Ryan loves you. He wouldn't be here if he didn't," Jayda said.

"He's going to leave me. I know it. I don't blame him. I couldn't be with me either," Yolanda said.

"Stop it!" Jayda said, grabbing Yolanda by the shoulders.

"No! You stop it! You don't have a clue how I'm feeling. You will never understand because you just can't relate. You're no better than I am. You killed your baby too. At least I did by accident. You intentionally killed your baby, for a man nonetheless," Yolanda blurted out.

Yolanda yanked away from her and stumbled towards the car as it pulled to the curb. Jayda watched as Ryan tried to help Yolanda into the vehicle. She looked at Shay and Jamison, who wore a face of shock at what Yolanda said. Hurt and embarrassed, Jayda started walking down the sidewalk. Shay and Jamison followed her.

"She's drunk. She didn't mean it," Shay said.

Jayda kept walking and didn't respond.

"Can I take you ladies home?" Jamison asked.

"Jayda needs a ride home," Shay said.

"No, I'll ride with you. Jamison, thanks for the dance. I'll call you tomorrow, I promise," Jayda said, finally stopping.

Shay kept walking to allow Jayda and Jamison privacy.

"I'm sorry the night ended the way that it did. I know Yolanda is going through something tough, so you need to be patient with her. She may never get over the loss of her child," Jamison said. "She's angry with herself. She really didn't mean those things."

"What she said about me—"

"I don't care about that," Jamison said, interrupting her. "You and I will get to know each other, and whatever you want to tell me about yourself, you can do that. I'm not going to judge you. Don't let what I do for a living fool you into thinking that I've never made bad decisions because I have. I just started making better decisions."

"See, you and I have something in common. You know just what to say," Jayda said.

"Yeah, we do," Jamison said.

Jamison pulled Jayda close to him. He hugged her, then kissed her. She didn't resist him. Instead, she passionately kissed him back.

"I'm going to walk you two to your car and then you are going to call me when you get home. Deal?" Jamison asked.

"Deal? Who says that?" Shay asked. "Come on, Jamison. We served her to you all buttered on a plate, and you're coming at her with that lame game?" Shay said.

"He's not lame at all. Deal," Jayda said, kissing him again.

Shay laughed. "Y'all so corny. But I love it."

On the way home, Jayda checked in with Ryan. He said Yolanda was asleep. She wanted to talk to her, but knew it was best to wait until the next day. She was very concerned for her friend. After the things she said about her relationship with Ryan, she wanted to know what was going on.

When Jayda got home, she thought about what her friend said about her. Yolanda's words were harsh but true. She reflected on the relationship she had with Khalil. It was a good relationship in the beginning but had turned volatile. She loved him, but she knew he didn't love her the same. She also knew she deserved better and could do better. Jamison was better. Just like a schoolgirl, thinking of Jamison put a smile on her face.

Chapter 15

Jayda rolled onto her back and kicked the covers off of her as her house phone rang. She had ignored it and remained asleep after it rang the two times before. She planned to sleep in after a long night out. She didn't call Jamison as promised and was eager to call him later. Instead of calling, she had sent him an "I'm home" text. She was too embarrassed to call him. She didn't want him asking her the hard questions that she really didn't want to answer.

Since it seemed the caller wasn't going to give up on reaching her, she stretched over and answered the phone.

"Hello!" she yelled into the receiver.

"Good morning. This is Officer Bland."

"Oh, good morning. I'm sorry about that. I was sleeping," Jayda said, sitting up on the bed. She was pleased to hear from him.

"Have you heard from or seen Khalil?" he inquired.

"No, I haven't. Isn't he locked up by now?" she asked.

"No. We haven't been able to locate him. He knows we are looking for him. Hopefully, he turns himself in."

"Really? He's never going to do that. I haven't heard from him since you all went to his mother's house. He called and threatened me, but I haven't heard anything from him since then."

"We are doing all that we can to locate him. You have a protective order in place, so—"

"A protective order isn't going to protect me from him," Jayda interjected. "I think he's laying low so he can just pop up and kill me or something!"

"Please calm down. I'm doing everything that I can. We have a warrant for his arrest. We're going to get him. I promise."

"Look, just get him," she said and hung up.

Just then, the doorbell rang.

"Who the fuck is it now?" she said.

She grabbed her robe and looked out the window. There was a delivery truck outside. She slowly opened the door after removing the three locks she had installed.

"Good morning. I have a delivery for you," an older man said.

He looked to be in his sixties, and from the huge smile plastered on his wrinkled face, he seemed to enjoy his job.

"Thank you," she said, taking the bouquet of chocolate-covered fruit and card.

"You're welcome and enjoy," he said, tipping his baseball cap at her.

He walked back to his truck, eager for his next delivery.

She smiled as she thought about Jamison and the cute gesture. He put a smile on her face. After closing and locking the door, she placed the vase of chocolate-covered fruit down on the table and sat on the sofa to open the card. She put her feet up on the coffee table and sat back. She opened the card and read it.

I'm sorry, baby. Please drop the charges. I can't go back.

I love you, Khalil

Jayda jumped up from the sofa. Grabbing the vase and the card, she ran into the kitchen and slammed them into the trash can. Then she tied the bag and took it out back to the dumpster. On her way back inside, she was grabbed from behind.

"Don't scream," Khalil said.

He held her in a headlock with one hand over her mouth. She attempted to get loose, but he held her tightly. She tried to scream, but he tightened his grip around her neck. The enormous amount of strength he inflicted on her at that moment convinced her that he could and would break her neck.

"Don't be stupid. Now walk," he said, forcing her into the house.

Once inside, he let her go and closed the door behind them. Jayda tried to run, but he grabbed her and pushed her against the counter. She frantically looked around the kitchen for something she could get her hands on to defend herself. She eased towards the counter, but he was on her. He grabbed her by the back of her neck and dragged her to the bedroom. She cried from the pain he caused from squeezing her neck.

"Khalil, please don't hurt me," she begged.

He threw her on the bed.

"Khalil, please don't hurt me," he mocked.

"You don't have to do this. I'll drop the charges. I swear," she cried.

"Why did you press charges against me in the first place? I told you I was sorry!"

"I know, I know. I made a mistake, but I can fix it."

"I love you, Jayda. I don't want to hurt you, but you fucked up. I can't even go to my momma's house. The police are watching the house. How do you plan on fixing this?"

"I can fix it. I can call and have them drop the charges."

"How?!"

"I'll tell them I lied. I'll say I did it to myself. I'll tell them anything you want me to. Please don't hurt me!"

"I could've done anything to you, but I didn't. I had to grab you like that so you wouldn't scream and run," he said.

He sat down on the bed and dropped his head.

"I'm sorry I hit you. I'm sorry I cheated on you. I'm sorry for everything. But I love you. After all of this, I'm a changed man," he sobbed.

Jayda didn't move. She watched Khalil shed tears. She had never seen him cry before. Never. Yet, he was crying for her. She didn't know if she should hit him over the head with the lamp or console him.

"You know I've been through a lot in my life. I'm still learning from my mistakes. I watched my dad beat my momma's ass every day. I know it ain't right, but I'm fighting my demons every day," he said.

Jayda slowly crawled on the bed towards Khalil, whose back was facing her, and placed a hand on his shoulder. He turned towards her with tears in his eyes.

"This relationship has to be over," she gently said.

"Why? I'm never going to hit you again. You got what you wanted. You called the police on me and everything."

"What do you mean by I got what I wanted? I didn't call the police to scare you into keeping your hands to yourself. This wasn't a scare tactic."

Khalil stood to face Jayda. "So, you wanted to send me back to jail? You wanted to put another black man behind bars?"

"You are abusive. I've let you get away with it too many times. I don't deserve for any man to put his hands on me. That isn't love. I deserve more. I'm done, Khalil."

He began pacing the floor.

"Please leave. I don't feel safe with you around," Jayda told him.

She sat on the edge of the bed. Just in case he decided to lunge at her, she could defend herself.

"Come on, Jayda! Who's going to want you? Look at you," he said, gesturing toward her.

"Look at you! You're a punk! You're a punk because you like to hit women. That's pretty low, don't you think?" she said.

"You're not that hot. I only talked to you because you had a pretty face and were a nurse. I thought you had a nice body until I saw you with your clothes off."

"You didn't have a problem with my body when you were fucking me. Now that I don't want you anymore, you have so much to say. Too bad for you that my confidence is way up."

Jayda couldn't believe what he was saying. All of her life, she heard people tell her that she had a pretty face and was smart. That meant her large size wasn't going to help her in any way. She weighed over three hundred pounds before her weight loss surgery. Now that she had lost the weight, she received many compliments from the same people who avoided saying anything about her weight before. Now she had beauty, body, and brains. She knew she would have extra skin after losing so much weight, but with the risk of possible complications, she opted not to have the skin removal surgery. Instead, she wore Spanx, dressed to the nines, and loved herself.

The sound of footsteps in the house startled them both. They looked towards the bedroom door. Khalil pointed his gun in the direction of the sound.

"Who is that?" he asked.

"I don't know," she said.

Suddenly, Officer Bland and two other officers appeared, charging in with their guns drawn and shouting commands.

Jayda threw her hands in the air and didn't move.

"Drop the gun!" Officer Bland shouted.

Khalil slowly lowered the gun and carefully placed it on the floor. Obeying the officer's commands, Khalil put his hands in the air. Jayda tried to process what was happening as things were happening so quickly.

"I didn't do nothing to her. Tell them I didn't hurt you," Khalil said.

Officer Bland recited the Miranda rights and placed Khalil under arrest without further incident. Jayda watched as it all unfolded in her bedroom. She was confused as to why Officer Bland and the other two officers were in her home. One of the police officers put away his weapon and walked over to Jayda. He reached for her hands and slowly lowered them to her side.

"You're safe now. Are you hurt? Do you need medical assistance?" he asked.

"No, I'm not hurt," she stuttered.

She stood to her feet with the officer's assistance.

"Get him out of here," Officer Bland said, shoving Khalil over to another officer.

"I want a lawyer!" Khalil shouted as he was being led out. "Tell them I didn't do anything! Jayda, you said you were going to drop the charges!"

Jayda placed her face in her hands and exhaled.

"You will have plenty of time to contact your lawyer when we get to the precinct," the officer said.

Jayda and Officer Bland followed the officers who were escorting Khalil out of the house. She followed them to the front door. She watched as Khalil was placed in the police car and driven away. She felt both relief and fear as Khalil was finally taken into custody. She didn't know what the repercussions were going to be once he was behind bars. He was a nasty person when he was angry, resulting in violence. The one thing that stuck in her mind was something Khalil once said. The first time he slapped her, he told her, "Bitch, if you ever call the law on me and get me locked up, you know what I'm going to do to your ass when I get out."

She snapped back to reality when she heard Officer Bland's baritone voice say, "If you hadn't left your phone off the hook, I wouldn't be here right now. I heard your doorbell ring, and something told me to stay on the line. We've been sitting on your house for the last three days. Good thing because we were finally able to find him."

Jayda didn't immediately respond. She closed the front door to her home and took a seat on the sofa before she hit the floor.

"I know this is too much, but I need you to come down and give a statement about the event that occurred today," he said, taking a seat across from her.

Jayda finally spoke. "I didn't know I left the line open. I was so exhausted when you called. I was out late last night. I just wanted to go back to sleep. You're right. All of this is just too much. I need time to process all of this. Can I come down another day to give a statement?"

"I know this is tough, but we need you to cooperate if we are going to keep him in custody," he told her.

"Please, give me a couple of hours. I really need to wrap my brain around all of this," she said.

After Officer Bland was confident that he had convinced her how important it was for her to meet with him sooner rather than later, he left. Now that she was alone, she had time to think. Usually, she would call Yolanda to talk it out. However, after the things she said to her the night before, she decided not to call her. She didn't want to call Shay just yet, either. She felt Shay would only confirm her fears of retaliation from Khalil. She thought calling Jamison would be a better idea. He was an attorney and could give her legal advice as well as support. Although she didn't call him the night before, she felt he wouldn't hold it against her. Her text still showed that she thought of him.

After she called Jamison and filled him in on what happened, he offered to come to her house and escort her to the police station. At the station, Jayda gave a statement with Jamison's help. She was advised to get a restraining order and to report any contact from Khalil. After they left the station, Jamison took her back home.

Jamison pulled in front of Jayda's house and turned off the engine.

"Are you in a hurry? I could really use some company right now," Jayda asked while rubbing her temples.

"I didn't have much planned for the day. I guess I could keep you company," Jamison said.

They smiled at each other and exited the car. Jamison walked slowly behind Jayda, allowing her to lead the way. She opened the door and quickly sat down on the sofa. Jamison closed and locked the door behind him. He looked around before taking a seat.

"So, you don't have a security system?" Jamison asked.

"No, but I will be getting one installed as soon as I can," Jayda replied.

She kicked off her shoes and began to massage her foot.

"That's a good idea. You're a single woman, and with everything that has been going on, it would be smart to protect yourself. Do you have a gun in the house?"

"I have a gun that my father gave me when I moved out. I haven't touched that thing since I moved here though. I don't like guns," she said.

Jamison sat down beside her. "Let me do that for you. I've been told I have that touch."

He reached for her foot. She reluctantly placed her foot in his lap.

"Lay back and relax."

Jayda rested her head on a pillow on the arm of the sofa. Jamison proceeded to massage her feet gently, applying just the right amount of pressure where needed. Jayda moaned as she felt relief by his hands.

"That feels good. Who taught you how to give such a good foot massage?" Jayda asked. "Oh, never mind. I don't want to ruin the moment."

Jamison laughed.

After her foot massage, Jayda sat up, feeling much better.

"Thanks for taking the time to help me with all of this." She reached for her purse. "I'm not sure what your hourly fee is, but I can pay you."

"No. There's no fee. I'm just helping out a friend. Believe it or not, I know what you are going through. I've been where you've been," he said.

"Oh, really? What do you mean?" she asked.

"I'm a survivor of domestic violence too," he leaned in and whispered.

"Wow. I've never met a man who admitted to being a survivor of domestic violence. You hear about those things, but you never see the faces of the men who have experienced it. Thank you for admitting that to me. That means a lot."

"I'm a man who stands in my truth. Being a domestic violence survivor doesn't make me any less of a man. I know that now, but I did struggle with it in the beginning. That's why it took me so long to get out of the marriage with my ex-wife. I didn't want anyone to know what was happening behind closed doors. To be honest, I was embarrassed."

"That's why so many men don't speak out? Women feel the same way. We feel ashamed too. I still feel that way," Jayda shared. "I thought people would think I was weak. I even lied to my best friends. But, for some reason, I kept taking him back."

"You kept taking him back because you loved him. I stayed because I loved her."

"You know my story, so tell me about yours. But only if you're comfortable telling me."

"The short version is that we met in law school. She was beautiful, intelligent, and at the top of her class. She came from a good family with a good upbringing. We dated and decided to move in together after graduation. After moving in together, I saw a different side of her. She became demanding and controlling. If I put the toilet paper on backwards, it would be war. After pressure from her father, she wanted to get married. I didn't want to get married at that time, but I did. At the same time, we were starting our careers. Life became stressful, and she became irate and violent. It started with name-calling and saying disrespectful things to me. Then she started throwing things at me and hitting me. I was raised never to hit a woman no matter what she does. So, it took that one time she hit me, and I found myself on the verge of hurting her. That's when I walked away from her and the marriage."

"I'm sorry you went through that. I wish people knew that domestic violence doesn't only happen to women. It can happen to men too."

"I guess this is what's going to bring us together. I know you're just getting out of a bad relationship. You're probably not ready yet, but I want to be here for you."

"You're right about that. I don't want anything serious right now. I'm still trying to get rid of Khalil for good. Besides, you already put me in the friend zone, remember?"

"Right. We must be friends before we can be anything else. Don't you think?"

"Yeah, sure. I think you're a nice guy. We have a few things in common. Let's see where it goes. Friends?" she asked, holding out her hand.

"Most definitely friends," he answered, shaking her hand in agreement.

Chapter 16

Shay sat on the edge of her bed, contemplating whether she should listen to the little devil on her left shoulder or the little angel that sat on her right shoulder. She twisted her hair between her two fingers and bounced her right leg up and down. She hadn't spoken to or heard from Rob in three days. She saw a local news report that he was at the local training camp and was negotiating a huge deal. Rob declined her offer to escort her to Yolanda's father's retirement party because he had plans. She had suspected he was dealing with another woman when he suddenly stopped sleeping over. Their time together was starting to diminish, leaving her with fewer opportunities to get pregnant.

After another failed attempt to reach him by phone for the fifth time, she'd had enough. She went to her bedroom closet and pulled down a shoebox from the corner of the top shelf. She removed the pair of high heels from the box. Underneath the shoes, and tissue paper, was an envelope. She pulled out the envelope, counted the bills inside, and set one thousand dollars to the side. After placing everything else back in the box, she put the box back in the closet where Jayda or Yolanda could find it if she needed more bail money.

Shay logged into an application on her cell phone and located Rob through the GPS cell phone locator. She had installed the same app on his phone weeks before without his knowledge. At any time, she could log in and get an accurate location on him. Just as she thought, he was at the same address that she had tracked him several times before—the same address he was at whenever he was missing in action.

She had to be his one and only in order to get him comfortable enough to catch him slipping. So far, she had been unsuccessful. She was going to cash in before anyone else had a chance to, no matter the cost. Since meeting him, she hadn't been involved with any other men. She couldn't risk a toss-up of who fathered her child. She needed the paternity test to be ninety-nine-point nine percent accurate.

Shay grabbed her car keys. Before walking out the door, she placed the money under the salt shaker on the kitchen table. She thought about her children but knew they would be fine with her parents for a night or two if things went left. She also knew what she was about to do wasn't smart. It wasn't her best judgement, but she didn't care. A dangerous game was in play. Her intention of using Rob to get a check was her ultimate goal, but she found she had developed feelings in the process. Those feelings resulted in her actions. He had good dick, good conversation, and made her a few promises once he made it. But he never put a label on their relationship. Label or not, she was riding out for him.

She left the house and jumped into her car. Flooring the gas, Shay sped down the street. As she followed the GPS, she fumed at the thought of what she may find once she arrived at her destination. Several scenarios ran through her mind and how she would respond. Each scenario began with Rob being caught with another woman and ended with her in handcuffs. She didn't see any other outcomes. When she was only two minutes away, she thought about turning the car around. Then she thought about Rob pleasing another woman while she waited for her turn.

"You don't have to answer your phone because I will pull up!" Shay shouted.

She turned the corner so fast that she felt the car almost tilt on two wheels. She looked down at her phone to confirm that she was heading in the right direction. The app provided the exact location of the phone. She pulled up to a small brick duplex in a neighborhood where she wouldn't rent a room. There weren't many homeowners left in the neighborhood, and properties were rented out to low-income families. Many yards didn't have grass, and the dilapidated houses were an eyesore. Not to mention, there were too many people hanging out on the streets and porches in the middle of the day.

She slowed down once she reached her destination. Shay checked her phone to confirm which door she was going to kick down, then she made a U-turn and parked on the street in front of the duplex. She left her car running for a quick exit. Dressed in black sweat pants, a black hoodie, and boots, she slicked her hair back into a tight bun and secured it with a rubber band. Exiting the car, she walked down the driveway toward the house. She wasn't sure which door was his, so she chose the first door on the right as her target.

As she got closer, she saw Rob's car parked alongside the house, confirming that she had picked the right door. Seeing his car angered her. She was infuriated that he would go out of his way to tuck his vehicle out of sight. This too confirmed that he was up to no good.

She walked up the three steps leading to the front door of the house. She turned towards the street, held on to the rusted metal railing, and started horse kicking the front door with her boots.

"Open the door! I know you're in there! Face me like a man!" she shouted as she kicked the door. "Climb out the pussy, Rob!"

Suddenly, the front door swung open while she was in mid-kick, knocking her off balance, but she recovered quickly. She let go of the rail and turned around to find a shirtless Rob standing there.

"What the fuck are you doing here?" he seethed.

He stuck his head out the door and looked around.

"Where's your bitch? Who the fuck lives here?" she asked, breathing heavily. "I've been calling your ass for days, and you're laid up with the next bitch."

"Your ass better calm down. Don't be coming around here with all that drama. Get the fuck out of here!"

"So, you're just going to act like I didn't just catch you cheating on me? I'm not going anywhere. Where is she?"

"Where is who?"

"Your bitch."

"Come on, Shay. You're out here doing the most for nothing. Look at you, embarrassing yourself like this. You're too old for this shit, ain't you?"

"Now you want to throw shots. I wasn't old when you were all up in this pussy, now was I?" She paused. "Yeah, that's what I thought."

She tried to get past him, but he blocked her and pushed her back.

"Stop!" he said.

"Why are you doing me like this? What did I do?" she asked.

"You didn't do anything until now. I told you before that I can't be associated with this type of shit. You have disrespected my mother and me. You can't just show up here and make false accusations, speaking on shit you don't know anything about. I'm done."

"Your mother? I don't believe that. If this is your mother's house, then where is she? I know you have a bitch up in there. She must be a punk. Because if it were me, I would've been out here!"

"You need to leave. I don't have to prove shit to you. Don't you need to go home to your kids or something? What type of mother are you?"

Shay took a step back at his harsh words. She knew he was speaking facts. His words stung and snapped her back to reality. Once again, she found herself allowing a man to drive her away from what was important—her children.

"Fuck you, Rob!" she said. "And fuck the hoe you have up in there too, punk bitch!"

She hawked and spat in his face. Rob wiped his face and quickly moved towards her.

"Hold on, son," a woman said, stopping him.

An older woman appeared in the doorway. She was clearly his mother as they bared the same resemblance.

"Young lady, I've listened to you curse and disrespect yourself long enough. I will not tolerate you provoking my son. What you just did was disgusting. I wouldn't fault him if he slapped you because you deserve it. But I raised him better than that. I don't know who you are or where he found you, but it's best that you crawl back to where you came from. Until you learn some respect, you're not welcome here."

"I'm sorry, ma'am," Shay said, lowering her head.

"Oh, so you do have manners," his mother said.

"I apologize. I thought he was with another woman. If I would've known this was your home, I would've never come here like this," she said.

"Well, I guess you and my son aren't as close as you thought," she said.

Shay watched as the woman walked away. She was ashamed of her actions. Rob didn't say a word. He closed the door, leaving her standing outside. When she turned around, she noticed a crowd had formed, and people were laughing at her. She lifted her head and walked back to her car. She felt like a fool. Her pride and her feelings were hurt. All she wanted was to go home and hide with a glass of wine to wash away her shame.

Chapter 17

Yolanda, wake up," Ryan said, lightly arousing Yolanda from her sleep.

Yolanda was still in her dress from the night before. Ryan managed only to remove her shoes once he was able to get her in the house and into the bed. Yolanda resisted, forcing him to strong-arm her a time or two. He never wanted to force her to do anything that she didn't want to do. In that instance, she was sloppy drunk. Therefore, he had to force her into the car and the house.

"Good morning," she said, rolling over on her side to see Ryan.

"It's one o'clock. I didn't want you to sleep the day away," he said.

"Why did you let me sleep in so late?" she asked.

She tried to sit up but eased her aching head back down on the pillow. She winced in pain and grabbed her forehead. Ryan handed her two aspirins and a glass of water.

"I figured you would be in bad shape once you were awake. Do you know how much you had to drink last night?" he asked.

Yolanda took the aspirins and a few sips of water.

"I don't remember. I didn't make a fool of myself, did I?" she asked.

"You were drunk. You said some mean things to Jayda last night."

"Oh, no. What did I say?"

"I'm not getting in the middle of that. You and Jayda can hash that out on your own. But I think you have some apologizing to do."

"I'm your wife. You're supposed to be on my side."

"That's why I'm staying out of it. I didn't survive the three of you by sticking my nose where it didn't belong."

"At least tell me how bad it was. I didn't call her fat or anything like that, did I?"

"No, but it was bad."

Yolanda's stomach flipped. She shot up and ran into the bathroom to empty her stomach. Ryan didn't follow her. He didn't hold her hair and offer her a towel as he had done many times before. Instead, he waited in the bedroom for her to return.

After a few minutes, Yolanda returned with her face in a towel. As she climbed back in the bed, she could feel Ryan's piercing eyes on her. She met his eyes, and the two of them stared at each other, each one communicating their true feelings without saying a word. They begged the other to understand. Ryan was the first to look away, hanging his head.

"What's wrong?" Yolanda asked.

Ryan lifted his head and gently placed a hand on her thigh.

"I don't know why you are choosing to let your life spiral out of control," he said softly.

"You've withdrawn from this marriage, and now you have turned into an alcoholic and pill popper.

Pain welled up in her chest. She swallowed hard. As she embraced the throbbing pain in her head, she felt she deserved it. She could only imagine the things she had said or even done the night before. Fortunately, for her, she had no recollection of the end of the night. She gritted her teeth in anticipation of what she knew was coming.

"I was thinking it's time for me to do something about this," he continued. "We both lost our only child. I know it doesn't seem like it, but I've been struggling with it too. My issues haven't been as evident as yours though. I think it's my fault that you are the way you are. Instead of being here for you, I have poured myself into my work. That took me away from you and the pain of losing Ryanna. I abandoned you and left you to deal with her death alone. For that, I am sorry."

Yolanda swallowed over the lump that had formed in her throat while he was speaking. She watched him as he waited for a response.

"I don't know what you want me to say to all of that. I guess we're both dealing with things the way that we feel we need to. You are dealing with things your way, and I'm dealing with things my way. There's nothing to apologize for," she told him.

"I think it's best that I take some time off work so I can be here with you more. At least until you decide to return to work. That way, you won't feel lonely, and maybe you will stop drinking so much."

"I get drunk to wash away the pain. I can't live like this, not with this pain. I can't breathe. The pain starts in the soles of my feet and rushes to my head. The thought of her is killing me. It takes the life right out of me. I want her back; I want to be with her. I don't see any other way out of this pain but to be with her. I'm coping by taking the medication, and the alcohol… well, I don't know what I would do without it."

"You'll survive just like me."

"Look at you. You're the strong one; I'm the weak one. You have all the answers just like Jayda, who I'm sure is out there somewhere letting Khalil fuck her and beat the shit out of her. Then she's going to come around here acting like her shit don't stink. I hate people like y'all. Too worried about face value."

"Jayda is your best friend, and I am your husband. Is that what you think of us? We are the ones who have been here for you through the thick and the thin. Jayda and Shay have been a blessing to you…to us. I consider them more like sisters than just friends. You should think more of those that are in your corner, Yolanda."

"Ryan, please. Just let me be. Let me wallow in this pain and misery. I'll come out soon enough."

"See, that's the problem! I'm not going to let you be like this. This isn't living. Do you think Ryanna would want you like this? Does this make you a proud mother?"

"I'm not a mother anymore. I failed at it. And I don't need you around here babysitting me. I want to be alone sometimes."

Yolanda turned away from Ryan. She didn't want to discuss her issues or the issues that he had with her. She wasn't feeling like herself and didn't want to say anything else that could hurt him.

"They say hurt people, hurt people. I see that's true. I'm not going to let this ruin us though. I love you, Yolanda. I love you so much that I'll let you fight me and scream at me until we get through this. I know we will get through this together."

"Let me help you," he continued. "You're depressed. We can see your doctor and change your prescription. What you're feeling could be a side effect of the medication you're taking. You don't want to die," he said.

"What else is there for me to do? Our baby girl is gone and I can't give you another one. I'm nothing now. I fucked us both. At least you can start over again. Find you someone who can give you children and go on to live your life with your new family," she said.

"Is that what you think? I'm with you. We are family. There isn't another woman that I love more than I love you. You will never have to worry about me leaving you, especially not because you can't have children. We decided to make that decision together. Who knew things would end up like this? But we will get through it."

Yolanda let out a slight chuckle.

"You make me sick. Always looking on the brighter side. I guess that's the white side of you. Shit is fucked up! We are fucked up in the game! We are not going to make it. You don't think I know you resent me now. Say it! I killed your daughter. Say it!"

"No, I'm not going to do this."

"Say it, Ryan! I killed her."

"You need help. I'm calling your mother."

"Call her for what? She can't help me."

Ryan proceeded to walk out of their bedroom. Yolanda got out of the bed and followed behind him.

"I'm sorry."

Ryan stopped in his tracks and turned around when he heard Yolanda start to cry.

"I don't know what's wrong with me. My emotions are all over the place."

"Come here," he said.

Yolanda walked over and hugged him tightly. Ryan held her in his arms as they both cried.

"I should've done more to help you. I knew you were depressed, but I didn't think you would ever try to hurt yourself," he said.

"I miss her," she said.

"I miss her too," he said.

Ryan kissed her on the cheek, where tears had fallen. He wiped away her tears with the back of his hand and left her in the bedroom alone. When Ryan left, Yolanda let out a cry. She wasn't pleased with herself. She longed for her daughter. She longed to see her again, hold her, and hear her cries. For her, nothing and nobody else mattered. She was angry with God and the world for the loss of her daughter. More so, she hated herself for being the cause of her daughter's death.

As she sobbed, her head pounded. Suddenly, she regretted binge drinking. She felt a temporary ceasefire by consuming enough alcohol to make her forget the majority of the night before, and now she was paying for it. Like any pain that she felt, she felt she deserved it and more. As her and Ryan's relationship seemed to unravel, she felt it was nothing that she could do about it. She didn't feel she deserved him. Him still loving her seemed unreal. She wanted him to blame her for what happened. Him leaving the marriage seemed to be more of the right thing to do.

Ryan hadn't closed the door behind him, and she could hear him banging around in the kitchen. She knew he was probably preparing her a meal. She didn't feel she deserved it at all. As much as she wanted to join him in the kitchen, she physically didn't feel up to it.

Rolling over on the bed, she picked up her cell phone from the nightstand and scrolled through the numerous missed calls and text messages from Shay and her mother. She took note that Jayda hadn't called or texted her. She decided to call Shay to gauge the temperature.

"Hey, YoYo!" Shay screamed into the phone.

Yolanda yanked the phone away as Shay's loud voice pierced her ear.

"Damn. Why are you so loud? My head is killing me," Yolanda said.

"That's what you get for acting a fool last night. What's going on with you, girl?"

"I'm trying to end this pain in my heart to be honest. But nothing seems to be working."

"Awww, YoYo. I know you're still grieving, but the bottle is only going to pause the pain. It won't stop it. Have you thought about going to grief counseling? You know Jayda or I will go with you. We all could use it."

"That sounds like a good idea. I have to do something before Ryan leaves me."

"What's going on between the two of you?"

"What goes on between couples who lose a child?"

"You haven't been yourself. You attacked Jayda last night, and you of all people got sloppy drunk."

"I guess you can tell me how to handle all of this. I've never felt pain or a void like this in my life. I don't feel that I deserve Ryan. I push him away, and he stays. I've been treating my only friends like shit, and you still love me."

"That's what friends are for. You're going to be alright. I know it's tough, but I don't want you to get too deep into a depression. It's going to be hard to pull yourself out. I'm not used to seeing you like this. You're always so strong and positive."

"No one would ever understand until they are in my shoes. It's easy for you to give me all of this good advice. I hear you, but I can't make any promises."

"I can respect that."

"Hey, have you spoken to Jayda today? I heard I owe her an apology for last night. You know I didn't mean whatever it is that I said."

"Yeah, sure you didn't. By the way, Jayda is going to have to tell you herself what happened to her today. You're not going to believe it!"

Yolanda sat up in the bed.

"What happened to her? Is she alright?"

"She's fine now that Jamison is with her."

"What happened, Shay?"

"Call her on the three-way. Let her tell you."

Yolanda made a three-way call to Jayda just as Ryan returned. He quietly entered the room with a plate of food and handed it to Yolanda, then he left her to her conversation.

"Hello? Hello?" Jayda said on the line.

"Hey. Shay is on the line too," Yolanda told her.

"Hey, ladies," Jayda said.

"You're not busy with Jamison, are you?" Shay asked.

"No, we're not busy," Jayda replied.

"I want to apologize for anything that I said last night. I was—" Yolanda began.

"Say no more. It's okay," Jayda said.

"Well, that was easy. You don't want me on my knees?" Yolanda asked.

"Come on. I accept your apology. We're good," Jayda said.

"Yes! Now that the two of you have hashed out your issues, tell YoYo what happened to you," Shay said.

"What happened?" Yolanda asked.

Jayda filled Yolanda in on the day's events. Shay commentated, filling in the gaps that Jayda seemed to miss. Yolanda couldn't believe that Khalil was finally behind bars for abusing Jayda. She really couldn't believe Jayda finally came clean about the nature of the abuse she had experienced with Khalil.

"I'm so glad you are safe and that you are with Jamison," Yolanda said.

"Yeah, he's awesome. He came right over when I called, and he went to the police station with me."

"My man Jamison. You can thank me for that," Shay said.

"Thank you, Shay!" Jayda and Yolanda said.

"Well, ladies, I've kept Jamison waiting. I'll call you later," Jayda said.

"Hey! We all need to get together soon. We have some things to talk about, ladies. Especially you, Yolanda," Shay said.

"Of course, we do. Just let me know when. I love y'all," Jayda said.

"Love you too," Yolanda said.

"Right back at you," Shay said.

Jayda ended the call. Shay and Yolanda remained on the phone.

"Did you hear that?" Shay asked.

"That's me eating. Ryan makes the best omelets," Yolanda said.

"Not you and all that smacking you've been doing. I'm talking about Jayda. She sounds different; she sounds happy. I think Jamison could be good for her," Shay said.

"He is a good man. I just hope she's really done with Khalil. She deserves better than that," Yolanda said.

"I think our girl got her groove back," Shay said.

"I hope she did. Now, if only I can get mine back," Yolanda said.

"You will, YoYo," Shay said.

"I hope so," Yolanda said.

"I have to check on these kids. They done got all quiet. Let me see what they're doing," Shay said.

"Okay, talk to you later," Yolanda said.

Yolanda felt exhausted from forcing herself to hide how she felt and putting on a smile for her friends. The temporary feeling of importance quickly faded away.

She walked into the bathroom and looked into the mirror that reflected her pain. She shifted her weight as she contemplated her next action. She believed death would bring her closer to her daughter. Only death could stop the pain in her heart and the longing she had for her daughter. Only death could kick down the doors of guilt.

She pulled a bottle from the medicine cabinet and read the label. It was the remaining pain medication prescribed to her from when she had her daughter. The irony brought tears to her eyes. She viewed it as a sign that she was doing the right thing.

"God, please forgive me," Yolanda whispered as she squeezed the bottle in her hand, then twisted off the cap.

Before she gave herself a chance to change her mind, she turned the bottle over in her hand, causing the pills to spill out into her palm. She turned on the water, closing her eyes, listened to the water flow. Then she filled a glass with water. She began to stuff the pills one by one into her mouth. She swallowed and gagged as she stuffed more pills into her mouth, washing them down with water.

"Yolanda?" Ryan called out.

Startled by his voice, she rushed to finish the pills. In haste, she dropped the glass in the sink, causing it to shatter. Ryan rushed into the bathroom.

"What are you doing?" he asked.

He looked at the remaining pills in her hand and the broken glass in the sink.

"What the hell are you doing?" he repeated.

Yolanda let the pills fall from her hand and said, "I don't want to do this anymore. I want to be with my baby girl."

"No, baby. Please don't do this to me!"

Ryan grabbed her and swept her mouth with his fingers. Yolanda choked.

"I want to be with her. I want that more than I want the breath in my body."

"Come on, baby! Don't do this to me!" Ryan said.

Ryan pulled her towards the toilet and placed two fingers down her throat. Yolanda began to vomit. He repeated his actions. After the third time, she went limp in his arms. He laid her on her side on the floor and rushed to call for help.

Chapter 18

Jayda arrived at the hospital. She found Ryan, Shay, and Yolanda's family in the lobby. She ran up to Ryan, who stood to greet her.

"What happened? Is she alright?" Jayda asked.

"I don't know. We are waiting for the doctor to come back," Ryan said.

"Oh, my God! Please let her be alright!" Jayda said.

Jayda looked around the waiting room.

"Hi, Mr. and Mrs. Clarkson. Hi, Nicole," she said.

Everyone greeted Jayda between their sobs.

"Ryan, what happened?" Jayda asked. "I was just on the phone with her, and then this happened."

"She swallowed a bunch of pills. She tried to kill herself," he informed her. "I can't believe this! I can't lose her too," he snapped.

"Why would she do something like this?" she asked.

Starting to feel weak, Jayda sat down in the nearest chair, which happened to be beside Nicole. Nicole put her arms around Jayda and hugged her.

"She's going to be alright. I know she is," Nicole said.

"You have the nerve to ask why?" Shay snarled.

Jayda looked up and saw Shay standing over her and Nicole.

"Look at you hugged up with that. Both of you should be ashamed of yourselves. Jayda, you know exactly why she's in here," Shay said.

Jayda stood to her feet to face Shay eye to eye.

"How am I the blame for what she did? I didn't make her do this? How dare you make such an accusation! What's the matter with you?" Jayda said.

"Ladies, please don't do this here," Ryan said.

He grabbed them both by the hand and moved them to another area away from the family.

"I need you both to be strong. Please don't turn on each other now. Yolanda is going to need both of you. So, whatever problem you two have, you need to fix it," Ryan said.

He let go of their hands and left them alone.

Jayda didn't understand why Shay treated her like the enemy and blamed her for Yolanda's condition. She was hurt by her words, especially in front of Ryan, Yolanda's parents, and Nicole.

"What the fuck do you think you're doing? Are you high or something?" Jayda asked.

"No, I'm not high. This is all your fault. If you hadn't tried to get her to lie about what happened to Ryanna, she wouldn't be here. She felt guilty. How could you do something like that to her? You were supposed to be a friend to her when she needed you most. A real friend would've told her to do the right thing the first time. She's not like you. She doesn't pretend to be something she's not. You're so busy trying to act like you're so perfect, but your life is just as fucked up as the rest of ours," Shay said.

"I've never said I was perfect. I did what I thought was best for her at that time. You know as well as I do that she isn't built for prison. I didn't want my friend to go away behind something I know was a mistake. This justice system is against us, and you know that. They would've made an example out of her," Jayda said.

"You are not the fixer almighty! You can fuck up shit too! For someone like you to give any advice on anything dealing with a child is almost insulting. You're not a mother. You don't have those motherly instincts."

"How dare you talk to me like that! You think you know it all. What type of parent are you? You're the type of bitch that chases behind dick and leaves her kids on her mother. The same type of bitch that stays getting locked up behind a man because you don't know how to be a woman."

"I am a mother, and that's something you'll probably never be. How many abortions have you had, and by how many men? A mother carries and gives birth, not kill their babies. Like I said, you giving any advice about kids is insulting."

"Who the fuck do you think you're talking to?"

"I'm talking to you! It's about time one of us stands up to you. I think it's best that you leave. Yolanda doesn't need you around right now."

"You can't tell me to leave. It's not about you. I'm here for Ryan and Yolanda. How you feel doesn't matter to me. Yolanda and I were friends long before you came along. If you think she would allow you to come between us, you must be crazy."

"You'll be surprised."

"Step aside, bitch. Don't think I won't put these hands on you, friend or no friend, because you are completely out of line."

Jayda started to walk away when Shay said, "I wonder if Yolanda would want you around if she knew about you and her father?"

Jayda stopped walking. She felt the knife that Shay twisted in her back. She turned around to face her again.

"You swore you would never speak of that?"

"Yes, I did. And I meant it. But if you don't fall back, I'll tell her," Shay threatened.

"After everything I've done for your sorry ass, you think you can threaten me with my past? Remember, you won't be only hurting me."

"See, that's the problem right there. I don't owe you shit. I've done just as much for you as you have done for me. I'm willing to tell the truth to expose you for who you really are. You're not perfect. You have more dirty secrets than Yolanda and I put together."

"I can't believe you right now!"

"It's snow season, bitch! Now leave before I tell them what happened between you and old nasty Mr. Clarkson. We have an audience too."

Jayda's eyes watered as her heart broke. Her best friend was in the hospital fighting for her life, and as much as she wanted to be there for Yolanda and her family, she thought it was best that she left. There was no way she could risk Shay telling her secret.

Jayda wiped her tears and walked back to the lobby with Shay close behind her. Before she could speak, Ryan rushed up to them.

"She's going to make it!" he said.

"Thank God!" Jayda said.

"We can go in and see her soon. They're going to have to keep her for a while, but she's okay," he cried.

Jayda embraced Ryan, then looked at Shay and rolled her eyes. Shay shot her a threatening look.

"Thank God she's okay. I have to go. I was called into work. I'll check on her later," Jayda said.

"I was hoping you could be here for her," Ryan said.

Jayda looked at Shay, who glared back at her.

"I'm sorry, but I have to go. I'll check in with you later. I'm so sorry," she told him.

Jayda left the hospital in tears. She couldn't believe how Shay approached her, forcing her to leave the hospital. And the most hurtful of all, she threatened to expose her secret. She didn't know what to do with all of that. She always had Shay and Yolanda to lean on. Now those relationships were threatened.

It had been many years since she had tucked away the memory of that night, and she prayed it would never come back to haunt her. But she never expected betrayal. On her way home, she thought about the one mistake she made that could end her friendship with Yolanda.

Jayda pounded her fist on the steering wheel, blaring the horn. Cars maneuvered into the other lanes to avoid her reckless driving. Tears fell from her eyes as she screamed and pounded her fist. Thick streaks of mascara rolled down her face with her warm tears. Her heart felt as if it was shrinking in her chest. The pain that came with the shrinking feeling made it hard for her to breathe. As much as she wanted to curse out Shay, Jayda knew to tread lightly because she had a bullet in the chamber.

"Shit!" she screamed.

She maneuvered her car to pull into the right lane when a loud horn startled her. She whipped her head around to see that a truck was in the right lane. She almost lost control and collided into the truck. That shook her up enough to snap her back to reality. She slowed down and tried to pay closer attention to the other cars on the road.

She hit the button to roll down her window, letting in a cool breeze. The wind blew through her hair, sending tresses slapping into her wet face and sticking. She turned up the radio to drown out the conversation on repeat in her head that she just had with Shay. Shay dug up a grave that was buried many years ago with no headstone or grave marker.

Jayda was in disbelief. She watched how Yolanda was spiraling out of control. She was so caught up with what she had going on in her life that she didn't take the time to stop and check on her. She knew this because she helped her friend in a time of need. The help she provided wasn't the help that could give her longevity; it was helpful for the time being. Her advice and her advice alone was the cause of her friend's grief.

She wanted to fix everything, including her friend. Had she taken a step back and dealt with things differently, things might've turned out differently. Maybe Yolanda wouldn't have tried to end her life. There was much to think about. She was on the run from her past and pulled back in due to the present events.

Chapter 19

During the rest of the ride home, Jayda thought back to the night she made a huge mistake. It was a Saturday night and Yolanda's turn to host their weekend sleepover. The girls loved it at Yolanda's house because her parents usually turned in early and didn't hover over them. Jayda, who had a crush on Yolanda's father, would often make inappropriate jokes about him. Yolanda didn't like it but would laugh it off with a warning to Jayda to stay away from her father.

Jayda was eighteen and at her highest weight. She and Shay were dating brothers at that time. The brothers were supposed to come over that night, and the two of them were going to sneak out to be with them. Instead, only Shay's boyfriend came. Jayda later found out her boyfriend was with another girl. Jayda had waited weeks for the opportunity to be with him again, but she was let down. That night, Shay gave all the details on the sexual encounter that she had, while Jayda was getting turned on by it.

As the other two slept, Jayda tossed and turned as she yearned to be pleased by a man. She tried to take her mind off of sex, but she couldn't. She tried calling her boyfriend again, but he said he was in bed and couldn't get over to her. After she hung up, Yolanda's father crossed her mind. Earlier, she had seen his print through his pants and was surprised at how big his penis appeared to be. She crept out of the bed and downstairs. The house was dark, and she was sure Yolanda's parents were in bed.

She knew Mr. Clarkson sometimes went out to the garage late at night to work on his car. So, she crept out to the garage. It was dark, but in the corner was a light. Jayda walked slowly towards the corner of the garage, where there was a small sitting area. She could see an empty bottle of alcohol on the table.

She stood in the dark watching as Mr. Clarkson masturbated to porn on the small nineteen-inch television. She watched as two men double penetrated a woman. Something she had never seen before.

At first, she was disgusted, but then she became turned on as she watched how much the woman was being pleased by the two men. A moan from Mr. Clarkson drew her attention to him. She walked around the car parked in the garage to get a better view of him sitting on the sofa. She moved closer until she was able to see him in full view. He had his penis in his hands, stroking it. Jayda felt wetness in her panties, and her nipples became erect. The throb she tried to get rid of was almost painful.

Jayda watched him intensely, imagining him inside of her. She wanted him inside of her. She was grown now and no longer the little girl that he had watched grow up. As she moved in closer, she didn't realize there were boxes stacked to the left of her. She knocked over the boxes, startling Mr. Clarkson.

He jumped up and called out. "Who's there?"

Instead of being afraid, Jayda felt bold.

"It's just me, Mr. Clarkson," she said.

"Why are you in here? Go back to bed!" he said, stuffing his penis into his pants.

"I don't want to go back to bed."

"Jayda, go back to bed! You shouldn't be in here."

"I don't want to."

She walked closer to him. She could smell the heavy scent of alcohol on his breath. He backed away. His red eyes widened as she rubbed her large breasts against him.

"I don't know what you're trying to do, but this isn't right. Forget what you just saw and go back to bed!"

Mr. Clarkson's penis was still erect and pressing against her stomach. He fumbled inside of his pants, trying to make his penis go down. Jayda reached inside of his pants and pulled it out. He pulled back from her, but she followed him. She squeezed his penis in her hand, amused by his thickness. He was rock hard and stiff in her hands. Then she began stroking him. She watched as he tried to fight the urge not to give in to her. She knew the alcohol was on her side, and she liked it.

"Wow, Mr. Clarkson. You're so big."

"This isn't right, Jayda. Please stop."

But he didn't move away. His breathing became heavy and fast.

"What's wrong? We're both grown. No one has to know about this."

He reached down, gently removed her hand from around his penis, and pushed her away from him.

"I can't do this. I've been drinking, but I know this isn't right. I'm a married man. This isn't going to happen. Now go!" he shouted, pointing towards the door.

"No! You're not attracted to me! Is it because I'm fat?"

"No. Your size has nothing to do with this. You're a beautiful young lady."

"Then prove it! You've cheated on Mrs. Clarkson before. What's wrong with me?"

"You don't have anything to do with my marriage. This is wrong. I can't do this." Throwing his hands up, he said, "Jayda, I'm leaving."

When Mr. Clarkson tried to walk past Jayda, she grabbed his arm and forcefully tried to kiss him. She could taste the harshness of the alcohol as they kissed. He turned his head away, but then began to kiss her back. That night, Jayda and Mr. Clarkson had sex in the garage. That wasn't something she was proud of. She was pleased that night but quite embarrassed after it happened. She had slept with a man old enough to be her father, and it was her best friend's father. The worst thing yet about that night was that Shay saw the two of them together in the garage.

When she and Mr. Clarkson were done engaging in the forbidden act of sex, Jayda swore never to tell a soul. Mr. Clarkson was regretful and apologetic for his weakness. Jayda rolled her eyes at him as he pleaded for her to keep their secret between them.

As she walked away from him, she thought about Yolanda and her mother. She began to feel guilty and realized that the risk she took wasn't worth hurting them. At that moment, she decided to bury the memory and never to do anything like that again. When Jayda opened the garage door to go back to the house, she looked up and saw someone standing there in the dark. She jumped back.

"I can't believe you just fucked Mr. Clarkson!" Shay blurted out.

Jayda closed the door behind her and pulled Shay aside. Shay laughed loudly.

"Shut up before you wake them up," Jayda whispered. "What are you talking about?"

"I just saw you fucking him. He was tearing that ass up too. I can't believe you."

Shay continued to laugh.

"Stop laughing. It's not funny."

"Oh, yes, it is. When Yolanda finds out about this, she is going to kill you. You're nasty!" Shay said, pointing a finger in Jayda's face.

Jayda grabbed Shay's finger and twisted it.

"If you tell, then I will have to kill you!"

"Ouch!" Shay yelped.

Jayda let go of her finger.

"I wasn't really going to tell. How could you do this to her though? She's our best friend. She's our sister. The Clarksons are good people."

"I know. I'm sorry. I don't know what came over me."

"As long as you promise this will never happen again, I won't say anything. You promise?"

"I promise I'll never do anything like this again. Thanks, Shay."

"I hope so. Because you're a nasty bitch."

Under the door, they saw the light to the garage go out. The two rushed upstairs and back to bed. Yolanda, who was still asleep, didn't realize the betrayal that had occurred. Jayda and Shay didn't say anything else to each other that night, and they never spoke of what happened until Shay threatened to expose her.

From a few houses down, Jayda noticed a vehicle parked in front of her home. She wasn't expecting anyone, and it wasn't a car that she recognized. She pulled into her driveway, then turned to look at the vehicle. It appeared that no one was inside. She looked around at her surroundings. When she felt safe enough, she walked to her house. She had her keys ready and entered the house quickly. Once inside, she disarmed her alarm system and reset it.

She could feel stress and strain settle into her neck and shoulders. She kicked off her shoes. From the fridge, she retrieved a chilled bottle of wine. Instead of using a wine glass, she opened it and drank straight from the bottle. She walked back to the living room and cut on the television. She thought about calling Ryan to check on Yolanda but decided to wait until she thought Shay wasn't around. She sat down and began to channel surf. She could hardly settle on something to watch because she was anxious to talk to Yolanda. A few minutes later, there was a knock on the door.

Jayda sat up but didn't move to open the door. It was late, and again, she wasn't expecting anyone. Then she remembered the suspicious car outside.

She went to the door and asked, "Who is it?"

"Ashley."

"What the fuck?" Jayda said, swinging open the door.

Standing there on her porch was Ashley, Khalil's new baby's mother. She stood there with her hands on her hip and her face twisted.

"Yeah, it's me."

"What the fuck are you doing here? And how do you know where I live?"

"Don't worry about all that. Just know I've been here before."

Jayda reached behind the door and grabbed the metal bat that she kept there for a situation just like Ashley. When Ashley saw the bat, she took a few steps back.

"And you were saying what?" Jayda said, swinging the bat in her hand.

"Khalil told me to come over here and ask you for the money I need for our daughter. I need to pay for daycare, and she needs diapers and milk. If it weren't for you, he wouldn't be locked up. He was taking good care of us."

"You tell Khalil that I ain't giving you or your baby shit! You made that baby with him, not me."

"He was giving us two hundred dollars a week. What am I supposed to do now?"

"I don't know what you're supposed to do. You need to figure that shit out. But I ain't the answer, bitch."

"See, I didn't come over here for all of this. You're supposed to be his girl, right? He does have two kids that he was taking care of. Did you even think about all of that before you had him locked up?"

"I don't give a fuck. That's Khalil's problems, not mine. We aren't together anymore. So, fuck you and fuck him."

"I know you have his money. All I want is my money. I know he left some money up in there," Ashley said, looking around Jayda into the house.

"Do you want to come in to look for it?" Jayda said, swinging the bat in Ashley's direction. "Come on in. You want the money so bad. Come get it."

"Fuck you. You just wait until Khalil gets out. He's going to fuck you up," Ashley said.

She cursed as she walked across the lawn back to her car.

"Bye, whore!" Jayda called after her.

Chapter 20

Thunder shook the house, awakening Jayda from her sleep. She had laid in bed thinking about Yolanda and Shay. She didn't understand how Shay could turn on her like that. She wasn't sure what brought about her nasty disposition towards her. She finally found sleep once her mind stopped racing. Another loud clap of thunder roared in the distance. Jayda rolled over to glance at the clock; it was a little after four o'clock in the morning. Rolling onto her back, she stared at the ceiling. She wanted to call to check on Yolanda but didn't want to wake Ryan too early.

Lightning lit up her bedroom. Through the temporary light, she saw her closet. Khalil still had a few things in there. She thought about what Ashley said about Khalil having money at her house. She sat up in the bed and thought about where he may have stashed money that he didn't want her to find. He was never the flashy type. She didn't see him with a lot of money except once. When they first started dating, he did things to try to impress her. He flexed his muscles in the streets and with the men he worked with in front of her. He also took her to where he often did his pick-up, showing her how much he trusted her. One time, they picked up a large duffel bag on their way to the beach. She assumed there was money in the bag that he placed in the trunk with the rest of their bags.

When they arrived, he dumped the contents of the money onto the hotel bed. That night, they fucked on top of the money. They didn't care when the money fell to the floor or stuck to their sweaty bodies. It turned them on. She turned over so she could get on top, the bills sticking to her ass and back. It turned her on when she felt the money fall off her as she bounced on Khalil's penis. They even used the money to make it rain on each other.

Afterwards, he asked her to count the money, bundle it, and let him know how much it was while he ran out to get them something to eat. She gathered all of the money and did as he requested. She didn't know that was also a test to see if she would steal from him. He knew exactly how much money was in the bag. She passed another test. That was the first and last time she had seen Khalil with any real money.

Jayda thought about it and then began to search her closet. After an hour of combing the closet and her bedroom, she turned up with nothing. She thought hard. He spent a lot of time at her home alone. She was sure he would've taken any money or anything of value with him when he left. She was right. She didn't find anything anywhere in the house.

Suddenly, the lights in the house flickered. She could hear the wind forcing leaves and debris against her home. The storm was picking up. She, like many people, didn't like thunderstorms, and especially when she was alone. She lit a couple of candles that were around her bedroom to ensure she would have light in case the lights went out. Laying back down in bed, she listened to the storm.

She picked up her phone to check the battery status. Seeing that she had a couple of social media notifications, she checked them. There were a few messages from some friends of theirs asking about Yolanda and what was going on. She didn't know how word had spread so fast. Then she thought about Shay. She immediately went to Shay's page. Shay was known for posting everything on her social media pages with no regard for other people's privacy. She always used the excuse that since she didn't name names, it didn't matter what she posted. That went for when it was something related to Yolanda or Jayda, as well.

On Shay's page was a post asking for prayers for Yolanda and Ryan. She didn't say why, but that was enough to get people to inquire about what was going on. Shay being Shay, she was sure to exclude mentioning Jayda purposely by stating that she and Ryan were by Yolanda's side. To add insult to injury, she added the hashtag *#weareallsheneeds*.

Jayda became infuriated. Shay had declared war on her and their friendships. She wouldn't usually reply to a post that rubbed her the wrong way. She would just keep scrolling. This time, however; Shay had gone too far. Jayda clicked on the comment button and quickly began to type a response to Shay's post.

Shay, you are out of line yet again. Everything is not for social media. But since you felt the need to throw shade my way, I must say that if YoYo only has you, she is in serious trouble. Stop trying to flex your muscles and seem stronger than you really are. I'm still here for you and especially my best friend YoYo. #alwaystheweakestlink.

She read over her comment and thought about not sending it. Then she thought about how Shay made her leave the hospital without seeing Yolanda and how Yolanda must've felt when she came out of recovery and did not see her.

"Now, bitch," Jayda said, posting the message.

Jayda thought about Shay's response and wondered if she would out her on social media. If she did, she would deal with it. She wasn't happy about what happened, but if that was what stood between her and her best friends, she would have to find a way to tell Yolanda. She prepared herself for Shay's response and decided to tell Yolanda what happened between her and her father once she was strong enough to hear it. One thing was true; Jayda regretted what she did. As an adult, she realized how her insecurities led her to such a bad decision.

She said a prayer for Yolanda and vowed to see her first thing in the morning. She wasn't going to allow Shay or anyone else to keep her from her best friend. It was Jayda and Yolanda before Shay came along. There was no way she was going to let her come between the two of them. If anyone had to go, it was going to be Shay.

It was still early, and Jayda had to get some sleep. She checked social media one more time to see if there were any new comments on Shay's post. There weren't. While she was holding her phone, it rang. The caller ID showed Unknown. She usually didn't answer unknown or private numbers. It was very early in the morning, much too early for those types of calls. Then she thought about Yolanda. It could've been Yolanda trying to reach out to her. Not wanting to miss an opportunity to speak to her and apologize for not being there for her, she answered.

"Hello."

"What's up?" Khalil said.

"Khalil?"

"Yeah, it's me. Don't hang up."

"What do you want?"

"You don't ask how I'm doing, or do I need anything. Just snitch on me and throw me to the wolves. Typical of weak-ass bitches like you."

"I'm not here for none of this. Bye."

"No! Please don't hang up."

"Why shouldn't I? You haven't changed. You're still disrespectful. You're not supposed to be even contacting me."

"You're right, but I called to make sure you were safe."

"Khalil, why wouldn't I be safe? Now that you're not here kicking my ass, I would consider that safe. Oh, unless we're talking about you sending your baby momma over here to ask me to give her money for your baby. Are you crazy?"

"I thought you would look out for my daughter and son while I was locked down. Since you're the one who put me here, your ass should do right by my kids. That ain't why I'm calling you."

There was a pause. Khalil lowered his voice almost to a whisper.

"I don't have much time on this phone. Just be careful. I owe some people out there, and they made it clear that they want theirs. They know where I stayed, and they know about you. After all of this, I still don't want to see anything happen to you. I'm working on a few things, but my hands are tied in here. So, watch your back. If anything happens, just call this number that I'm going to text you, and I'll find a way to call you back."

"What do you mean? What do I have to do with what you owe someone? I don't have anything to do with that."

"It doesn't matter. That's how this shit works. They might think you're holding for me. They could come after my paper."

"What paper? I ain't never seen you with any real paper except the one time, and that was years ago. What have you gotten me into?"

"You're going to be fine. Like I said, just watch your back. I'll calm this shit down as soon as I can."

"Khalil, what the fuck am I supposed to do with that? I guess that means you don't have what you owe these people, right?"

"Do you think if I had it I would be calling you? I told you that I didn't have much time to talk. Just listen to what I said. Text that number if anything happens, and I'll take care of it. I got to go. I'll check back on you."

"Khalil!"

He hung up.

"Oh, my God."

Jayda's hands began to shake as she tried to process what Khalil said. She thought about her life being in danger behind him. She suddenly didn't feel as safe as she had felt moments before his call. Her phone chimed, notifying her that she had received a text. It wasn't a local number, but she knew it was the number Khalil said he was going to send her.

The weight she was feeling moved her to tears. She needed her girls at that moment. She needed Yolanda to help her put things into perspective and Shay's street smarts and connections to find out what was going on with Khalil. She wanted to call Shay so bad, but she didn't want to be the first to call. Jayda felt that Shay owed her a huge apology. Her hands were only tied because she allowed them to be.

She began to cry. It seemed as if her world was crashing down around her, and she had no one to turn to. Her support system was non-existent. If it were anyone else, she would tell them exactly what to do. Being that it was her, she was chasing her tail with no options.

Chapter 21

Hours passed as Shay, Ryan, and Yolanda's family waited for Yolanda to be admitted to the hospital. Shay sat beside Ryan feeling like a million bucks because she had knocked Jayda off her perfect pedestal. It was a long time coming. She wanted to get back at Jayda for years but could never find the right time to pull the trigger to hit her target. The day she walked in and saw Mr. Clarkson fucking Jayda, her heart grew envious of her.

Shay had been performing porn star quality blowjobs on Mr. Clarkson for months. He had refused to have intercourse with her but allowed her to blow him. She didn't feel guilty because he was married. She only felt guilty because it was her best friend's father. Mr. and Mrs. Clarkson were practically separated after discovering that he had an affair with a woman closer to his age. Mrs. Clarkson was much older than Mr. Clarkson. They slept in separate bedrooms, and from what Yolanda told them, they hardly talked. But, on the outside, they kept up appearances.

That night, she was going to do what she had done many times before. She assumed Jayda was with her boyfriend as planned and not in the garage. To her surprise, Jayda was getting what she couldn't have. She watched as Mr. Clarkson stroked in and out of Jayda's round ass. She listened as Jayda moaned and watched while she clawed at the sofa's fabric as he plunged deeper and deeper inside of her. Shay was infuriated at the sight of her best friend and her man crush engaging in such an intimate act. She didn't understand why he would have sex with Jayda and not her.

She wanted to tell Yolanda what she saw in order to put an end to it but knew that she would also be telling on herself. There was no way Yolanda wouldn't have confronted her father as she had done many times before when he had affairs on her mother. If Yolanda confronted him, Shay's secret could get out, and that she couldn't have. Instead, she confronted Mr. Clarkson herself about having sex with Jayda. He denied it initially until she described to him what she had seen. Only then did he know that she saw them. He apologized and cut her off completely.

She expected Jayda to put up more of a fight when she told her to leave the hospital. Jayda was not one to back down from a fight, but Shay used the only thing she knew that would make her draw back her claws. And it worked. Although Jayda left, she knew it wasn't the end of the fight. Jayda was going to make her pay, but Shay was willing to gamble for Yolanda's sake. She truly felt it was Jayda's fault that Yolanda was in her predicament. Selfishness was the only reason she could think as to why Jayda gave Yolanda such bad advice.

It was time for Jayda to learn a lesson and realize that she was not the queen. Shay didn't want their friendship to end, but she wanted the dynamics to change. She wanted them on even ground. She didn't want to feel like the third wheel in their friendship. Like anyone else, she wanted to be respected and thought of equally. Then there were times when Jayda made her feel close like a sister. Someone like Shay didn't understand that spectrum. She yearned and needed consistency, and that was what Yolanda provided.

Ultimately, she wanted to sit Jayda down so she could undo the damage she felt she had done, which resulted in Yolanda's attempted suicide.

The doctor came out and called for Ryan. He and Yolanda's family hurried towards the doctor, and there was a short discussion.

Then Ryan turned to Shay and said, "Wait here," before they all disappeared through the door.

After saying a prayer for Yolanda, Shay sat back and began to bounce her leg nervously. To distract herself, she decided to scroll through her social media. It wasn't long before she discovered Jayda's comment on her post. She laughed out loud at the comment.

"Weakest link my ass."

She started to type a reply but decided against it. She didn't want to have a spat on social media with Jayda when she was only trying to knock her down a few pegs. She knew Jayda was definitely in her feelings and decided to ignore her instead.

After Ryan and Yolanda's family were able to visit with her, it was Shay's turn. Ryan allowed Shay to visit with Yolanda alone. Shay was taken to the back where Yolanda was, and a nurse stood close by as Shay walked towards Yolanda.

She looked terrible. Shay's eyes watered as she fought back the tears. Yolanda was pale, had dark rings around her eyes, and didn't look anything like the Yolanda she knew. She wondered how she could look so different from the last time she saw her. Then she realized Yolanda was severely depressed and managed to hide it from everyone. She didn't recognize her. Gone was the perfectly bronzed face and wide smile. Before her was a woman in pain. At that moment, she regretted forcing Jayda to leave. She needed her help. She didn't know what to say or do to help her friend. Together, they would've figured it out as they always did.

Yolanda lay on her side in the fetal position. Her eyes were closed, but she wasn't asleep.

"Hey," Yolanda said in a raspy voice.

"Hey. How are you feeling? I mean…" Shay's voice trailed off.

"I know what you mean. I feel like shit."

Shay placed her hand on Yolanda's shoulder and then rubbed her back as tears fell from her eyes before she closed them.

"Where's Jayda?" Yolanda asked.

"She's not here, but I'm here. That's all that matters right now."

"Did anyone call her?"

"Yeah. She was here, but I told her to leave."

"Why?"

"I didn't think you wanted her here. This is all her fault. She didn't deserve to be here."

"What are you talking about?" Yolanda said, moving Shay's hand off her shoulder.

"Jayda hasn't been a good friend to you. She had you lie about what happened to Ryanna, and she let you get your tubes tied after having one child. Now you don't have any children and can't have any more if you wanted to. If it weren't for her, you wouldn't be here."

"Do you listen to yourself sometimes? I tried to kill myself, and you come in here like God Almighty placing blame on Jayda. Jayda has been nothing less than a good friend to me, a sister. What you did makes you less than a friend."

"What?" Shay asked.

"You know I needed the both of you here, if possible. I'm fucked up, Shay, and seeing the two of you could've given me some hope that things will be at least alright. No one tells me what to do. Any decisions I've made are because I alone chose to make them. It's my fault I'm here and no one else's. I don't know what you said to her to get her to leave, but I know it must've been something pretty bad. Shame on you."

"I'm sorry. I thought I was helping you."

"Helping me? You were helping yourself. I don't know what issues the two of you have, but I hope you resolve it. We are supposed to be friends, best friends. If that's the case, I need both of you."

The room fell quiet.

"Miss? Her visit needs to be over soon," the nurse said.

"Do you want me to call Jayda so you can talk to her before I go?" Shay asked.

Yolanda nodded her head weakly.

Shay pulled out her cell phone and called Jayda. She prayed she would answer her call, but the phone rang and went to voicemail.

"Jayda, I'm sorry. Yolanda wanted to talk to you. Call back, please."

Ryan returned to the room.

"They said we have to end our visit," he said.

"I know. I'm ready," Yolanda said.

Shay tried to hug Yolanda, but it was awkward. It was as if she didn't want to embrace her back.

Instead, she whispered in Shay's ear. "Fix it."

Shay left the hospital in tears. She felt terrible because she managed to hurt both of her friends with one selfish act. She felt alone for the first time in a long time. She felt like she had lost her two best friends, and she didn't know how to fix what was broken between them.

Instead of driving to her mother's house, she decided to call Rob. She missed him. They spoke briefly and sent texts, but he avoided seeing her in person.

"Hey, what's up? I was thinking about you," Rob said, answering the phone in a high-pitch tone.

"Is that right? So, why did I have to call you?" she asked.

"I called you twice. Did you check your voicemail?"

"No. I was at the hospital."

"Are you alright? The kids alright?"

"Yeah, we're okay. It's Yolanda."

"Everything okay?"

"It will be."

"Good. Because I'm trying to see you tonight. I have news for you."

"What?"

"I got signed!"

"Really?"

"Yes! Your boy is going pro!"

"That's great, Rob!"

"So, you coming through or what?"

"Luckily, my mom offered to keep the kids tonight. So, yeah, I'll come over."

"Naw, I have a suite. I've been up here celebrating. All I need now is you."

"Okay. Text me the address and room number. I'm on the way. I have to swing by Jayda's house first."

"Alright."

It had begun to rain heavily as a storm was moving in. Since Shay didn't have an umbrella, she dashed out towards the street where she had parked. She had found a good parking spot just as she arrived at the hospital. Using her large handbag, she shielded herself from the cold rain, but she still was soaked with the wind blowing. She hit the key fob to unlock the doors to her car, and the headlights came on. Shay reached her car and jumped in quickly.

"Shit!" she said.

She reached into her glove department for a stack of napkins and began wiping her face, hands, and chest. The thin blouse she wore clung to her skin, exposing the outline of her breasts and curves. She removed her wet shoes and placed them on the passenger's side floor. Then she flipped down the visor to look at herself. Her naturally curly hair had started to transform into natural curls from the straight pressed look. Her waterproof makeup proved to be of quality as there wasn't a smear on her face. After patting her face dry and tucking her hair behind her ears, she started her car and headed for Jayda's house.

The car's windshield wipers were moving at the fastest speed possible, yet it couldn't keep up with how hard and fast the rain was coming down. Shay decreased her speed on the highway and moved into the slower lane as the rain picked up. As visibility became worse, she thought about pulling over, but she was only half a mile from Jayda's exit. She held on tightly to the steering wheel. It was late, and there weren't many cars on the highway, allowing her to feel somewhat safe driving slower than the posted speed limit.

As she approached the exit, the rain slowed down, calming her. She took the exit and slowed down as she drove around the sharp curve. Suddenly, there were bright lights and a siren behind her. She looked in the rearview mirror to find a police car trailing close behind her. She looked down at her speedometer to see if she was speeding, and she wasn't.

"What the hell is he stopping me for?" she said.

Shay was met with a red light. Looking around, she didn't see any other cars around. She didn't want to pull over on a dark side street, so she decided she would pull over at the shopping center on the right. As she waited for the light to turn green, there was a knock on her window. Startled, she jumped and rolled down her window.

"Ma'am, I need you to pull over," the officer said.

"I am. I wanted to pull over somewhere safe. Can I pull over there?" she asked, pointing towards the shopping center.

The officer looked around.

"Pull over there," he said, pointing to a side street.

It was the very side street where she did not want to pull over. Her heart sunk. Something didn't feel right.

"Okay," she said hesitantly.

Shay rolled up the window and realized the light had turned green. Proceeding, she turned down the dark side street with the police officer behind her. She kept the engine running and placed the car in park. Then she picked up her cell phone and thought about who she should call just in case. She decided to call her mother. She prayed her mother would answer. If not, she was going to leave the line open so the voicemail could pick up everything. As the phone rang, she looked back to find that the officer hadn't exited his car.

"Come on, mom," she said.

"Hello?" her mother answered.

"Mom, I'm being pulled over by the police. Stay on the phone, please."

"Of course. Where are you?"

"I'm about five minutes from Jayda's house on Route 10."

"Okay, baby, I'm here. Everything is going to be fine."

"Mom, he's coming. Just stay on the phone."

Shay rolled down her window as the officer approached.

"License and registration," he said.

As he shined his flashlight in her face and around her car's interior, she reached for her purse.

"Do you have any weapons?" he asked.

"No, I don't have any weapons," she responded.

She slowly took out her wallet and handed him her license and registration from the glove compartment. As he reviewed the information, she got a good look at him. He was an older white man, small build, thick mustache, and dark eyes.

"Why did you stop me?" she asked.

"You were speeding back there."

"I wasn't speeding. I was actually driving slow because I couldn't see in the rain. Are you sure you pulled over the right person?"

"Ma'am, step out of the vehicle."

"I wasn't trying to be disrespectful. I just was saying that I wasn't speeding."

"Step out of the vehicle," he repeated in a firmer tone.

Shay unbuckled her seatbelt and stepped barefooted out of the vehicle. She closed the door behind her but stood near the open window where her mother would still be able to hear her. There was only a drizzle of rain. So, the windshield wipers scraping against the damp windshield made an almost fingernails against chalkboard type of sound.

"Are you aware that you were speeding back there? You could've caused an accident in this weather."

"Officer, I wasn't speeding," Shay told him once more. "You must've stopped the wrong car. I was having trouble seeing with all the rain, so I know I wasn't speeding back there."

The officer looked her over. When he shined his flashlight on her bare feet, she shifted.

"Why are you driving without your shoes? Where are your shoes?"

"Oh, my shoes are right there in the car. I got wet on the way to my car. My shoes were soaked."

Shay quickly turned around, thinking she should retrieve her wet shoes.

"Stop! Don't move!" the officer shouted, pulling out his gun and pointing it at her.

Shay immediately froze and put her hands up.

"What do you think you're doing?" he asked.

"I was just going to get my shoes," she told him.

"Did I ask you to get your shoes? Turn around and place your hands on the car." The officer placed his gun back in the holster.

"What? I didn't do anything," she said.

"Face the car and place your hands on the hood!"

Shay did as she was instructed. With her hands still in the air, she slowly moved towards the front of the vehicle. When she reached the front of the car, she slowly placed her hands on the hood.

"Officer, this isn't necessary," she said.

The officer walked behind her, and using his knee, he spread her legs and roughly began to frisk her. When he reached her breast area, he groped her breasts, making hard circular motions. Shay winced with pain. Next, he moved his hand to her midsection, running his hands along the waist of her skirt. As he began moving his hands up her thigh, she saw the headlights of an oncoming car.

"Stop it!" Shay said.

She quickly turned around and waved down a passing vehicle. Just then, the sky opened up, and a downpour fell upon them. The car stopped at the light. The officer waved the vehicle on, but they didn't move. Shay continued to wave at the car, signaling that she needed help. After a few seconds, the passenger's window rolled down.

"Are you okay?" a woman asked.

"I'm being harassed by this officer. I didn't do anything."

"Move on. This is a traffic stop," the officer said.

The woman looked at Shay and back at the officer.

"I'm not interfering with what you're doing, but with all the craziness happening in the world, I wouldn't feel right leaving this young lady out here in the dark alone with you. So, I'll just sit here until you're done. You wouldn't have a problem with that, would you?" the woman asked.

She then held up a cell phone, making it clear that she was recording.

The officer turned to Shay and said, "Slow down. The next officer may not be as kind as I am."

"Oh, is that right? Now I can leave after you held me against my will?" Shay asked.

The officer walked close to her. "I suggest you leave now, or I can make this stop turn into your worst nightmare," he said.

Shay brushed past him and opened her car door. Once behind the steering wheel, she quickly rolled up her window as the rain was pouring inside.

"Get home safely, ma'am," the officer called out as he walked towards his car.

After pulling off, Shay picked up her phone.

"Mom, are you there?" she asked.

"Yes. Are you okay?"

"I am now. A car pulled up, so he let me go. He touched my breasts! If it weren't for that car pulling up, I don't know what else he would've done."

"Shay, you need to file a complaint on that officer."

"Oh, I will. He had no right to stop me in the first place. I wasn't speeding."

"Honey, are you heading home now? It's late, and you need to get home."

"Yes, I'm on my way home now."

"The kids are fine. You just get home safely. Call me when you get there."

"Kiss them for me and tell them that I love them."

"Of course, honey. Don't forget to call me as soon as you get home."

"I will. Thanks, mom," she sighed. "I love you."

"No need to thank me. I love you too, honey."

Shay ended the call with her mother. She thought about turning around and heading home after the night she was having. First, Yolanda and then being sexually assaulted by a police officer. She tried to push what just happened to the back of her mind. She had another chance to be with Rob. Once he left, their time would be limited to none. So, she couldn't pass up the opportunity to be with Rob. She hadn't been with him for a while and wanted to see him. After their fight, she did all she could to get him to forgive her.

She kept driving towards the hotel. The night's events had shaken her up, but she knew she had yet to achieve her goal. It was one more opportunity for her to get the liquid gold. It was official. He was going to play professional football. The check she was going to gain for having Rob's first child would be worth it all.

Chapter 22

I was worried you weren't going to make it. Severe storm warnings were coming across the television while you were on the way here," Jayda said.

"Well, I'm here. It was rough getting here. There was some flooding under the overpass. There were at least two detours," Jamison said while following Jayda into the kitchen. "The candles smell great."

Jayda laughed. "Don't get the wrong idea. They were all that I had. I didn't want to lose power and be in the dark. That wouldn't be any fun, now would it?"

"That all depends," he replied jokingly.

"I tried to throw something together. I didn't cook, but I did have this."

Jayda displayed a plate with cheese, crackers, and grapes. She held up a bottle of wine.

"Looks good," he said.

Jayda smiled and proceeded to pour two glasses of the wine.

"Have a seat in the living room. Can you take our food, please? I'll bring out the drinks," she said.

"Sure."

Jamison picked up the plate and went into the living room.

Jayda reached into her pajama pants pocket and pulled out her cell phone. She saw a missed call from Shay. She thought about returning her call but didn't want her good mood ruined. She decided to deal with her the next day and enjoy Jamison's company. When Jayda went to join him in the living room, he was looking at the pictures above her fireplace.

"I see you love pictures of yourself. That one right there is huge," he commented.

"Umm, yeah. I worked hard to get where I am. I definitely wasn't born with this body," she said.

She handed him a glass of wine as she sipped from hers. While standing beside him, she pointed out the people in the photos other than herself. She didn't want to give him the wrong impression of her. She wasn't conceited or arrogant, but she would never show him pictures of herself when she was overweight.

Jamison seemed interested and asked very in-depth questions about her family. In return, she did the same.

"Are you and your dad close?" he asked.

"Yes, we are very close. I love my father. I'm his baby girl."

"How was it growing up as an only child? I know you were spoiled."

"It was nice at times. At other times, it was lonely. I had friends and cousins that I spent a lot of time with, but I did want a little sister. I use to play with my dolls and act like they were my sisters when I felt lonely. I would sit them around me and tell them all of my secrets."

"What secrets could a little girl have?"

"Petty secrets. I told them when I stole an extra cookie or when I got a bad grade. Things like that, nothing serious."

"How are you holding up? Really?"

Jayda sighed.

"Tonight has been one of the worst nights of my life. Yolanda is in the hospital, and Shay is blaming me. She and I are at a point of no return."

"I'm sure you two are going to patch things up. You've been friends way too long."

"I don't know. She did something I don't know if I can forgive her for."

"What did she do?"

She sighed and took a sip of her wine.

"Let's just say we have a childhood secret among the two of us. Something that Yolanda wasn't privy to. This information will hurt her and place our friendships on the line."

"Childhood secrets, eh?"

"Yeah. We all have them, but some are worse than others."

"Yes, we do. I'm sure you will be friends again. Forgiveness goes a long way."

A loud clap of thunder roared down from the sky, rattling the house. Jayda jumped back in her seat. Jamison wrapped his arms around her and pulled her in close. Jayda rested her head on his shoulder and wrapped her arms around him, holding him tightly. In Jamison's arms, she felt safe. She couldn't recall a time that she felt so safe in a man's arms other than her father. Even with Khalil, safe was never an emotion she felt while with him.

"Jayda, let's forget all about troubles and enjoy each other. Let this storm still us."

She agreed without responding.

For the next hour, she lay in his arms. She listened to his heartbeat and enjoyed the warm feeling that came with being in the company of a man who had no ulterior motives. They listened to the rain, the thunder, and watched the lightning flash that provided a temporary dim light to the room.

"Jayda?"

"Yes."

"This is us."

"What do you mean?" she asked, lifting her head to look into his eyes.

"I want to be with you. I'm not talking about in the capacity in which we've been seeing each other lately."

"Funny you say that. I was just thinking it seemed like you and I were brought together due to legal woes. You were there for Yolanda, and you were there for me. Now look at us. You came over because I needed you. I don't want you to get the wrong idea about me. I'm not a damsel in distress or some needy woman."

"I've never thought that. What I did for you and your friend was a service. I'm not talking about any of that. I want you to be my woman. I want to be your man."

"Jamison, I don't know what to say."

"Say you want the same thing."

"I do, but…" She hesitated.

"But what? Is it about Khalil?"

"I did just get out of a serious situation with him. Khalil and I will never be together again. I just don't want to rush into a new relationship too soon. Don't get me wrong. I feel the same way you feel. I can see us together. I think about you all the time, and you give me butterflies."

"So, why are you turning me down again?"

"Jamison, all I'm asking for is time. I want our beginning to be strong and without any of the drama that I'm going through."

"Are you referring to Shay? That doesn't have anything to do with us. That's between you two."

"I know."

"You know what, Jayda? I'm not going to pressure you. Evidently, there's something you're not telling me, and I'm not even going to ask."

Jamison walked into the kitchen with both of their wine glasses. Jayda slammed herself back against the sofa and mockingly choked herself. She thought about telling Jamison about the call from Khalil but decided it would only add more unwanted drama to their undefined relationship. On the other hand, she had feelings towards Jamison. He was everything she wanted in a man. He was handsome, charismatic, intelligent, respectful, and had a successful career. What more could she want in a man? She kicked herself for being so indecisive when the answer was clear.

Jamison returned with the glasses refilled and sat them down on the table. Then he took his seat next to her on the sofa, but not as close as they were moments before.

Jayda sat on the edge of her seat. She took a deep breath.

"I have something to tell you," Jayda said.

"You can tell me anything. There's no judgement here," he said, holding his hands up in the air.

"I'm only telling you this because I want to be with you. I don't need your help. I just want you to listen."

"Okay."

"Tonight, I received a call from Khalil that scared me. He apparently has some issues in the streets with someone, and he wanted to warn me."

"Is someone threatening you?"

"Something like that. He just told me to be careful and that he was going to handle it."

"You can stay at my place. I'll protect you."

"I said that I only needed you to listen. If we are going to be together, I want to be honest about everything. So, there it is. I have unresolved issues with Khalil that doesn't involve my heart."

"I'm not just going to sit by and wait to see what happens. If he called to tell you that, then it must be something serious."

"Knowing Khalil, it could be anything. He may owe someone money or something. I'm not sure. He's going to call again, and when he does, I'll find out what's going on."

"Let me know what's going on as soon as you find out. I'll do whatever I can to help you."

"There you go again. You have to be the hero," she said jokingly.

"Okay, okay. It's in my nature to protect. I can't help that."

"At least I know I'm safe as long as I'm with you."

"So, are we together now?"

"Starting right here, right now. This is us."

Jamison moved in slowly and passionately kissed Jayda. She was so caught off guard by the passion in his kiss that she began to feel lightheaded. When the kiss ended, Jayda slowly opened her eyes. She had never felt such passion before, and she didn't want it to end. So, she went in for another kiss, but Jamison stopped her.

"I don't expect anything to happen tonight. No pressure. I got my woman. I got what I need."

"I was planning on sleeping with you on our first official date. I just wanted another one of those kisses," she said, pointing to his lips.

He took her finger into his mouth and sucked it.

Jayda moaned.

"If you keep on doing these things to me, we may have to go all the way."

Jamison kissed her again. Surprisingly, the second kiss burned with the same passion and desire as the first.

"You are special," Jayda said.

"I won the prize. You're it," Jamison said.

"It's getting late. Do you want the sofa, or do you want to spoon?" Jayda asked.

Just the thought of having him in her bed caused her to throb with desire.

"Maybe I should take the sofa," Jamison said.

Jayda looked towards his pants and saw why he opted for the sofa.

"Oh, I see. This is going to be tough." Jayda stood. "I'll set you up out here, and then I'll go to bed."

"Sounds like a plan," Jamison said.

Jayda walked away quickly. She went to the linen closet to get a pillow and blanket for him. She made up the sofa as he washed the dishes that they had used.

"Thanks," Jamison said.

"No, thank you for cleaning up."

"I needed the distraction."

"Yeah."

"Goodnight."

"Goodnight. See you in the morning."

Jamison walked over to the sofa to settle in for the night. Jayda went to her bedroom. She checked her phone to see if Ryan had returned her call. There was only a missed call from Shay that she didn't plan on returning anytime soon.

As she lay in bed, she couldn't find sleep. Her mind raced as she thought about Jamison. He was it. All that she wanted in a man was in Jamison. Then

Khalil crept into her thoughts. She was done with him, but she wasn't sure if he was done with her. His issues were starting to become her issues. Then there was Shay. The threat that Shay posed was real. Too real for her to even think about at that moment because it overshadowed all happiness in her life. She planned to continue stuffing her secret down deep inside and taking it to the grave.

Chapter 23

Shay pulled into the hotel parking lot. She exited the car and walked quickly inside. She spent the ride to the hotel checking her rearview mirror for police cars and driving no more than the posted speed limit. She wanted to be off the streets and somewhere safe. She felt karma on her heels for what she did to Jayda.

She entered the hotel. The clerks greeted her with pleasantries even though it was well into the wee hours of the morning. She smiled and headed for the elevators. Rob was on the fourth floor of the hotel. When she arrived on the floor, she immediately smelled the pleasant scent of marijuana. She stepped off the elevator and headed towards his room. As she got closer, the smell got stronger. She knocked on the door of the hotel room.

"Hey, baby!" Rob said.

"Hey. What's going on?"

Shay stepped into the room, which was a mess. She looked around in disgust. A man and two females came out of one of the bedrooms.

"What the fuck is going on in here?" Shay asked again, turning towards Rob.

"We were just celebrating, and they were just leaving. I had my homies over for a little celebration, that's all."

The man and women walked past her and out the door.

"Do you think you should be smoking and having parties? You don't need negative attention right now," Shay said.

"I wasn't smoking. I had a few drinks, but I'm drug-free. I'm not going to fuck up my money over no damn smoke. I let my homies do their thing. It's all good," Rob slurred.

"Are you sure you only had a few drinks?" she asked.

His eyes were red, and his speech was garbled.

"I came home to celebrate with my people. I'm up, baby!"

"I'm happy for you. I know how hard you worked for this. Good thing you're not going to be far away. We can still see each other," she said.

"You're more than welcome to visit anytime you like, but call first," Rob said jokingly.

"Why would I need to call, when you'll know I'm coming because you will be paying for those flights?"

"No doubt. I've seen your crazy ass in action. You like to pull up on a nigga. I ain't playing that shit with you or no other females."

"How many bitches do you have?"

"There's you and only you."

"Stop playing with me, Rob."

Rob headed towards one of the bedrooms in the suite.

"I've been waiting for this all night. Come on, girl," Rob said.

"Let me lock the door. I don't know who you had in this room tonight."

Rob grabbed her hand and led her to the bedroom.

"I was among friends tonight. Now, I'm with your crazy ass."

Shay looked back at the door, wanting to secure it with the latch. She felt something in her gut. She felt something bad was going to happen. But something bad had already happened when the police stopped her. She was now safe with Rob, but she didn't feel quite that way. She pushed past her feelings so she could be with Rob.

Once in the bedroom, they both immediately undressed. They stood in front of each other, staring at each other's bodies. They hadn't been together in a while and were taking each other in with their eyes.

"I missed your pretty ass," Rob said.

"I missed you too."

"I know you did," he said, stroking himself as his soldier stood at attention.

Shay walked over to him. They began to kiss while moving towards the bed. Once on the bed, she slid down his body and took him into her mouth. Rob let out a moan. She sucked hard and fast as her hands gripped him tightly. Both moved to a rhythm that only the two of them could hear. She came back up to kiss him. He was more relaxed than usual. Usually, she took charge when they had sex, only to be interrupted for him to put on a condom. This time was different.

Rob rolled her over on her back and straddled her. She looked at him in surprise as he dominated her. He sucked on her nipples and licked her down to her stomach. He had never performed oral sex on her before, and she didn't expect him to. However, to her surprise, he went down on her, and it felt wonderful. She was surprised by the smooth but strong strokes of his tongue. He knew just how to get her there without messing around. Tears fell from her eyes as she reached her climax.

Rob straddled her again. This time, he inserted his penis inside of her. Her back arched as he deeply stroked her without a condom. The possibility of him slipping up and getting her pregnant heightened every sensation she felt. At the end, he released himself inside of her. His limp body fell on top of her. She lay there praying that her one shot was it. She fell asleep in his arms.

Shay blinked her eyes as she awoke from a deep sleep. She rolled over to find Rob wasn't in bed. Sitting up, she looked around the room. It was quiet. She wrapped the sheet around her and went to open the door. When she reached the door, she heard voices—unfamiliar voices. She slowly opened the bedroom door and peeked out. Rob was on his knees, hands tied behind his back and a gun pointed in his face.

She couldn't hear what was being said, but she did notice the man holding Rob at gunpoint. It was the same man she saw earlier that night leaving with two women. She slowly closed the door. She picked up the hotel phone and called the front desk.

Before the person who answered could finish their greeting, Shay whispered, "There's someone in our room with a gun. Call the police."

"Is anyone hurt?"

"Not yet. Hurry up and call the police."

There was no way out of the room except through the front door. She quickly, but quietly, put on her clothes. She needed somewhere to hide. There was a bathroom connected to the bedroom. She went inside, shut off the lights, and hid in the shower with the curtain drawn. She prayed no one would come looking for her. She could clearly see the man's face in her mind.

After a few brief moments, she heard a single gunshot. Shay gasped and threw her hands over her mouth. She tried not to scream or make any noise that would attract attention. Seconds later, she heard the bedroom door swing open forcefully, hitting the wall behind it. There was rummaging around in the room, and she could hear drawers being yanked open. They were looking for something. She prayed he wouldn't come into the bathroom. She listened nervously to the commotion in the next room.

When the bathroom light came on, she thought about her children and her mother. She didn't want to die, but she felt death before her. Light footsteps moved around in the bathroom. She stood very still and didn't breathe. The curtain moved back slowly. Just when Shay was ready to scream, a woman appeared. There was a familiarity in her eyes. In those seconds, Shay tried to recall her face. Just when she realized who the woman was, she motioned for Shay to be quiet. It was one of the women who was with the man she saw. But the woman wasn't a stranger; she knew her.

"There's nothing in here," the woman said, closing the curtain.

Shay held in her cry with her hand. She couldn't believe what was happening.

The woman closed the door behind her as she left.

Shay slid down the shower wall into a heap of silent tears. She knew she wasn't safe until the police arrived. So, she remained silent and continued praying more than she had ever prayed in her life. She even asked for forgiveness for what she did to Jayda. She was under the impression that karma had come around at lightning speed. Not just for Jayda, but for her past sins too.

"Police! Is anyone in here?" she heard a man say.

"In here. I'm in here!" she cried out.

Police officers stormed the bathroom, overwhelming her. She was helped out of the shower and into the main area of the hotel room. There were so many people asking her questions that she didn't know who to answer first.

"Everyone back up. Give her some breathing room," a woman ordered.

"I'm Bianca. Everyone calls me B. Are you hurt?" she asked.

"I don't think so."

"Do you mind if I make sure?"

"No, go ahead."

As Bianca examined Shay, she looked around the room for Rob.

"Where is he? Where's Rob?" Shay asked.

"He's being transported to the nearest hospital for treatment. Well, you seem to be okay. Your heart is racing. Probably due to what's happening right now," Bianca said.

Shay began to breathe rapidly.

"I can give you some oxygen to help you breathe."

Bianca placed an oxygen mask on Shay.

"These officers are here to help you. They're going to need you to tell them what happened here. You need to help your friend by answering their questions."

Shay nodded her head in agreement.

"Okay, then. You'll be okay."

There were people all over the hotel room. Taking pictures, standing around talking, and going through Rob's belongings. It was as if she were having an out-of-body experience. She heard the voices in the room but didn't understand the words. The sound of the gunshot replayed in her head.

She needed to call Jayda and Yolanda. She reached for her phone in her purse, but suddenly remembered that Yolanda wasn't able to help her, and Jayda wasn't taking her phone calls. She found herself alone once again. The ones who she knew would be right by her side with no questions asked were not available for her. She had other girlfriends that she could call, but she knew what came with that. She didn't want her business in the streets and rumors to get started. She didn't want to tell her mother either because it would be one more mistake she had made in her mother's eyes.

"What is your full name?" an officer asked.

"My name is Shay Bryant," she replied.

"Did you know Robert Gibbs?"

"Yes. We're friends."

"How well do you know him?"

"Well enough, I guess. We're in a relationship. We're not at the meet-the-parents stage yet. We were still getting to know each other."

"Tell me what happened here."

"Rob invited me here to celebrate his signing to his new team. When I arrived, he had already celebrated with his friends. There was a man and two women that didn't leave until I arrived. That was the same guy I saw standing over him with the gun. When I saw that, I hid in the shower. After I heard the gunshot, they came into the bedroom looking for something. The woman found me in the shower, but she didn't tell him. She protected me."

"Do you know this man and woman?"

"I've never seen them before last night. Rob didn't introduce us. We just saw each other in passing."

"Do you know what they were looking for?"

"No. I didn't see anything out of the ordinary."

"What time did you arrive?"

"Around two."

"What did you and Robert do while you were here?"

"We talked for a little while, and then we went to bed."

"Did he say anything to you about anything that might've happened earlier in the day? Like during the party?

"No."

"Can you describe the suspects?"

Shay could not only give a description, but she knew a name. Street code is do not snitch.

"I can try. I didn't get a really good look at them."

"We will need you to give a full statement."

"Okay."

After asking her a few more questions, the officer said, "If you think of anything else, please give us a call. We will be in contact with you if we have any more questions. Here's my card."

Shay took the card from the officer's outstretched hand.

"Can you write your full name, address, and best contact phone number here for me?" he asked, handing her a notepad.

Shay provided her contact information with shaking hands. The realization that she could've been killed started to come back. She thought about Rob. She didn't know his condition or where on his body he had been shot.

When she was done, she handed the notepad back to the officer.

"We'll be in contact with you."

"Am I free to leave?" Shay asked.

"Yes. Will you need a ride?"

"No. My car is outside."

Shay was escorted to her vehicle by a female officer, who she noticed took down her license plate when she pulled off. She cried the entire way to her mother's house. As much as she wanted to go to the hospital to check on Rob, she knew she needed to go to her children. Instead, she decided to take a detour to the hospital. She knew exactly what hospital they would take a gunshot victim. She raced towards the hospital. When she arrived, there was chaos as soon as she reached the emergency room. The local news station was outside the hospital reporting on the shooting. She raced inside, where she found his mother in the arms of a young man. She remembered his mother from the time she confronted him at her home.

"Excuse me. I'm a friend of Rob's. How is he?" Shay asked.

Rob's mother looked up and removed her glasses. She used a tissue to wipe her eyes.

"Were you with him?" his mother asked.

"Yes. I've already spoken to the police, and I told them everything I know. I didn't see exactly what happened. I hid from them. I was so scared. I didn't know what else to do."

"Thank God you weren't harmed too. We have to pray for my son now."

"Is Rob okay?"

"He's in surgery. They don't know if he's going to make it."

Shay immediately broke down.

Rob's mother took Shay into her arms, and they cried together.

After an hour, Shay's mother called looking for her. She did tell her mother that she was on the way to pick up her children. Again, she told her mother that she was on the way but had to make a quick stop.

"I have to go. Please give me a call when he gets out of surgery. Here's my number," she said, scribbling her number on a piece of paper.

"I will. You get home to your babies and hold them close. You never know when God will call them home," Rob's mother told her.

A chill ran over Shay's body. Somehow, she knew she would not be returning to see Rob.

When she arrived at her mother's house, she embraced her children. The thought of never seeing them again sent a ripple of pain through her chest. She hugged and loved on her children.

"Shay, are you okay?" her mother asked.

"Yes. I just needed my babies. I had a long night."

"Are you sure everything is okay?"

"Yes, mom. I just want to get my babies and go home."

Shay thanked her mother, and the children gave their grandmother a hug. Then Shay took her children home. She had a newfound enthusiasm for motherhood. Her children needed her presence as much as possible. Realizing just how short life was, she wanted to change for the better, starting with her family. Her friendships were on the rocks, and she needed to mend those relationships as well. She also knew something that she was sure Jayda and Yolanda didn't know. Their old friend was back, and she was more dangerous than ever.

Chapter 24

Yolanda sat in her room at the mental health facility, where she was transported after her attempted suicide. Her mother was able to get her into a private facility for evaluation. She was embarrassed that she survived and had to face her family and friends. She was angry that she failed at committing suicide. She wrestled with those feelings until she started talking about her feelings with one of the doctors she found a connection with.

Dr. Bradley was a female therapist and able to relate to Yolanda's loss since she had lost a child during childbirth. During Yolanda's sessions, Dr. Bradley was able to get her to understand that there was life after loss. Once she was able to get Yolanda to see and understand that fact, she was able to help her deal with her issues.

Yolanda sat on the twin-size bed positioned along the far wall in a corner. She set the cup of water down on the bedside table, then opened her mouth and moved her tongue side to side to show that she had swallowed her medication. The nurse smiled at her and wrote on her clipboard. This occurred twice a day like clockwork. The young woman smelled of sweet flowers. Yolanda knew the fragrance; it was a familiar scent. She fought through the fog to find the name of the scent, but it escaped her. This frustrated her. She closed her eyes and inhaled deeply to trigger her memory.

A soft knock on the door got her attention.

"Good morning," Ryan said, walking in with roses.

Yolanda didn't respond. After the nurse was done, Yolanda stood to her feet. She walked over to a chair that faced away from the door.

"I was hoping we could talk. I don't want to push you, but we really need to talk."

Ryan walked further into the room. Yolanda stared at nothing in particular, looking across the room.

"Yolanda, talk to me. You've had a cooling-off period, but now you have to talk to me," Ryan said, walking closer to her.

He slid a chair alongside her. He faced the chair the opposite direction towards the door. He sunk into the chair. Yolanda took in a deep breath, closed her eyes, and let her head fall back slowly as a smile spread across her face. Ryan smiled as well.

"I thought that would get your attention. I know how much you love this cologne. I thought if I wore it, I could get some type of reaction from you. I was right," he said.

The temporary progress he had just made quickly faded as she returned to her previous state. Ryan felt defeated as he tried to get through to his wife.

"I'm sorry I didn't listen to you. You tried to tell me, but I didn't listen. I was dealing with my own feelings—feelings I didn't know how to deal with. Being the man and being strong was what I thought I was supposed to do. I was supposed to pull you out of it, and we were supposed to move on with our life. That's what I thought I was supposed to do. I saw you falling apart and didn't do anything about it. I thought babysitting you until you were able to get out of the bed was going to fix it. I failed you. Please forgive me," he said.

"You didn't fail me. God failed us. Our children are supposed to be precious blessings from God. If that's true, why give and take away? That doesn't make sense to me. We tried so hard to get pregnant. We spent so much money, time, and effort to get pregnant. When I found out I was pregnant, it changed everything. The stakes in life were higher. I had more than myself to live for, more than myself to work for. I was going to be responsible for another little human," she said.

She smiled as she wiped away her tears.

"Just the thought of her little face warmed my soul. To give life only to lose it is not fair. Not at all. So, I question God. Why? Why give such a blessing only to take that blessing away?"

She paused.

"He still hasn't answered me. I want that answer one day."

"You can't be angry with God. You have to take some responsibility in this too."

"So, you're blaming me? I know what I did. It was a mistake. I'm not a baby killer! I didn't smother our baby on purpose."

"I'm not blaming you, but you are responsible for what happened. We are responsible for what happened. I share the blame with you. Yolanda, you're going to have to find a way to forgive yourself."

"Why? Why haven't you left yet? I know deep down inside you hate me for what I did. There's no way you can be around me and not see me as the person who killed your daughter. How can you pretend that you still love me?"

"That's enough! I do love you. When I look at you, I still see the woman that I married. You are the same woman that I still love. I'm hurt by what happened. I could do one of two things. I can blame you and let what happened destroy this marriage, or I can forgive you. I'm choosing to forgive you because I don't want us to end. Not like this."

"I don't want you to look up a year from now and resent me. Look at me. I'll never be the same."

"Neither will I. We have to get used to our new way of life. Together, we will get through this. You and I and the memory of our daughter will give us the strength we need."

"You always say the right things. You're right. Please be patient with me."

"Always," he said.

They were interrupted by a nurse.

"Good afternoon. It's time for her session with Dr. Bradley. You can stay or come back later if you like," the nurse said.

Yolanda stood and walked towards the door with the nurse.

"I'll be right here when you get back," he told her.

"Okay," she said.

Yolanda and the nurse walked to Dr. Bradley's office. The office smelled of vanilla, and it turned her stomach. It reminded her of the air freshener her mother sprayed around the house when she was a child. She never liked the smell of vanilla.

Dr. Bradley stood to greet her with cold hands as she entered the room.

"So, how are you feeling today?" Dr. Bradley asked. "Be honest."

Yolanda was in a fetal position on the black leather couch, facing Dr. Bradley. She bit her nails as she turned over onto her back.

"I feel different. I feel empty," Yolanda replied.

"Why do you feel empty?" Dr. Bradley asked.

"I don't know. It's just how I feel. Like I'm missing something inside of me. I'm broken."

"What part of you do you feel is broken?"

Yolanda returned to the fetal position.

"Deep down on the inside, I feel so empty. When my daughter died, I felt empty. There was a hole in my heart that hurt every day. I counted the days that I was without her. Two days, five days. Then it turned into weeks without my baby girl. The longer I lived without her, the more I wanted to be with her. I wanted to fill the void. I knew nothing on this earth could fill it. I know I made the wrong decision to take my life, but it felt so right at the time. Now the emptiness I felt before is much bigger and deeper. There's a larger void, and I don't know how to fix it."

"That's why you're here—to find the tools you need to help you. I think you have a great start in recovery. You're recovering from a great loss. You lost twice. You lost your daughter and then yourself."

Yolanda began to sob.

"It hurt so bad. I just want the pain to go away," she cried.

"Yolanda, sit up. Look at me."

When Yolanda didn't move, Dr. Bradley stood up and walked over to her. She kneeled before her and helped her to sit up. As she cried, Dr. Bradley watched her.

"Yolanda, do you believe in God?"

"Yes."

"So, you know He can fix this, right?"

"I'm so angry with Him. He took my baby from me!"

"God can fix this, but you have to let Him work."

"I prayed too many times. I prayed and asked Him to give me back my baby. I miss my baby so much it hurts!"

"Stand up."

Yolanda weakly attempted to stand to her feet.

"I can't help you if you don't help yourself."

"Stand up, Yolanda."

She slowly stood to her feet. Unsteady on her feet.

"Now, raise your hands above your head," Dr. Bradley said.

Still kneeling before her, Dr. Bradley placed a hand on Yolanda's stomach and one on her back.

"Now, I want you to let it all out. Cry out to Him! Scream! Shout! Just let it out!" Dr. Bradley told her.

Yolanda took in a deep breath and released a growling sound. Then she cried out in an ear-piercing roar. Dr. Bradley held her between her stomach and back, preventing her from falling over.

"Yes. Let it all out. Don't leave anything behind. Don't stop until you have let it out. Say all the things you need to say. Don't hold anything back. This is how you move forward. This is how you start to refill."

"I'm sorry, baby. I'm so sorry. I didn't mean to hurt you. I didn't know that was going to happen. God, please forgive me. Help me, Lord! I need you!"

Yolanda cried, screamed, stomped, and said what was on her heart.

Once Yolanda calmed down, Dr. Bradley dropped her hands from Yolanda's body.

She then looked up at her and asked, "How do you feel now?"

"I feel lighter."

Dr. Bradley stood to her feet, straightened her clothing, and smiled as she wiped away a tear.

"Good job."

Chapter 25

"Next time, I get to plan date night," Jamison said, rolling over onto his back. He rested an arm behind his head. "You are a tease. I thought we were supposed to be taking it slow. You're making it hard for a brother with this game. This isn't fair."

"This is fair. You rolled the dice, and you got a chance to feel my girls," Jayda said, jiggling her breasts. "Don't be mad that your roll on the dice put that mouth to work. I ain't mad at all," Jayda said.

"I see. Now it's your turn to roll the dice."

Jayda picked up the two dice from the game they purchased from an adult store. They initially went to the store to browse but ended up making several purchases—some as a gag and the rest for pleasure. Jayda rolled the dice.

"Kiss. Ear. That's easy."

Jamison grinned. "Too easy."

Jayda leaned over and softly kissed Jamison's ear, then slipped her tongue inside. He flinched a little as she slid her tongue in and out of his ear.

"Okay," he said, letting out a laugh and playfully pushing her away.

The doorbell rang.

"Are you expecting company? It's pretty late," Jamison said.

"No, I wasn't expecting anyone," Jayda said as she stood to go to the door. "Who is it?" she called out.

"Hey, Jayda. It's Alonzo."

Jayda took a step back from the door. She knew it couldn't have been the Alonzo that knew Khalil. The same Alonzo she treated at the hospital. She didn't know why he would be ringing her doorbell.

"What do you want? Khalil isn't here," she said.

"I know. That's why I'm here. I need to talk to you for a minute."

She heard Jamison moving in behind her.

Turning to him, she said, "It's okay."

She opened the door and stepped outside, leaving the door partially open.

"What are you doing here?" she asked.

"Khalil owes me some money," Alonzo told her.

"I don't have anything to do with Khalil's debt. We're not together anymore. He's locked up, so I don't think you will be getting your money anytime soon."

"See, that's the problem. I need my money."

"What do you want me to do about that? That's between you and Khalil."

"Khalil said you were the one who hooked him up with the pills. I figured you could do the same for me. It'll clear his debt, and we won't have a problem."

"I've never done anything like that for him."

She looked back at the door, wondering if Jamison was listening.

"I know you and your girl at the hospital know a few doctors that could use some extra cash. Get me the same deal you got for Khalil."

"I can't help you."

"If you can't, then get me my money. He owes me seven thousand."

"Seven thousand dollars?"

"Yeah. If you ask me, it's easier to put me on. But that's up to you."

"Alonzo, how do you think I have that type of money to pay you?"

"Because you're the reason Khalil is locked up and why he fucked up my money. I'll be back, and when I come back, you better have my money or my connect. If not, then I'll have to pay a visit to your job."

Alonzo turned to walk away.

"Wait!"

Alonzo turned around.

"I don't have a connect or seven thousand dollars. I'm not getting involved in Khalil's bullshit. You're going to have to take this up with him."

"Bitch, why do you think I'm here?"

Jayda looked surprised. She thought back to the conversation she had with Khalil and realized this was what he warned her about.

She turned around and went back inside the house.

Jamison was walking towards her.

"I was about to come back out to check on you," he said.

"You were about to come back out? Did you hear us talking?" she asked.

"I couldn't hear what you were saying, but I could tell it was pretty intense. Is everything okay? Who was that?"

"I'm fine. It's a friend of Khalil's. He's upset about what happened."

"Are you sure everything's okay?"

"It's okay."

Jayda kissed him.

"Game over by the way. I don't want to get you too worked up," Jayda told him while playfully pushing Jamison back into the house.

"There's a good movie I wanted to watch with you," he said.

Once inside, Jayda locked the door and set the alarm system.

"Okay, I'll be right back," she said.

Jayda went to the bathroom, closed the door behind her, and locked it.

"Oh, my God!" she whispered.

She paced the small floor and then sat down on the toilet. She wished she could call Khalil, but there were no inbound calls to the jail. She had to either visit him or wait for him to contact her again. Her mind raced as she thought about all of the things Alonzo would probably do to her if she didn't comply with his demands. She had never been in a situation like this before. She knew drug dealers didn't play about their money and would kill for lesser amounts of cash. Alonzo had been to her job and her home. She wasn't safe if she didn't come up with something and fast.

Sadly, Jayda felt she may have deserved to be in the predicament that she now found herself in. Despite everything she had been through with Khalil, she knew she had a much bigger price to pay for what she had done in her past. Right then, it was time to face the music.

The thought of what she did sickened her. She jumped up, flipped the toilet seat open, and vomited into the bowl. She had mentally blocked out what happened for many years. The memory of what led to what happened started to resurface after her fight with Shay. No one in the world but her, Shay, and Mr. Clarkson knew what she had done.

She felt the overwhelming urge to free herself of the secret she had kept for so long. She walked out of the bathroom and straight to Jamison, who was sitting on the sofa waiting for her.

"I need to talk to you," Jayda said.

"Sure, let's talk," he said.

He picked up the remote and turned off the television.

"What's going on with you?" he asked.

"Hold on," Jayda said.

She left the room and returned quickly. Jayda sat down beside him.

"I need a friend right now. I need an ear. I'm not looking for advice nor judgement. I just need to tell someone what happened. I need to be free from this," she expressed.

"I'll just listen," he replied.

Jayda exhaled and handed Jamison a check.

"What is this?" he asked.

"I need to talk to you in confidence. It's that serious."

Jamison ripped the check in half and said, "Don't insult me."

"Here it goes. Again, please don't judge me," she said.

"This is a no-judgement zone," he said.

"The reason why Shay and I aren't speaking is because I had sex with Yolanda's father, Mr. Clarkson. Shay threatened to tell Yolanda if I didn't leave the hospital that night."

Jayda paused to assess the damage. Jamison wore a poker face. She couldn't tell what he was thinking.

"Say something," she said.

"Damn, I don't know what to say. Mr. Clarkson? Yolanda's father?"

"Yes, I did it. Believe it or not, Mr. Clarkson was fine back in the day. We were all crushing on him, but there is no excuse for what I did."

"Wow, I can see how that could cause a problem among friends," he said.

"I just wanted to get that off my chest. I'm a shitty person and a shitty-ass friend. I don't deserve to be friends with Yolanda. If she knew what I did, I'm sure we wouldn't have been friends this long. Now Shay is using what happened to push me away from her. I don't know what to do."

Jamison scratched his head.

"What are you thinking? I'm a slut now?" Jayda asked.

"No, of course not. I'm just shocked, that's all. Give me a second to digest this information." He paused. "When you said you had something to tell me, I thought it was going to be something else, but not this."

"Damn it. I knew I shouldn't have talked to you about this. Now you're going to think differently about me. If you're not feeling this, I understand."

"No, that's not it at all. I'm just surprised. You all seem so close. I didn't think you and your friends had something so painful between you. I understand your dilemma. I can even give a little advice."

"Do you think I'm a bad person?"

"No. You are the same beautiful woman I thought you were."

"You're just saying that to make me feel better."

"Jayda, how can I judge you? We've all done some questionable things in our lives. What happened between you and Mr. Clarkson was wrong. He knew better than to have sex with his daughter's friend. You should've been like a daughter to him."

"It's not all on him. He was drunk, and I came on to him."

"He was a grown-ass man. That's some pedophile shit."

"No! I was old enough to know better. I've never blamed him. He tried to stop me, but I wouldn't let him."

"There's no excuse for what he did, and I don't know if I will ever look at him the same."

"Please don't let that cloud your judgement about him. It happened only once, and he regretted it almost immediately. Although we never discussed what happened, I know he still feels awful about it. We just put it behind us and moved on as if nothing happened. Now Shay is forcing me to swim in my shit. That's the only reason all of this is coming up."

"That's tough. I would say truth is the best policy, but it will cost you a lifelong friend."

"As for Shay, I guess we aren't as close as I thought. She wasn't always like this. She seems to be keeping tally of all my fuck-ups. She always has something slick to say, or she'll throw something I've done wrong in my face."

Jamison sat back on the sofa.

"You're a strong woman. I know you'll figure it out."

"I'm not trying to weigh you down with my issues. It's just that I don't have anyone else to talk to right now. Majority of my life, I've had Yolanda and Shay. I never thought we would find ourselves in the positions we're in right now. We know how wicked Shay can be to others, but now I'm her target. Yolanda has always been the strong, level-headed friend who kept us all in check. And I was the one who seemed to know all the moves on the board."

"I know you just wanted an ear, so I'll be that anytime you want me to."

"I knew I could talk to you. You know what? I actually feel better. Thanks for listening."

"You can talk to me anytime about anything. We're still getting to know each other. That means we must know the good, the bad, and the ugly about each other.

"For the record, my life isn't normally this complicated. I'm just a simple girl doing what I love to do, and that's taking care of people. I love my job as a nurse, I love my family, and I love my friends."

"Jayda, you have to take care of yourself before you can take care of others."

"I know that."

Jayda let his words resonate with her. Her heart felt lighter, but she knew there were tough decisions to be made. Jayda's need for approval and Shay's need for acceptance clashed. She didn't know if or when she would speak to Shay again. She had no desire to see or speak to her. She needed to know what Shay planned to do with the information she had on her. If she was going to out her to Yolanda, she wanted to do it first.

Jayda and Jamison settled in to watch a movie. She felt safe in Jamison's arms. She knew he would protect her if he had to; she could feel it. Although nestled in his arms, she could still feel the world's weight upon her shoulders. That outweighed how she felt with Jamison. It was all temporary. Soon, her world would come crashing down around her. She owed a drug dealer money for her ex-boyfriend's debt. Her secret about Mr. Clarkson would be revealed, and she would lose Yolanda as a best friend because she had sex with her father. Jamison would see just how fucked up her life was. Becoming emotional at the thought of all of the things going wrong in her life, Jayda began to cry. She used the touching scene on television as an excuse for her tears. She had to come up with a plan and fast.

The house phone rang. Both Jayda and Jamison turned their heads towards the kitchen.

"That's a first. I forgot you had a house phone. I never heard it ring," Jamison said.

"It doesn't ring that often. You know you have to have that old trusty landline. When the world is in a crisis, do you think that cell phone is going to work? No, it isn't. As long as I have my house telephone, I'm good," Jayda told him.

The phone rang a few more times.

"Are you going to answer that?"

"Maybe I should. Pause the movie for me."

Jayda jogged to the kitchen to answer the phone.

"Hello?" she answered.

"Hello. May I speak to Jayda Price?" an unfamiliar voice asked.

"This is she."

She listened to the person on the other end in horror.

"No! Where is he?" she yelled.

Jamison rushed in the kitchen to check on Jayda.

"What's wrong?" he asked.

Jayda dropped the phone.

"My father, he's gone."

Chapter 26

raise God! Praise God!" Pastor Grayson shouted into the microphone.

The organist played triumphantly as altar call began.

"If there's anyone who doesn't know Jesus and that He died on the cross for our sins, come up! He died so that we may have life and have it more abundantly! Do you want to be saved? Come up! Amen. Amen."

Pastor Grayson gestured for the congregation to stand and those desiring to be saved to come to the altar.

The choir began singing, "Come to Jesus." A few started making their way to the altar. The Holy Spirit was in the building. People were speaking in tongues and shouting. Pastor Grayson spoke a great word that touched many souls, especially Yolanda's. Her heart ached as she stood beside Ryan. She had so much pain. The pastor preached on giving all of your pain, troubles, and problems to God. He spoke on how we try to fight battles that are meant for God.

"Give it all to Him!" the preacher shouted. "It's not your battle; it's the Lord's! Don't worry about your neighbor. Make your way to the front for prayer." Pastor Grayson stepped down to begin praying for those who had formed a line in the center aisle.

Yolanda felt the need for prayer but didn't move towards the altar. She prayed silently, while many wept in the distance. There were shouts and cries among the people. She moved to tears as the spirit moved within her.

Pastor Grayson had initially requested that the congregation stand, close their eyes, and bow their heads. When Yolanda looked up to see what Ryan was doing, she saw that he had quietly made his way to the altar. He was pretty close to the front of the line. She decided to join him, as she knew they both needed prayer. She made her way to him, took his hand, and stood beside him. He was weeping, and she wept with him. When their turn came to be anointed with oil and prayed over, Pastor Grayson laid a hand on each of them and immediately began to speak in tongues. Yolanda could feel the power through him. She screamed and cried as the ushers helped hold her up. She could hear Ryan speaking in tongues.

"God! Yes, Lord. Do it! Fix it! It's done!" Pastor Grayson shouted. "God heard your cry. He has done something special in you and for you. God loves you, sister. God is always in control, sister," he said.

After the pastor finished praying over them, Yolanda opened her eyes. She saw differently. It was as if a blindfold had been removed from her eyes. She saw life, hope, and felt love again. Her heart was no longer heavy with grief. It was an amazing feeling. She looked to her husband, who looked at her ever so lovingly, and fell into his arms.

"I love you, baby. I'm sorry," she said.

"I love you too. I forgive you, and please forgive me," he said.

"I do," she replied.

They walked back to their seats feeling renewed.

After church, the two of them headed home to finish cleaning out the former nursery. She wanted to donate the things from the nursery, but first, she had to build the courage to enter the room. It was part of her healing process.

Standing outside of the nursery, Yolanda slowly opened the door and took a step inside. Once inside, she found that most of the things had already been removed from the room. The crib, dresser, and changing table were all gone. The room had been returned to the original color of Snowbound White. Instead of getting upset or crying, she felt grateful. She was grateful that Ryan had spared her the responsibility of returning the room to a guestroom. There were a few boxes in the middle of the floor. She knelt and opened one of them. Inside the box were a receiving blanket, hat, and booties. She smiled and lifted the receiving blanket to her face. She covered her face with the blanket and inhaled the scent.

The pain she was scared to feel didn't fill her up. Happiness filled her up instead. She thought about her daughter's face and the memories she had with her. The assurance that she would see her again pressed her forward. They planned to turn the room back to a guestroom, but she wanted to leave a piece of Ryanna in there. She looked around and saw the abstract wall art that read "LOVE IS" propped against the wall. She had purchased it during her pregnancy and thought it would be a nice addition to the nursery. It was a piece of art that Ryanna would be able to keep as décor going into her teen years.

"Yes," Yolanda said, picking it up.

She walked over to the spot on the wall where the art used to hang. In Ryan's fashion, he left the nail that had secured the art in the wall. Yolanda shook her head, then she placed the art on the wall and smiled.

"I love you, Ryanna. You will forever be in my heart," she said, as she admired what would be such a small thing to someone else.

Yolanda looked at her watch and realized it was almost time for her appointment. She finished moving boxes out to the hallway. Once she was done, she showered and prepared for her appointment. When she came downstairs in her robe and with her wet hair tied in a towel, she was greeted by her hairstylist Lulu. Lulu was a salon owner and mobile stylist, who was building a celebrity clientele with her amazing talent and services. She was skilled in styling hair and makeup. She was your one-stop shop for the beat.

As she walked down the stairs, she watched as Lulu set up her workstation.

"Hey, Lulu. Thank you so much for making a house call," Yolanda said.

"Hey, girl," Lulu said.

They greeted each other with a hug.

"It's been a while, so don't fuss. I've been going through some things."

"I know. That's why I'm here to get you back to your fabulous self. I'm going to do your lashes and brows today. I see you've been roughing it. We'll get that out of the way too."

Yolanda sat down in the chair.

"Let's see what we have here," Lulu said.

She removed the towel and allowed Yolanda's wet hair to fall freely.

"What did you want today? I brought my bundles with me in case you wanted a sew-in."

"I want something different."

"We can go shorter. You have the face for a nice tapered look."

"That's what I was thinking. Cut it all off."

"Now, I'm not going to cut it too short because I need some hair to work with. But I got you."

"I know you do."

"Sit back and relax."

While Lulu styled Yolanda's hair, she made small talk about her children and the latest gossip at the shop. Yolanda laughed at some of the stories that Lulu shared with her. When she was done, she proceeded to do Yolanda's lashes and brows.

"Wait. Let me see my hair," Yolanda said.

"Wait a minute. I want you to see it all at once. Let me work, YoYo."

As she worked on Yolanda's makeover, she asked, "So, what's going on with your girls?"

"Who? Jayda and Shay?" Yolanda asked.

"Who else am I talking about? I saw the two of them going back and forth on social media."

"What are you talking about?"

"It looked as if it had to do with what happened with you. I'm not sure. That was strange to see because I know how close all of you are. Then I saw that Jayda and Shay are no longer friends. I guess somebody blocked somebody."

"And you know all of this how?"

"You know I was investigating that shit. It had something to do with you, and I wanted to make sure you were alright."

Yolanda shook her head.

"I'm good. The two of them have their moments just like all friends. It's nothing."

"Are you sure?"

"Yes, I'm positive."

"I also heard your girl, Shay, had something to do with that guy who was all over the news after being shot."

"What?"

"Yeah, the one that was supposed to be playing football. I heard he was fucking with Shay's ass, and she set him up. She was there when it went down. How was he the only one shot and nothing happened to her?"

Lulu paused and took a closer look at Yolanda.

"You didn't know?"

"No. This is the first of me hearing about all of this. Where do you get your information?"

"The news, the streets, and the salon. Facts are she was there, and he was shot. Everything else is speculation. I'm surprised she didn't tell you."

"I haven't spoken to anyone. I've been focusing on me."

"Now, can you focus on your friend because I'm hearing some bad shit out here?"

"Don't believe everything you hear."

"Of course not, but facts are facts. Oh, and I heard that Jayda got Khalil locked up. About time she stopped letting him dog her out. Good for her. I heard he owes a lot of money out here in these streets. You know how that goes."

"How do you know more about my sisters than I do? I have got to see what's going on."

"And another thing, people use that word sis too damn much. Sista, sister, sis, sus. That shit means nothing to some. Everybody is not your sis, you feel me? When bitches come at me with that sis shit, I be like, *No, I'm just your beautician. We are not friends.*"

"Yes, I know what you mean. What would I do without you, Lulu?"

"I'm just the messenger. I just wanted to make sure you knew what was going on. I know since your daughter passed away; you've been a little out of touch."

Yolanda took in a deep breath. "Thanks for the update."

Lulu continued to fill Yolanda in as she thought about Jayda and Shay.

"Oh, have you seen Koshie?" Lulu asked.

"Who?" Yolanda asked.

"I think you two used to be friends. She came to the shop a couple months back asking about you."

"It's been so long. No, I haven't."

"I didn't say much, but she was asking your cousin about you. You know I fired him three times in the past six months. You need to talk to him. He can't keep sleeping with the clients."

"What did he tell her?" Yolanda asked, ignoring all that other stuff Lulu was talking about.

"From what I could hear, he wasn't trying to tell her much of anything. He basically said he hadn't talked to you in a while, which we all knew was a lie. That's what got my attention. That Koshie chick was really trying to get some info out of him, but he curved her. She really wanted to see you. I thought she found you by now."

"I guess we'll catch up soon."

Yolanda tried to maintain her composure. She was shaking and didn't want Lulu to notice.

Yolanda thought about all the missed calls from her cousin Drew. He had sent many urgent text messages, but she didn't return any of them. Now she knew why.

"All done. Girl, I put the sauce on it! Ryan, come see your wife!"

"Let me see first."

Yolanda reached for the mirror, but Lulu pulled it back from her reach.

Ryan walked into the room. The look on his face made Yolanda grab the mirror from Lulu.

She looked at herself in the mirror.

"Wow! I love it!" Yolanda said.

"Thanks, Lulu. Now, it's time for you to go so I can be alone with my wife and that new haircut," Ryan said.

"You look so beautiful," Lulu commented.

"Thanks to you," Yolanda said.

Ryan walked over to Yolanda and kissed her.

"You're looking really good, woman," he told her.

"Thank you, baby!" Yolanda said.

Lulu began to breakdown her workstation. "Let me go so you two can have some privacy."

Yolanda stood and walked over to the mirror on the wall to get a better look at her makeover.

"Nice," she said.

"More like sexy, if you ask me. Not that you weren't sexy before, but there is a little more edge there," Ryan side, walking up behind her.

Ryan kissed Yolanda on the neck. She closed her eyes and moaned. He continued kissing her along her neck and bare shoulders as he removed her robe. Underneath, she had on a bra and panty set.

"Is it too soon?" he whispered in her ear, then he sucked on it.

"No, it's just right," she moaned.

Chapter 27

As Jayda sat at her computer, someone began ringing her doorbell repeatedly. After grabbing the baseball bat from behind the door, she opened her front door to find Yolanda standing there. Before she could greet her, Yolanda walked right in.

"Hey, I've been looking for you," she said. "I went to your job, and they said you were out on leave."

"Hey!" Jayda said. "I didn't know you were home." She paused for a moment, noticing Yolanda's new cut. "Damn, that style looks good on you!"

"Thanks. I've been home for a few days. How come you haven't been answering your phone?"

"My phone is in my bedroom on the charger. I'm working on something right now and didn't want to be disturbed. Did Lulu do that? That cut is everything!"

"Yes and stop changing the subject."

"How come no one told me you were home? The last thing I knew was that you were in a treatment center and couldn't have visitors. How are you?"

"I'm much better. The question is, how are you? How's Shay? From what I hear, you two have something ugly going on."

"What did she tell you?"

"She didn't tell me anything. She's at work. I'll talk to her this evening. What's going on between the two of you?"

"Lulu?"

"It doesn't matter who told me! Talk! Tell me what's going on."

"Calm down, please. Let's sit down."

Yolanda followed Jayda to the dining room. Jayda retrieved a wine glass and poured a glass of wine for Yolanda.

"I hope that's for you because I'm taking a break from spirits. But help yourself," Yolanda told her and then said, "This is not the time for the two of you to be fighting. You won't believe what I'm about to tell you."

"What's going on?" Jayda asked.

Yolanda took a deep breath. "Koshie is home, and she's been looking for me."

"Yeah, that's what I thought. I received a friend request from her. I wasn't sure if she was in or out. Why was she asking around about you? Do you think she knows what we did?"

"I don't know, but we have to be careful. We have to stick to our story, no matter what."

Jayda downed the glass of wine she had just poured.

"I can't do this. It's too much going on all at once," Jayda said.

"Are you worried about Shay? You two are going to smooth it over. You've been friends way too long," Yolanda said.

"No. My father died," Jayda said.

"Oh no! I'm so sorry to hear that, Jayda. What happened to him?" Yolanda asked.

"It happened suddenly. I was here with Jamison, and then I received a call from the hospital that my father died."

"When?"

"Last night. It all happened last night." She began to cry.

"Jayda, I know how much your father meant to you. Anything you need, please don't hesitate to ask. Have you started making the funeral arrangements?"

"I didn't have to. My father already took care of everything. He had a burial plan for years. He didn't want me or mom to go through what he went through with my mother. I only have a few small things to take care of, but other than that, there's nothing else for me to do."

"It's good you don't have to make all of the plans for his burial." Yolanda sat back in the chair and shook her head. "Damn, I came in here like a storm and didn't even know you lost your father. I'm so sorry about that."

"It's not like you knew what happened. We have been out of touch lately. There's a lot that we need to talk about. Shay is out of control. I don't want to see or talk to her."

"This may not be the right time, but I need to know what's going on with you two. She's going to tell her side. So, I'm giving you a chance to tell yours."

"She's a dirty bitch. You know that. We've seen how dirty she can play. This time, she's coming for me and our friendship."

"What can she possibly do to come between our friendship? We've been friends the longest. Nothing can come between us. You know that."

Jayda took a deep breath.

"Right now, I want to lay my father to rest and figure out what I'm going to do with the rest of my life. I have Jamison by my side, and then I have this dark cloud hovering over me. Khalil just won't go away."

"Speaking of Khalil, is he in some type of trouble? I heard he has debt out here in the streets. Did you know that?"

"You wouldn't believe what he has gotten me into. This man is coming around here asking for money that he owes him. At least Khalil found it in his heart to warn me, but what can I do about it? The fucked-up part is my father dying may have saved my life. I'll have the money to pay Alonzo to leave me the fuck alone."

"Has he threatened you?"

"Yes."

"You need to call the police. Have you told Jamison what's going on?"

"Hell no! He can't find out. I'm going to handle it."

"Between you and Shay, I don't know which one of you is worse. Did you hear about Shay?"

"No. I told you that I haven't spoken to her, but I did see on the news that Rob was shot."

"Lulu said that people think she set him up. She was there when he got shot."

Jayda chuckled. "I wouldn't be surprised if she did. You know she can't be trusted. She's been working him for months now, trying to get pregnant so she can get some of that football money. Now look."

"She's our girl. She needs us," Yolanda said.

"I have my own problems. My days of running to Shay's rescue are over. After what she did, I will never forgive her. I'm done, YoYo. If you still want to deal with her, do so at your own risk, but don't call me when she starts tripping on you."

Yolanda stared at Jayda and then looked at her suspiciously.

"Naw, something isn't right here. What does Shay have on you? Whatever it is, it must be serious."

"Please! I'm telling you; she's turning on the only people who have been there for her. She is reckless, careless, and doesn't care who she hurts."

"I'm surprised by you two. Now is the time where our friendship is needed more than ever. We are supposed to be tight, not ripping each other apart. What happened to that bond we shared? What happened to us being more like sisters than friends? Where is the love?"

"I don't know, but you can start by keeping Shay away from me. I have my father's funeral to plan, and I need to pay off Khalil's debt. Until then, I can't deal with this."

Yolanda shook her head in disbelief.

"I need you and Shay. I'm at my lowest. If the two of you won't do it for yourselves, then do it for me."

Jayda sighed and slouched down in her chair, pouting out her lips.

"She needs to apologize first. Then I may entertain the thought of forgiving her. I'll do it for you."

"Thank you."

Jayda's phone rang. She picked it up and smiled, then answered without excusing herself from the conversation. Yolanda rolled her eyes as she listened to the one-sided conversation.

"Hey, Jamison… I'm still in shock. Thank God, my dad was thoughtful. He knew I wouldn't be able to do this… Sure, I would love your company. See you later. Bye."

Jayda ended the call with the widest smile.

"That man just does something to me. With all that I'm going through, he is my peace in the storm," Jayda said.

"Are you in love with Jamison? When did this happen?" Yolanda asked, surprised.

"I don't know, but I really like him. We're taking it slow. I don't want to mess this up."

"Slow is good. Just pace yourself and follow your heart. He's definitely an upgrade from what's-his-name," Yolanda said jokingly.

"Who?" Jayda replied and fell out laughing. "Girl, I needed that laugh."

"Me too. I need more laughs," Yolanda told her.

"I feel you."

"I'll call Shay. We will be over tomorrow since Jamison is coming over today. I don't want you alone during this time. You were right there with me every step of the way when my baby girl died, and I'm going to be right here for you."

Jayda began to cry.

"I don't know where I would be without you in my life. You are my angel. I love you so much," Jayda said.

"I love you too," Yolanda said while sniffling. "See, it's all love. All we're missing is Shay. Then we will be complete."

"Girl, bye. Don't push your luck," Jayda said, pushing Yolanda towards the door.

Chapter 28

The alarm on Shay's phone sounded. Rolling over in bed, she dismissed it. She didn't know if she wanted to call into work and visit Rob instead. Since she couldn't afford to miss too many days from work, she decided to go in.

The local news and other networks reported on the shooting as well as the condition of Rob. From the latest report, he was robbed and shot. His condition was critical. She feared her name being released in the media as more details began to emerge. She didn't want anyone to think she had anything to do with the shooting since she was the one left alive. It could be hard for someone to believe she wasn't involved in what had happened to him.

Why would they leave a witness behind?

She planned to drop off her children, go to work, and then visit Rob in the hospital. As she proceeded to get herself and the children dressed, she listened to the local news. She wanted to stay up-to-date with what was being reported. Before she headed out the door, she heard a report on Rob. It was breaking news.

"Now, an update on Robert Gibbs. It is with great sadness that we report the passing of Robert Gibbs. He was the victim of a robbery and shooting, and he succumbed to his injuries early this morning. Sadly, Robert Gibbs didn't get a chance to begin his professional football career," the anchorwoman reported.

Shay froze; she couldn't move. As the anchorwoman moved on to the next news story, she still heard the report on Rob repeating in her head.

He's dead.

She couldn't believe he died and that she found out through the local news first. She had given his mother her phone number, but she hadn't called her. Shay felt her knees start to buckle as the thought crossed her mind that the night

Rob was shot, he engaged in unprotected sex with her for the first time. There was a possibility she could be pregnant with his baby. She no longer wanted to be pregnant. There was no benefit anymore. There wouldn't be any big checks coming her way. The plan she had died with Rob.

"Mommy," her daughter, Tyra, said.

Tyra tugged at her mother's dress.

Shay heard her daughter, but she couldn't find her voice to answer her. She tried to open her mouth, but nothing came out.

"Mommy, let's go. I'm going to miss breakfast," Tyler told her.

Finally, Shay found the strength to respond. "Okay, let's go."

She felt sick. She needed to sit down.

"Go and make sure all of the lights are off for me."

Tyra ran off to do as her mother requested.

"Are you okay?" Tyler asked.

"I'm okay. My stomach just hurts a little. Give me a minute," she said.

Shay gathered the strength to stand. She put on a fake smile for her children, all the while feeling sick to her stomach and fighting the urge to cry. After dropping her kids off at school, she headed to work.

During the drive to work, she thought of the last night she and Rob spent together, and tears filled her eyes. She quickly wiped them away as they fell. When she arrived at her office, she pulled into the parking lot. She checked the clock and noticed she was about fifteen minutes late. She ran late at least a couple of days out of the week, but she hadn't worried about it since no one had said anything to her. She slipped into the office quietly in hopes that no one noticed her tardiness.

Looking down at the street from her sixth-floor office window, Shay observed the people below. Crowds of people shuffled up and down the street, going to work and meetings in the business district. She tried to figure out how she could be so coldhearted towards Robert's death. She felt some grief, but she was still able to come to work.

She rubbed her hand over her belly and said, "Not now."

Knock, knock, knock.

Turning around, Shay said, "Come in."

The manager, Mr. Haskins, opened the door and peeked his head inside.

"Good morning, Shay. Do you have a moment?" he asked.

"Sure. Come in," Shay said, sitting down behind her desk.

Mr. Haskins walked in followed by Mr. Powell, who was most notably known as Mr. Pee. The smile on her face disappeared.

Mr. Powell derived the name Mr. Pee from smelling like urine. He thought Mr. Pee was a nickname the staff had given him to shorten his name. He and Shay didn't have the best relationship. Mr. Powell walked into the breakroom one day and overheard Shay make a joke about him as he was leaving. Once she thought Mr. Powell had walked out of the room, she said, "He knows he wants to eat more than that little entrée. Who does he think he's fooling? His belly ain't sitting on his knees for nothing." Ever since that day, he had it out for her.

"What can I do for you?" she asked the men as they took a seat in front of her desk.

Mr. Haskins loosened the knot in his tie and cleared his throat.

"Shay, it's been brought to my attention that you were late again this morning," he said, looking towards Mr. Powell.

Shay cut her eyes at Mr. Powell.

"Yes, I was a little late, and I plan on staying late to make up that time. I always do," she responded. "I had a rough morning. I found out a friend of mine passed away. Maybe you heard about him—Robert Gibbs."

"Yes, he was a great football player in college. He would've done well had he lived to play professionally. Sorry for your loss," Mr. Haskins said.

"Thank you," she said.

"I wasn't aware the two of you were friends. Sorry," Mr. Powell said.

Shay didn't respond.

There was a pause in the conversation as the two men looked uncomfortably at each other.

"I understand that this may be a very difficult time for you, but there's something we need to talk about. You've seemed to be distracted. Prior to all of this, of course. You've been late to work several days over the last few weeks, late for meetings, and your absences have long been a problem. Your floor is out of control. These people need supervision. That's your job—to supervise your staff. You can't do that if you're not here. Our biggest issue is that you've been handling fewer cases, resulting in Mr. Powell having to handle your responsibilities," Mr. Haskins said.

"Mr. Haskins, when I'm here, I'm working. We have at least four positions that need to be filled out there. That would alleviate some of these calls being escalated once they are filled. And might I add, our turnover rate has greatly decreased since I've been here. At least two of the four positions are direct results of promotions," she said.

"You're right. But there are other issues out there, and we need someone that can do the job consistently. They need to report to work on time and as scheduled," Mr. Powell chimed in.

Shay shifted in her chair but kept a poker face.

"Shay, we are asking you to resign. Please put in your resignation by Monday," Mr. Haskins said as he stood to his feet.

"What? I'm not going to resign," she said, sitting up in her chair. "I've been in this position for the last five years with impeccable performance, according to my evaluations. I have improved the quality of our services. My staff works as hard as they do because of me, not Mr. Powell," she said.

"This isn't up for discussion," Mr. Powell said, standing to his feet.

Shay sat back in her chair and crossed her legs.

"So, the two of you think you can come in here and intimidate me into resigning. This isn't personal, by the way. It's business. I think the two of you should take a seat," she said.

The two men looked at her in dismay and proceeded to leave the office.

"Rebecca is who you intend to place in my position, correct?" Shay asked.

The men stopped walking and turned to face her.

"Well, she is the next person in line for this position," Shay continued. "Oh, and might I add, she's qualified, right? Is sucking dick now a qualification? Because I didn't have that on my résumé nor was it a job requirement. Mr. Haskins, did Rebecca suck your dick so good that you plan to move her into my position?"

"I beg your pardon?" Mr. Haskins said.

"I beg your pardon," she mimicked. "If you fire me or force me to resign, I'll go straight to Human Resources and report the numerous times I saw you and Rebecca come out of your office with smeared lipstick on the front of your pants. There are about a dozen others that have witnessed the same. I have proof. I have pictures and videos. By the way, you should replace that broken blind in your office window. A lot can be seen through there," she said.

Mr. Haskins tightened his tie and glared at Mr. Powell as he walked out, slamming the door behind him.

"And you, I have a file on you documenting all of the company policies you have broken as well as a few laws. I can pass it along on my way out. It wouldn't serve any purpose to me anymore. It's up to you," she said.

Mr. Powell didn't respond for a couple of minutes.

"You will need to be here on time each day. No more long breaks, last-minute call outs, and don't undermine my authority in front of staff," he snarled.

She sat back in her chair and logged onto her computer.

"Now, get the fuck out. I have work to do," Shay said.

Mr. Powell left the office in a hurry, also slamming the door behind him.

Shay breathed for what felt like the first time. She opened and closed her clammy hands, then wiped them on her skirt.

She looked over at her cell phone and noticed a notification. Picking up her phone, she saw a text from Yolanda, and a smile immediately spread over her face.

"Oh, my God! YoYo!" she said.

She quickly read the message requesting, but somewhat demanding, her presence at Jayda's house to console her in her time of need. Her smile turned into a frown.

She dropped her phone on her desk and said, "Damn it."

Chapter 29

Jayda, you should try to eat a little," Jamison said.

Jayda picked around her plate of sushi. "I'm not hungry. I keep thinking about my father all alone in that cold funeral home. I can't wait to see him tomorrow."

"I'll be there once I get out of court."

"Jamison, you've done enough. You don't have to be there tomorrow for the viewing. I know you have a big case that you're working on. My family will be there. I will be fine."

"I know you will be fine. But you're my woman, and I need to be there to support you."

"And you're my man."

Jamison stood up from the table.

"Today, you have declared us a couple! We are a couple!"

"Yes, Jamison, we are a couple. I couldn't ask for a better partner and friend."

Jamison walked over to Jayda and extended his hand out to her. She took his hand and stood with him.

"Jayda, as your man, I promise to love, protect, and care for you," Jamison said.

"Jamison, as your woman, I promise to love you as you love me," Jayda said.

"That's fair, I think," Jamison said cautiously.

Jayda gave Jamison a quick kiss on the lips and tried to walk away, but Jamison pulled her back in by the waist.

"Get back over here," he said.

He kissed her deeply.

Jayda slowly opened her eyes after the long kiss.

"I love you," Jayda told him.

"I love you too," he replied.

They stared into each other's eyes. Without saying a word, he lifted Jayda up, and she wrapped her legs around him as they kissed passionately.

"Wait a minute. I have a nail appointment in a couple of hours," Jayda said between kisses.

"I only need an hour," Jamison said.

"An hour?" Jayda asked.

Jamison lowered Jayda down on the sofa as they continued to kiss. While kissing her, he slowly removed her bottoms and her top. Jamison then kneeled before her and partook of her sweet peach as he parted her legs wide and high. Jamison's tongue danced slowly across her center. He spoke a language that was new to her as an explosion of pleasure erupted inside of her. She clawed at the fabric under her and let out sounds of pleasure. Just when she was ready to tap out, Jamison did something unexpectedly. He lowered her legs down around his neck to position her peach in his face. He then stood to his feet and flipped her upside down to continue his dance on her peach.

She was shocked that she was in that position, but she fell into position like a pro. She eased Jamison's bulging penis out of his pants and took him into her mouth. She found his nicely-sized, veiny penis to be more than adequate for her. They both moaned as they enjoyed each other and pleased the other.

Jayda stopped and kissed the tip of his penis. He got the message. He then lowered her down until she stood in front of him. He removed his shirt and pants. For the next hour, they made love. Jamison delivered strong strokes that hit the spot each time, giving her an orgasmic experience. He fought back his orgasm with each stroke, heightening his experience. After the first time they made love, Jayda didn't want the feeling to end.

She felt safe, loved, and protected with Jamison, who was almost too good to be true. In comparison to Khalil, she didn't understand why someone like him would come into her life. She had kissed many frogs, but none like Jamison. Being with him scared her. He was a loving person and the sex was great. She liked that he was a gentle, pleasing lover.

"Wow! That's what I'm talking about," Jamison said.

"Listen to you," Jayda said.

"What? I knew it was going to be good, but that was damn good."

"You were alright."

"Alright?"

"I'm just playing. It was amazing."

"You are amazing."

Jayda sighed.

"What's wrong?" he asked.

"I'm not deserving of all of this. How can I go from being with a convicted felon to a lawyer overnight? Like really, that doesn't happen in real life."

Jamison reached for Jayda's face and turned her to face him.

"When a man finds a wife, he finds a good thing. Not the other way around."

Jayda smiled. "I've heard that before. You're just a special guy, and I'm still in awe of all of this."

"I hope we didn't move too fast. I know you're grieving, but this wasn't a mistake."

"I'm not saying that. I'm saying that you and I are too good. I'm just waiting for the bottom to fall out. I'm expecting to find out something horrible about you or find out you're not the nice guy that you portray yourself to be."

"I'm everything that I say I am. If I ever show you anything different, you can get a refund. I know what I'm signing up for. You've been hurt. You probably never had a man show his love for you the way that I do. I'm never going to put my hands on you. That isn't love. You have to realize that. Nothing you experienced in your past relationship is going to occur with us."

"I hear you, Jamison. I'm just processing."

Jamison gave her a quick peck on the lips and asked, "Don't you have an appointment?"

"Yes, but I need a few minutes."

Jamison gave a small chuckle and folded his arms behind his head.

She pressed her legs close together as she tried to push down the sensitivity running through her core. She and Jamison had made love for the first time. It had been a long time since she looked at herself in the mirror and smiled at what she saw. After she showered, she wiped the steam from the mirror and saw herself differently. She wasn't covering up scars or wiping away tears. She smiled because she truly felt loved and protected by Jamison.

The fumes in the nail shop swirled around Jayda's nose. Jayda let out a cough.

"Do you want a mask?" Porsha asked.

Porsha was Jayda's nail technician.

"No, I'm fine. You're almost done now," Jayda said.

"Why are you so quiet today?" Porsha asked.

"My father passed away. I'm trying to prepare for the funeral, as if there is a way to prepare yourself for something like that."

Jayda was flooded with emotions at the thought of her father.

"Oh, Jayda! I'm so sorry for your loss. I know how close you two were."

"It was so sudden. I just wasn't ready to lose him. Now both of my parents are gone, and that feels just crazy."

"Life has a funny way of showing up. We lose our loved ones, we lose jobs, we get sick, and we lose everything. That's why you have to have faith in God."

"I hear you, girl. That's what's getting me through it. God and Jamison."

"Who is Jamison? I knew you were glowing."

Jayda closed her eyes as she thought about Jamison and began telling Porsha about her new love.

"Jamison is love. He is everything I ever wanted in a man. So much that he scares me."

"You deserve better than Khalil. If this Jamison loves you the way you need to be loved, good for you. You know what? Today is all about you. You're going through a lot right now. The least I can do for one of my best clients is to give you the P-Special on me."

A tear fell from Jayda's eye, and she let out a small laugh.

"You don't have to do that, Porsha."

"No. I got you, friend. Right now, I can only imagine how you are feeling. You are mourning your father's death, and then you finally found a man who loves you. That can be a bit confusing and conflicting. Your father would be happy to know you are in good hands with Jamison. Anybody is better than Khalil in my eyes."

"Stop it. I made a huge mistake with that one."

"Today is about your needs. Today, you need some pampering. Please let me do this for you."

Jayda gave it some thought and then agreed to the P-Special that included the deluxe spa treatment.

"I was waiting for a friend who is already running late. I'd love to have the P-Special. Thank you so much, Porsha."

"Is Shay or Yolanda coming by?" Porsha asked, massaging Jayda's hands.

"No, another friend of mine."

The door chimed, alerting them that a customer had arrived. Jayda didn't bother turning around to see who had come into the shop.

Porsha looked up and greeted the person.

"Hi. How can I help you?" Porsha asked.

"Hi. I'm here for that girl right there," Sophia said, pointing at Jayda.

"Someone is here to see you," Porsha said, nodding towards the door.

Jayda turned around.

"Hey, Sophia! You're just in time," Jayda said.

"You can wash your hands now," Porsha said.

Jayda gestured for Sophia to follow her to the back of the shop where the sinks were located, while Porsha went to get the pedicure station ready for Jayda.

"Hey, thanks for coming," Jayda said.

"You know I got you, girl. Sorry about your father, Jay."

Jayda didn't respond.

"Did you bring it?" Jayda asked.

"Yes, it's right here," Sophia said, handing Jayda an envelope.

"Thank you! As soon as I get the insurance money, I'm going to pay you back."

"You better. Now that we're out of the pill game, I got to find a new hustle. This is most of the money I had saved up. Here, and be careful dealing with Alonzo."

Sophia handed the bag to Jayda, and Jayda carried the money over to her purse, placing it inside. Then she and Sophia hugged.

"Thank you," Jayda whispered in her ear.

"Love you, girl. I have to get going. Someone is out, and I have to cover her shift," Sophia said with a wink.

"I'll be back soon."

"I know you will. Take all the time you need. We're loving all the extra overtime!" Sophia said on her way out the door.

Jayda smiled as she watched Sophia leave.

"Are you ready?" Porsha asked, seated at the pedicure station.

"Yes," Jayda replied.

Jayda walked over to Porsha. She removed her shoes and enjoyed the P-Special. By the time Porsha was done, Jayda was so relaxed she could've taken a quick nap. She felt relaxed and lighter.

"Thank you for everything you've done for me today. I feel so much better," Jayda said, hugging Porsha.

"You're welcome. I'm glad I could do something to help lift your spirits," Porsha told her.

"That, you have done."

As Jayda drove home, she prayed her meeting with Yolanda and Shay would go well. She didn't want to fight with Shay in front of Yolanda. Shay was petty enough to tell her secret. She told herself that kissing Shay's ass would be mandatory in order to keep her in check, no matter how much it killed her. Challenging her would provoke her. She would have to deal with Shay another time.

"Incoming call from…" Jayda's car notified her.

Jayda pressed the button to accept the call, although she didn't recognize the phone number.

"Hello?" she answered.

"Sorry to hear about your pops. My condolences," Khalil said.

Jayda turned her nose up.

"Thank you, but how did you know?" she asked.

"It's my business to know what's going on with you. I left you there holding the bag. I have to make sure you're safe. How are you doing?"

The softness and sincerity in his voice almost made her smile, but she quickly remembered his short temper.

"So much for keeping me safe. One of your savages came to my house looking for money that you owe him. He threatened me."

"Alonzo came to my house?!"

"No, fool. Alonzo came to *my* house. Why did you tell him about our arrangements? You put me and my job in jeopardy!"

"I'm sorry about that. Why the fuck did he come to the house? I don't fuck with him like that."

"Apparently, you do. He threatened me. He said you owe him money. I'm going to pay him, and you're going to pay me back my money."

"What the fuck? I don't owe him shit. Our business been done."

"I don't know what you have going on but I don't want to have anything to do with it."

"I do have a tab but not with him. Don't pay him."

"My job and safety are on the line. What else am I supposed to do? I'm going to handle it. Not for you but for me. I don't trust you. For all I know you could be getting payback. I'm only doing this because you put me in danger."

"I always knew you had it in you. That was why I fucked with you. You tried to act all classy and shit."

"Khalil, I don't have time for you. Just pay me back my money."

"I ain't paying shit I don't owe."

"Fuck you! I'm gone."

"Why are you so quick to get me off the phone? You know how hard it is to make calls up in here?"

"I don't care."

There was silence on the phone.

"I'm hanging up," Jayda said, reaching to end the call.

"Since you got some new dick, you think you can hang up on me now? You grew some balls or some shit! Don't forget, Jayda!"

Jayda paused.

"What are you talking about?"

"I know you have some lame coming to my house. You probably got me locked up so you could be with him."

"You're locked up because you are abusive!"

Khalil laughed.

"I was done with your ass anyway."

"Well, good. I'm done with your ass too."

Jayda ended the call.

Her hands stuck to the steering wheel as she realized how sweaty her palms had become. She noticed that she would have some type of physical reaction whenever she spoke to Khalil. Although he was in jail, he still made her nervous.

Chapter 30

O h, no!" Jayda shouted.

She had just watched a funny video on her cell phone while sitting on the sofa with her feet on the ottoman. She played video after video of hilarious animal and human interactions. She tried to lessen her anxiety as she waited for the arrival of Yolanda and Shay. She was not sure if Shay had agreed to join them. She had about an hour to prepare herself.

Jayda finalized the funeral arrangements the day before and only needed to show up on the day of the funeral. Each time she thought about the funeral, she became nauseated, and a feeling of emptiness filled her. She had to shake it off and be strong. She promised herself that she would be strong, and then she would allow herself to break down. She knew if she allowed herself to feel, she wouldn't have the strength or mind to handle the issues at hand: Alonzo and Shay.

The video she was watching was interrupted by a call from Jamison. Jayda smiled as butterflies rushed her stomach.

"Hey, Jamison," she answered.

"Hey. How are you?" Jamison asked.

"I'm well. Especially after being with you."

"So, I guess I'm not the only one thinking about how amazing we are together."

"Amazing is an understatement."

"Is that right?"

"Yeah, that's right."

"I hear you, but your tone doesn't sound quite right."

"It's just that I haven't properly grieved my dad yet. I feel guilty about it. But I know if I allow myself to break down now, it's not going to be good. I have a lot ahead of me in the next couple of days, and I have to have the mind and strength to get through it. I just feel a little guilty, that's all. Oh, it didn't help that Khalil called me today."

After those words left her mouth, she wished she could reach through the line and yank that last sentence back.

There you go getting too comfortable, running off at the mouth. That man doesn't want to hear about Khalil.

"I understand you feel that you always have to be strong. You did just lose your father. It's okay to cry. It's okay to grieve your loss. That doesn't make you weak or incompetent. We all grieve differently. I guess you have to grieve in your own way. Don't worry about what others think. You do what you need to do."

Jayda closed her eyes as she listened to Jamison's comforting words in his sexy voice. She also took note that he didn't acknowledge that Khalil called her.

"Jayda?"

"Yes, I'm here," she said, snapping out of a daze.

"Did you meet with your friends yet?"

"No, not yet. They should be here in about an hour or so."

Just then, the doorbell rang.

"Speaking of friends, I think they're here. Early!"

"I'll let you go then."

"Okay, bye."

Jayda hung up the phone and dropped it on the sofa. Then she jumped up and stomped to the front door. After slowly opening the door, she looked over both Yolanda and Shay, then settled her eyes on Yolanda. Yolanda smiled widely at her and winked her eye.

"Hey. I know we are early, but we're here," Yolanda said joyfully.

"Yes, you are early. I wasn't ready for guests," Jayda said.

"Are you going to let us in? I have food," Shay said, holding up two large bags.

Jayda acknowledged Shay by sucking her teeth and rolling her eyes. She moved back and invited them in with a wave of her hand.

"I just didn't expect you two so soon. I was trying to relax before you came," Jayda said, locking the door behind them.

"Kill the attitude, Jayda. We come in peace and with food," Yolanda said. "There should be plenty of leftovers. The last thing you need to worry about is cooking. Oh, and Shay and I have arranged for a week's worth of meals to be delivered following the funeral service. If you need more, we can arrange that too. Anything else you need, just ask."

"I'm sorry to hear about your dad. He was like a father to me," Shay said.

Shay gestured as if she wanted to hug Jayda but decided against it. Jayda wanted to punch Shay in the mouth before, but now she wanted to embrace her friend. She thought about it and decided to concede. Holding out her arms, she invited Shay to an embrace. Shay's face relaxed and moved in quickly for a hug. Jayda and Shay embraced and held on to each other for a moment.

"Yes! Thank you, Jesus!" Yolanda shouted, clapping her hands. "I thought I was going to have to fight the both of you to get you to talk to each other again. Unfortunately, you had to come together like this."

"Not so fast. We still have something we need to talk about," Jayda said to Shay.

"Yes, I know," Shay responded.

"Well, I guess I can call Ryan while the two of you talk." Yolanda headed down the hallway. "Play nice!"

"Wait!" Shay said. "I have something to tell you."

Jayda cut her eyes at Shay. She readied herself to pounce on her as soon as the wrong words left her mouth.

"I saw Koshie the night Rob was killed. She was one of the women at the hotel. She saved my life. She protected me," Shay told them.

"What?" Yolanda said. "How come you didn't tell us?"

"We weren't talking, remember?" Shay said.

"She saved your life?" Jayda asked.

"Yes, she did," Shay said. "I don't think she knows."

"But she friend requested me and went looking for Yolanda. What do you think she wants?" Jayda asked.

"I don't know, and I really don't want to find out. If she was part of the robbery and homicide, I can only imagine what she would do to us if she knew what we did," Yolanda said, then added, "I think we all should keep our distance from her. If any of us have contact with her, play it cool and let the rest of us know."

"Should I accept her friend request? I don't want to make things seem suspicious. Let's not raise any red flags," Jayda said.

"Yes, accept it. Feel her out a little. If she wanted revenge, trust me, she could've had it," Shay said.

"Okay. You two hash it out. I'll be back," Yolanda said as she left the room.

"I think we should sit down," Jayda said.

They took a seat in the living room beside each other.

"Don't talk too loud. I don't want her to hear us," Jayda said.

"First of all, I'm sorry for how I treated you at the hospital. I was so angry with you over how you and Yolanda handled Ryanna's death. I blamed you for everything that was happening with her. That's why I acted so stupid that night," Shay explained.

"That was fucked up! There's no way I would've treated you that way. We are supposed to be sisters, right? So, where did that type of wickedness come from? I know you didn't agree with how I advised her, but you made that known. I didn't want her to go to prison for a mistake. I would've done the same thing for you. What is really the issue with us?" Jayda asked.

Shay took a deep breath.

"Tell me," Jayda said.

"Truth is, I held your secret for years. Your secret was my secret. The night that you got Mr. C to have sex with you was the night our friendship changed."

"What do you mean?"

"I too had a fling with Mr. C. My fling was a little different from yours. He actually had sex with you. I tried to get him to have sex with me, but all he wanted was oral sex. He told me it was wrong for us to be having sex, but he didn't have a problem with me getting on my knees. That was because his wife wasn't doing it. I was so mad at you. You got something I couldn't get from him."

"You were jealous? I get it now. You do know that was the first and last time that ever happened?"

"I believe you."

"What I did was so wrong. I own that. I was insecure, and my self-esteem was non-existent at that time in my life. He had sex with me out of pity. That didn't feel good at all; trust me. I regret my actions every day. I betrayed my friend, and she doesn't even know it. Shay, I'm sorry if you felt that I stepped on your toes. I had no clue what was going on with you. We were both crushing on him."

"I know. It's that little girl inside that held on to resentment towards you. I'm sorry, Jayda."

"I'm sorry too."

"I missed you, friend."

"I missed your crazy ass too."

"Sorry about Rob. I never got around to talking to you about that. We weren't talking at the time."

"I know, and I don't want to talk about that right now."

Jayda and Shay hugged and cried on each other's shoulders.

"All is well except Yolanda," Shay said.

"What do you mean?" Jayda asked.

"We made up, but she doesn't have a clue why we really fell out in the first place."

"Oh, no. I'm not telling her about that. Let the past stay in the past."

"It's up to you. But, if your truth is revealed, I'll also reveal mine. She'll have to kill us both, and we know she can't live without us."

They shared a laugh.

"You sneaky bitches!" Yolanda said, popping out from behind a wall.

"Yolanda!" Jayda said, standing to her feet.

"I knew one of you fucked my father. I knew Shay would do it, but not you, Jayda!" Yolanda said.

Jayda broke their embrace, startled by Yolanda's interruption.

"I'm sorry. I was young, dumb, and insecure. My self-esteem had to be dragging on the floor to do what I did," Jayda cried.

"Oh, I can't believe you!" Yolanda shouted. "Shay, you've always been a whore. I expect something like that from you," she added.

"Now, hold on. You're not going to stand in my face and call me a whore," Shay said.

"My father isn't perfect. He's had his share of affairs. I know that. But I never would've thought you would do something like that, Jayda," Yolanda said.

"I'm sorry. It happened once," Jayda said.

"Once? It should've never happened," Yolanda said.

"You're right. I'm so sorry," Jayda said.

"I'm sorry too," Shay said.

"We never meant to hurt you like this. I always wanted to tell you, but I didn't know how. I promise you it happened one time. And as for Shay, come on. You know what she went through as a child. We can't hold our childish behaviors against each other. We have all done some stupid shit, but look at us now," Jayda said.

"Yeah, look at us now. Fake friends and fake love. I don't need it," Yolanda told her.

Yolanda gathered her things and walked out of the door with Shay and Jayda running behind her.

"No, don't leave!" Shay shouted.

Yolanda backed out of the driveway and sped off.

"Now what?" Jayda shouted at the sky. "All of my dirt is out in the open. Is this what you wanted? You wanted to unburden me? There, you did it. I lost my father and now this. What the fuck did I ever do to you?" she yelled to the heavens.

Shay pulled Jayda into the house as she continued screaming obscenities. It was like she was on the verge of a breakdown.

"Jayda! Calm down. We can fix this!" Shay said.

"Fuck it. My life is one fucked-up picture. I guess God is punishing me. That's how I feel. No matter what I do, I can never outrun trouble. I smile when I'm really hurting. Why do you think I let Khalil hit me for so long? I deserved it. I betrayed my best friend. That's my hell!"

"Oh, Jayda," Shay said as she held her friend in her arms and cried with her.

Chapter 31

"Dad! Where are you?" Yolanda called out.

She went to the kitchen and placed her purse on the counter. Her dry throat reminded her that she needed a drink. She had left Jayda's house and went directly to her parents' house to confront her father. She opened the refrigerator and found it fully stocked. That wasn't anything unusual. What was unusual was not finding any beer. She grabbed a bottle of water and quickly gulped it down.

"Dad!" she called out again, wiping dripping water from her mouth with the back of her sleeve.

The garage door opened, and her dad walked in.

"What's wrong, baby?" her father asked.

"How could you have sex with my friends?!"

Mr. Clarkson walked over to her and grabbed her by the arm. Although she resisted, he managed to pull her into the garage and slammed the door behind them.

"Let me go! You're hurting me!" she said, trying to yank herself free.

"Don't you ever come into my home questioning me about anything that I've done. Do you want to hurt your mother? We've come a long way in our marriage. I've done some things that I'm not proud of, but your mother and I have dealt with those things. Who are you to bring up my past?"

"You fucked my best friends!" Yolanda yelled.

"Don't you talk to me like that! I've raised you, girl. I've taken care of you, and you are going to respect me in my house."

"You're talking about respect. You had sex with my teenage friends! Address that. Explain it."

"Yolanda, I think you should go."

"I'm not going anywhere until you explain how you could do something like that to me. What could you have seen in them? They were little girls."

"Don't you dare imply that! They were eighteen. You all were in your senior year."

"They were my friends! Do you have any sense of right and wrong?"

"What happened between myself and your friends was during a time when alcohol and women were a huge part of my life. I wasn't a good person back then. Your friends were consenting adults at that time. That was still no excuse. I'm ashamed."

"You should be," she cried. "They are the only two real friends that I have in my life. They are my sisters. All of you betrayed me. I know you've had affairs on mom, but I never thought you would've had sex with Jayda and Shay. I'm so disappointed in you. I don't even know what to think about you."

"I'm sorry. I'm a changed man. The man that I am today is much better than the man that I was back then. I'm devoted to your mother and our marriage. And I'm still your father."

"I just need time to think about all of this. I have to go."

"Your mother doesn't need to know about this."

"You telling me?" She shook her head and began to walk away.

"Yolanda, get back here! I'm not done talking to you. You came here like a woman to talk, so let's talk about it."

Yolanda stopped walking and turned to face her father.

"Come here, baby."

"No. I don't want you to touch me."

Mr. Clarkson walked slowly towards her.

"We have to forgive people even when we don't want to. You have to forgive your friends. They love you. We all made a mistake. We realized that and never made that same mistake again. That's all we can do about it now."

"It's disgusting. Every time I think about it, I want to throw up!"

"Don't think about it. Forgive and forget, especially in this situation. I understand where you're coming from, and I'm sorry. Please forgive me."

"It's going to take some time for me. This isn't something you just get over, dad."

"I know. Can your old man get a hug from his baby girl? Come on, baby girl, I need you."

Yolanda slowly walked into her father's waiting arms. She sobbed and cursed him. He consoled her as a father should.

"I could use a drink right about now," Yolanda said.

"Sorry, I can't help you with that. I gave up the beers."

"That's good. Hopefully, you don't make any more mistakes."

"Come on."

"I have to go. I'm emotionally drained. After everything that has happened today, I just took ten steps backwards. As if I don't have enough to deal with. Every time I look at you, I will think about you, Jayda, and Shay together. Disgusting! It's hard enough just to wake up and put my feet on the floor after losing Ryanna."

"Sit down," he said.

"I don't want to sit. I want to go home," she told him.

"Calm down first. I don't want you driving like this. Just take a seat and calm down. I won't bother you."

"Okay," she said.

She walked to a nearby chair and sat down.

"Where's mom?"

"She's at church. She should be here soon. Are you going to tell her?"

"No! That would surely put her in the grave. I would never hurt her like that. You've hurt her enough."

"You're right. I have. I'm spending the rest of my days trying to make it right. In my drunken state, I allowed some inappropriate things to happen. I'm not proud of any of this. It disgusts me."

"Dad, I don't know who you are. I hate you for what you did to mom and me!"

"I'm your father—the same man who fed and clothed you. You will not speak to me like this. No matter what, I've been the best father I knew how to be. I was young when I met your mother. She was older than I was. I wasn't ready for all the things that she was ready for. I just knew that I had this sexy older woman in my life. We fell in love and then we had you. I had to grow up fast. Your mother understood that. She was patient with me. I owe her my life. I promised her no more pain, and I meant that."

Yolanda slouched down in her seat and threw her head back.

"That woman sure does love you," she said.

"And I love her," he replied.

"I know."

"And I love you too."

"I love you too, dad."

"Now, are we done discussing this? Because I have some hard praying to do before your mother gets here."

"Yes, for now."

"I'm going in the house. You can let yourself out."

Yolanda decided to leave. On her way home, she tried to clear her mind of the things that she found out about her father and friends. She never thought her father could be so weak. Not her friends. That was low. She needed to get home. She wanted to lay in Ryan's arms, where she knew she would find comfort.

Yolanda entered her neighborhood. As her mind raced, she tried to apply the skills she learned in therapy. She rounded the corner to her street. Suddenly, a woman and her dog walked out in front of her car. She slammed on her brakes, missing the dog by inches.

"Oh, my God! Are you alright?" Yolanda said, jumping out of the car.

The woman pulled out her earplugs.

"You almost hit us!" the woman yelled.

"Are you okay?" Yolanda asked.

She kneeled to check the dog for injuries. The Labrador Retriever licked at Yolanda.

"I'm fine, but you almost killed my dog. How fast were you going?" the woman asked, holding the leash.

"I wasn't speeding. You didn't stop at the crosswalk. You should be more careful," she said.

"I'm a pedestrian. You need to watch out for me," the woman said.

Giving the leash a yank, she proceeded across the street.

"Really?" Yolanda said, watching as the woman continued to cross the street with her dog.

As she got back into her car, a thought crossed her mind. She remembered the importance of forgiveness. She thought about how she couldn't understand how Ryan forgave her for the death of their daughter. She didn't beg for his forgiveness; he gave it to her. She tried to compare Jayda and Shay's sin to her sin, and there wasn't a point in doing so. She was taught that a sin was a sin. Yes, her two best friends had betrayed her, but they were the same two friends that she loved and cared about. She couldn't imagine finding a friend that could compare to them.

"Lord, help me find it in my heart to forgive them," she prayed.

Chapter 32

The sun beamed down on the cemetery. It had to be the hottest day of the year. The humidity had caused Jayda's hair to frizz. She pulled her hair up into a bun and wiped the sweat from her neck.

Along with other family members, Jayda stood beside her stepmother, Cheryl, in front of her father's casket and tightly held her hand. After the prayer, the crowd began to thin. Jayda looked around for Yolanda. She saw her at the church and was hoping to have a word with her.

"Hey, Jayda," Shay said, startling her. "Hey, Ms. Cheryl."

"Hey. Thanks for coming," Jayda said.

"Hi, there," Ms. Cheryl said. "I remember when you girls used to come over and eat dinner at the house. Quentin loved having you girls over. Where's the other girl?"

"She's here somewhere," Shay said, looking around.

"Mom, get in the car with the air conditioning. It's too hot out for you," Jayda said. "Mitchell, can you please take my mom to the car? I'll be there in a second," she called out to her cousin.

Taking Ms. Cheryl by the arm, Mitchell led her to the car.

"Thank you," Jayda said.

"No problem," Mitchell said.

Shay put an arm around Jayda as they began to walk. Jayda wiped away tears as they fell.

"That was hard," Jayda said. "I held up better than I thought I would. I had to be strong for my mom."

"You're one of the strongest people I know. Even the strong get weak at times. And it's okay."

"Thank you so much for being here for me. I thought we would never talk again."

"Me too. I was such a bitch."

"Yes!"

They laughed.

"Now, we have to get our friend back."

"I don't think she will ever talk to us again, especially me."

"Yeah, she's going to need time to process all of that."

"YoYo is a good person. She'll eventually find it in her heart to forgive us. And if that's all she's offering, I'll take that."

"I'm offering more than that," a voice said from behind them.

Jayda and Shay turned around quickly.

"YoYo," Jayda cried.

"You know I couldn't let you go through this alone," Yolanda said.

Yolanda hugged Jayda and then pulled Shay in.

"Thank you, Jesus," Jayda cried with her eyes to the sky. "I thought you were never going to talk to us again."

"I wasn't, but then I remembered what I learned about forgiveness. Ryan forgave me for what happened. If he could forgive me, then I had to forgive the two of you. No sin is greater than another," Yolanda said.

"Are we back? The three of us?" Shay asked.

"It's always been the three of us. But I have to be honest. I don't consider the two of you my friends. This thing between us showed me that everything I thought about you and our friendships isn't true," Yolanda stated.

"How could you say that? Our friendship and love for each other have always been real. We made a mistake. We aren't the same people we were when we were eighteen and nineteen years old," Shay retorted.

"Yeah, you can't just throw away all these years of friendship," Jayda said.

"Why not? You aren't who I thought you were. And, Shay, you're *just* who I thought you were. You never hid your promiscuity and the lengths that you would go to get what you wanted from a man. That much I did know about you," Yolanda said.

Shay's mouth tightened, and her eyes narrowed.

"Hold on," Jayda said, placing a hand on Shay's arm.

"So, we can forgive a man for lying and cheating on us repeatedly, but we can't forgive our girlfriends?" Shay said.

"Oh, I forgive the both of you and my father. Our relationships have changed. What did you expect?" Yolanda said.

"I expected you to understand," Jayda said.

"What I understand is that you are not who I thought you were," Yolanda shot back.

This time, Shay pulled Jayda by the arm when she began to move closer towards Yolanda.

"This isn't the time or the place for this," Shay told her.

"Well, I couldn't leave you hanging today. I do still care about you. Plus, I had to pay my respects," Yolanda said.

Jayda and Shay stared at their friend, unable to recognize her. She wasn't that caring and understanding friend; she was cold. The three women stood there, no one recognizing the other. The three of them had a sense of unfamiliarity among them. That natural bond was no longer there. Their chemistry had gone horribly wrong.

"I just need to know if we are friends or not. It seems like you're talking in circles," Shay said.

"No, we aren't friends. However, we can try to build trust again. I have to trust my friends, and I don't trust you. It's going to take time. Hopefully, we can come close to what we had," Yolanda said.

"Jayda, say something. Do you hear her?" Shay asked Jayda.

"I understand. I betrayed your trust, and so did she. We're sorry for hurting you and betraying your trust," Jayda said. "I don't know what else to say."

"We can still hang out and talk sometimes. Things definitely aren't going to be the same," Yolanda told them.

"We can give you all the time you need. That's only fair. We can't expect you to get over it overnight. All I ask is that you put forth a real effort and give us both a chance," Jayda said.

"That's why I'm here, and that's what I'm doing," Yolanda said.

"Thanks," Jayda said.

"Thanks? She doesn't want to be friends anymore," Shay said.

"She does. She just needs time, and we're going to give her that," Jayda said.

"Okay, okay," Shay replied, throwing her hands in the air.

"I'll meet you at the house so I can help with the repast. If that's okay with you," Yolanda said.

Jayda smiled. "Yes, I would love that."

The ladies began walking towards their vehicles. They froze when they saw who was heading towards them.

"Excuse me, Jayda," Khalil said.

Fear wrapped around Jayda's chest. She felt all the blood wash from her face, and her ears began to tingle. Shay moved closer to Jayda and stood right beside her with her arms folded across her chest. Surprisingly, Yolanda walked up to Khalil and stood in his face.

"What the hell are you doing here? Jayda has a man, and she doesn't need you in her life," Yolanda told him.

"I'm here to pay my respects to the old man. As you can see, I have a woman. I don't want her," Khalil said, walking around Yolanda towards Jayda.

With him was Ashley, who had her arm hooked around his and was smiling as if he was a trophy.

"You shouldn't be here," Shay said.

Jayda looked around for Jamison, who was wrapping things up for Jayda at the gravesite.

"You're not welcome here," Jayda turned and said.

Jayda laughed and folded her arms as she looked at the two of them standing arm in arm. Ashley wore a smug look on her face. She smiled, showing her six gold teeth.

"I just wanted to pay my respects to the old man. He was a good person, and he helped me out a lot," Khalil told her.

"And you had to bring her to do that? How did you get out so soon?" Jayda asked.

"That's none of your business. I'm a free man," he said.

"I have a restraining order against you," Jayda said.

"Not anymore. That restraining order expired. Didn't your lawyer boyfriend tell you that?" he said.

"Can I talk to you in private?" Jayda asked.

Jayda yanked Khalil by the arm and pulled him aside, outside of earshot from the others.

"I paid Alonzo. I would ask you for my money, but I know you don't have it. So, I'll just count it as a loss. We're done," she said.

"He played you. I told you I didn't owe him. That's between you two."

"You still ain't shit."

"Do you still love me?" he asked.

"I don't love you anymore. I have a man who loves and respects me. You have Ashley over there."

"I've always had Ashley. And thanks for doing that for me. That's a very, very small price to pay when you send someone to jail, don't you think? I had many other ways of making you pay, but I'll consider us even," he said.

Khalil took a step towards her. She took a step back.

"With all my family and friends out here, you'd be a fool to put your hands on me," she warned.

Jayda saw Jamison coming her way. He didn't look happy.

"I think you should go. We're done," Jayda said.

She walked to meet Jamison. When she reached him, he wanted to go for Khalil, but she stopped him.

"It's okay. He came to pay his respects to my father," Jayda said.

Jamison watched Khalil and Ashley walk to their car before he spoke.

"I don't want him around you. You need to file another restraining order," he said.

"Did you know he was getting out?" she asked.

"No, but I knew it would be soon. Sorry. I didn't follow up as often as I should've."

"It's okay. You've been so busy with your cases, with me, and everything I have going on. I couldn't expect you to follow Khalil's case. We know he's home and that he's moved on apparently."

Yolanda and Shay joined them.

"Did you know he was out?" Shay asked.

"No," Jayda said.

"You need to be careful. I don't trust him," Yolanda voiced.

"You and I both," Jayda said.

"I'm going to make a few calls and see how this happened. Can you two please stay here with her?" Jamison asked.

"Of course," Yolanda said.

"We're going to the car. I know my mom is ready to go," Jayda said.

They walked to the limo where Cheryl was raising hell with the driver.

"We're not leaving without my daughter," Cheryl yelled at the driver.

Jayda rushed over.

"Mom, what's wrong?" Jayda asked.

"He was trying to drive off with me. I told him I was waiting on you," Cheryl said.

"Sir, what's the problem?"

"Ma'am, we have to go. I have another funeral right after this one," the driver explained.

"Mom, get in the car. We're leaving now," Jayda said.

She waved at Jamison, signaling that it was time for them to leave. Jamison jogged to the car.

"We'll meet you at the house," Shay told Jayda.

Jayda got into the limo with her mother as they waited for Jamison.

"Mom, are you okay?" Jayda asked, slipping off her shoes.

"No. My Quentin is gone. Although we weren't together, he was still my Quentin," her mother said. "I loved that man."

"I know, mom. He loved you too," Jayda said.

Jamison sat in the limo and ended his phone call.

"Ladies, I'm sorry," Jamison said.

"That's alright, handsome," Cheryl said with a wink.

Jayda smiled at her.

"Jayda, I just talked with the clerk, and she said Khalil was released on time served," Jamison said.

All Jayda could say in response was, "Wow."

The repast was full of familiar faces. Some people she hadn't seen in years, like her father's old drinking buddy, Mr. Perry. Every Friday, Mr. Perry and her father would have drinks together after work. They would talk all night while playing cards—just the two of them. Mr. Perry suffered a stroke years ago, leaving him wheelchair-bound. Now, he was walking with the assistance of a walker.

The outpour of love for her father was amazing. Jayda made sure to greet and thank everyone that was there. She noticed Yolanda and Shay fell into place with hospitality. She didn't expect them to do anything less. They also helped serve food and clean up.

Mr. and Mrs. Clarkson were also in attendance. Jayda noticed Mr. Clarkson eyeing her. She knew Yolanda had to have confronted him because he was acting slightly uncomfortable. Mrs. Clarkson gave her condolences to Jayda while Mr. Clarkson hung back. Jayda understood.

Jamison was a big help. He was there to catch her when she thought she would fall. He knew just when to sweep in and save her. She loved that about him. He was watching even when she didn't think he was.

Jamison pulled Jayda into the bedroom.

"Thank you so much," Jayda said.

"No need to thank me," Jamison replied, then kissed her.

Shay and Yolanda busted in the room.

"I knew it! I knew the two of you was a love connection," Yolanda said.

"I think somebody is in love," Shay said.

"You can thank me later, Jayda," Yolanda said.

"Yes, I'm in love with Jayda," Jamison admitted, picking Jayda up and twirling her around in his arms.

"And I love me some you," Jayda said, kissing him.

Just for a moment, all seemed well. Jayda was in love, and she had her friends' love and support. There were no longer secrets among them. Everything was out in the open. Alonzo was paid, and Khalil seemed to have moved on. Jayda was looking forward to life unchained. So far, it felt good.

Chapter 33

It had been a while since Jayda had seen Shay or Yolanda. There were a few conversations here and there, but nothing like it used to be. Jayda's feelings were hurt, but she understood why things had come to what they were. They didn't have their usual nights out nor did they visit each other. She missed her friends dearly.

After her father's funeral, they all seemed to isolate themselves. At the repast, they were in sync as usual, but when it came time to end the day, their goodbyes seemed final. It was very awkward for her. She told herself that she wasn't going to push or force anything. It was best they focused on healing themselves. One thing she knew, things would fall back into place in time.

During her time alone, Jayda focused on herself and her new relationship with Jamison. For the past month, she sought counseling. She needed to deal with her personal issues. She had lost both parents and suffered abuse. She needed to heal. All those things were a part of her, and she needed to know how to deal with her problems. She didn't want to bring all of that baggage into her new relationship. She wanted to present the best version of herself to Jamison and her friends.

Jayda kept up with her friends via social media. Yolanda posted mainly about her and Ryan and all of the things they did together. Yolanda and Ryan had taken a trip to France. Jayda didn't know anything about their trip until it was posted on social media, and she felt some type of way about that. Once upon a time, she would've been one of the first to know their plans. Now, she was informed about these things via social media posts.

Shay's posts seemed to be more about her children, which was different for her. She would normally post a thousand selfies of herself or sexy men. It was clear her focus had shifted, and she too seemed happy. She didn't know if Shay and Yolanda were talking, but she was sure they weren't talking to her. In her heart, she knew her friends were fine. Yolanda and Ryan were thriving following their tragic loss. Shay was more focused on being a mother. Jayda focused on herself and her new relationship.

It was time for Jayda to return to work. She was slowly putting her life back together. She planned to return to work and then reach out to her girls. She didn't want to go too long without trying to reach out. "One stop at a time" was her motto for getting her life back on track. She figured she had probably hurt Yolanda the most. So, that was the first relationship she would try to mend.

Jayda stood in front of the mirror, admiring her nakedness. She smiled at her reflection and didn't turn away in shame. Khalil had body-shamed her so much that she had started hating her own body. Now, she embraced her body. In her reflection, she saw beauty and happiness. No longer did she see scars and pain.

"Hey, sexy. What are you doing?" Jamison asked, rolling over in bed.

"Hey you," Jayda said. "I'm just getting out of the shower."

"Why are you up so early?" he asked.

"Did you forget? I'm going back to work today," she said.

"Oh, yeah. Give my brain time to catch up."

Jayda joined him in bed, lying on his chest.

"Are you ready?" he asked her.

"Yes, I'm ready to get back to work. I'm just ready to get back to my routine. You know what I mean?"

"I do. I know how much you love being a nurse. It's a big part of who you are."

"Now, I just need to get my girls back. I miss them so much. I see they are all happy and everything. I want to be a part of that too."

"I know you miss them. I also know there was real love between all of you. You will be close again. It's just a bump in the road. All friendships have them, and this is your bump."

"That's what I keep telling myself. I'm trusting God on this one."

"That's right, baby."

Jamison moved in for a kiss from Jayda, but she placed a finger on his lips, stopping him.

"We don't do that. Please brush your teeth first, sir."

Jamison laughed. "I thought you said you loved me?"

"I do love you. What I don't love is morning breath."

She kissed him on the cheek.

"I have to get ready," she said, leaping out of bed.

"Are you coming back over tonight?" Jamison asked.

"If you want me to," she said while dressing for work.

"I'd like to have you here every night."

Jayda paused. "Come on, not every night. But most nights."

"Hey, get used to the idea of living together. You're going to be my wife."

"I can get used to that," she said, displaying her ring finger.

"I have a few more hours before I'm due in court. I'm going back to sleep. Have a good day at work, babe."

"You too. Love you."

"Love you too."

Jayda arrived at the hospital with bells and whistles. She was happy to be back to work. Nursing was her passion. Caring for others gave her life. With each patient, she was filled with joy and compassion. It took a special person to care for others. That was something she knew she could do well. The staff and doctors all greeted her with a warm welcome.

"When you finish, come to the breakroom," Sophia said as she sat at the nurse's station.

"I have to discharge my patient, then I'll be right there," Jayda said, reading over a chart.

"It's been slow but steady today. You chose a good day to return. Yesterday would've had you walking back out the door. It was so chaotic," Sophia said.

"Just the way I like it," Jayda replied jokingly.

Jayda returned to her patient's room and read over the discharge instructions. A young woman came into the emergency room with her parents, after spraining her ankle during a run. After completing her work, Jayda headed to the breakroom to meet Sophia.

Jayda opened the door to the breakroom.

"Surprise!" everyone screamed.

"Oh, my God!" she said, her hands flying to her chest.

"Welcome back, Jayda. We missed you!" Sophia said.

Jayda was overcome with emotions.

The small room was filled with balloons and food. She looked around at everyone who was there. In the crowd, she saw Yolanda and Shay.

"My girls!" she sobbed.

She rushed over to them and wrapped her arms around them.

"What are you doing here? How did you know?" Jayda asked.

"Sophia called us. I wanted to be here," Yolanda said.

"You know I wasn't going to miss being around some fine, rich doctors," Shay whispered.

They laughed.

"I miss you so much. I need you two," Jayda cried.

"I miss you too. I miss the both of you," Yolanda said.

Shay folded her arms across her chest. "I've been fine without you two getting on my damn nerves."

"Stop playing. You know you miss the amigos," Yolanda said.

"Yeah, I miss you, bitches. But our break has been good. I think I came out a better person, mother, and friend. We needed this time to reflect."

"I agree. I've grown."

Jayda wiped away a tear. "I'm so not the person I was a month ago," Jayda said.

"Jayda, can you come over? Some of us have lives to save. Hurry up," Sophia said.

"I'll be right back," Jayda told Yolanda and Shay.

Jayda greeted a few people on her way to the opposite side of the room.

"Can I get everyone's attention, please? I know you have lives to save and an ER to run," Sophia began.

The room fell quiet.

"Jayda, we welcome you back. We also give our sincerest condolences on the loss of your father. We wanted to give you something special," Sophia said.

She handed Jayda a blue Tiffany's box. Inside was a necklace and a double heart pendant engraved with her father's initials.

"Thank you. This is beautiful," Jayda said.

People quickly began to help themselves to the food. The crowd started to disperse, leaving a few people in the breakroom. Jayda took the time to talk to her girls and catch up. It felt like it used to.

"I have so much to tell you, guys," Jayda said.

"Me too," said Yolanda.

"And you know I always have the tea," Shay said.

"So, can we agree that this is the start of a new beginning, a new friendship?" Yolanda asked.

"Hell yes. I'm all in," Jayda said.

"To new beginnings," Shay said, raising a cup of punch in the air.

The void in Jayda's heart quickly filled with joy. Her first day back to work was her best day. She thanked God and her father for bringing her and her friends back together again. Life was good at that moment.

Jayda was with a patient when Sophia came rushing in.

"There's a patient in room twelve that needs your assistance," Sophia said. "Hello, I'm Sophia. I'll be filling in."

Sophia took over with taking the patient's vitals. Jayda didn't move. She didn't understand what Sophia was doing.

"What are you doing?" Jayda asked.

"You are needed in room twelve, stat," Sophia said through gritted teeth.

"Okay…"

Jayda walked four doors down. She entered the room, and there was Khalil. He was lying on a stretcher, bleeding through his bandages. She had the urge to rush in and treat him herself, but then anger set in. She slowly walked into the room.

"Jayda," he groaned in pain.

"Khalil," she said flatly.

"That bitch stabbed me. She really tried to kill me."

"What did you do to her?"

"Just like a woman. You always take each other's side. Why did I have to do something for her to do this to me?"

"Because I know what you did to me."

Khalil coughed and moaned.

"That doesn't sound good."

"Help me. Don't let me die. They just put me in this room and left me here."

"Now you want my help?"

"You're a nurse. You're supposed to help me. Don't let me die."

"Did you tell them what happened?"

"I told them that crazy bitch stabbed me."

"Who stabbed you?"

"Ashley."

"Where is Ashley?"

"She should be locked up. I don't give a fuck about her. Don't let me die. Please, don't let me. Do something."

"You're not going to die. The doctor is coming. Just hold on."

"I'm sorry that I hurt you. I didn't mean to give you hell, Jayda."

"You didn't mean to, but you did."

"If I make it through this, I promise I'll treat you better."

Jayda looked at him. "What the fuck do you mean? You beat my ass, cheated on me, had a baby and put me down every chance you got. You turned into a monster. Now, why would I want you back?"

"I really fucked up with you. I love you, Jayda. You were the best thing to happen to me."

"What are you talking about? We are never going to be together!"

"Please," he said.

Khalil began to cough violently. Blood sprayed from his mouth.

Jayda pulled back his bandages to assess his injury. There were several stab wounds. Some bled profusely. She couldn't tell how much damage was done without further tests. She had heard the call put out for the surgeon. Noticing blood pooling on the sheets under him, Jayda rechecked him. This time, she tilted him over and saw a wound on his back. She went into action, calling for assistance. A team moved in and immediately began to work on him. Khalil was rushed into surgery, leaving Jayda with unanswered questions.

Chapter 34

Jayda slid on her pajamas for the much-needed girls' night that was underway. She could hear Yolanda and Shay laughing in the living room. Although she didn't know what they were laughing about, she laughed along with them. When she was done, she joined them.

"Those are so cute," Shay commented.

Jayda modeled her pajamas for them.

"You didn't say to wear your cutest pajamas to this party. I would've picked something else to wear. I was just trying to be comfortable," Yolanda said.

"I'm the host. So, let me be cute," Jayda said.

Jayda planned a full night of food, wine, and girl talk. They had so much to catch up on. The women spent the next hour sharing where they were in their lives. Jayda and Jamison's relationship flourished into something beautiful, and they were thinking about moving in together. Shay accepted a much-needed job offer. She was finally in a better financial situation as a single mother. She also revealed that she and her children's father were talking about being a family again. She assured them that she was being cautious in stepping back into that situation again. She felt it was worth a try. Yolanda and Ryan were back on track. She saw a therapist weekly, and they also were attending couples counseling. Although they couldn't have children the natural way, they were open to adoption.

As the night went on, the ladies settled in for a movie. During the movie, Shay and Jayda fell asleep. It was shortly after midnight when Yolanda heard a noise from the kitchen. Not sure if she was hearing things, she muted the television. Sure enough, she heard the sliding of the patio door. Slow and steady.

Yolanda felt panic. She shook Jayda and Shay awake.

"What?" Shay asked.

"Get up. Someone's in the house," she whispered.

"What?" Jayda asked, rubbing her eyes.

"Someone is in the fucking house," Yolanda repeated.

Shay jumped to her feet.

"Oh, my god!" Jayda said, attempting to stand, tripping over her pillow.

Yolanda stood beside Shay, helping Jayda to her feet.

"I have a gun in my bedroom," Jayda said.

The three women moved quietly and slowly to make their way to the back of the house. Suddenly, a shadow appeared from the kitchen.

"Hey, bitches!"

Koshie walked out of the shadows and displayed a gun.

The women stopped.

"What the fuck are you doing in my house?" Jayda asked.

"What are you doing here?" Shay asked.

"So many damn questions. Do you know how hard it's been to catch all three of you together? Thanks to Shay, who loves to post her life on social media, I knew all of you would be here tonight. You shouldn't make such things a public post. Anyone could just pop up on you. Thanks, Shay."

The women looked at each other and then tried to run.

"Stop! I'll shoot!" Koshie shouted. "Get back in there."

She guided them back into the living room with a wave of her gun. The women were all scared and holding on to each other as they followed her orders.

"Take a seat. I want to share too. You were all in here sharing and caring. It's my turn now," Koshie said.

The three women sat down on the sofa.

"I'm the one you want. Let them go," Yolanda said. "They didn't have anything to do with what happened."

"Look at you. Now you want to do the right thing, huh? Too late for that now," Koshie said.

"Oh, revenge was ever so sweet," Koshie continued, laughing as she spoke. "You three are creatures of habit. Easy for a bitch like me to handle. You don't know the meaning of friendship. *I* was your friend. I loved you like sisters. We had so much fun together. I could be myself around you. Sadly, it took a real test of friendship for me to find out who my real friends were. Did you really think you were going to get away with it? You did, didn't you? Sorry, but not sorry. I could've taken the rap for you, but you didn't give me that choice. I knew you had plans for college and a promising future, unlike myself. I knew that. As a friend, I would've done that for you. But, no, you left me behind. You didn't even have the common courtesy to write or visit me. You could've at least pretended that we were friends."

"We were your friends," Jayda said.

"Shut the fuck up, Jayda! You still have low self-esteem, even after losing all of that weight. I heard you hooked up with Khalil, a known womanizer. He likes to smack a woman around sometimes, right? I heard he was kicking your ass," Koshie said.

"What is this? You call yourself picking us off? We're still standing," Shay said.

"Shay, you haven't changed at all. You always knew where to find that bag. You led me right to a baller. I knew I could depend on you. You thought you were going to get a come up with Rob, but I made sure that would never happen. You will always be a broke-down bitch," Koshie said.

"That's enough. Do whatever you came here to do," Yolanda said.

And Miss Goody Two-Shoes YoYo; you were supposed to do the time, not me. I saved the best for last. I wanted you to hurt the worse, and I believe I have accomplished that. I have the one thing you will never have. I have your husband's baby," Koshie said.

"Bitch, you're crazy!" Yolanda shouted.

"Yes, I am. Years of being locked down will do that to a young woman! While you were locked away dealing with your issues, poor Ryan was left all alone. I came by for a visit. I told him that I was an old friend who had traveled a long way to give my condolences. He was kind enough to let me in to leave a card and flowers. He was drinking a beer, so I slipped him a little something to make him more comfortable. I was able to get him up, if you know what I mean. It didn't mean anything to me. I had only one chance of getting pregnant and look at God. It worked. I am carrying Ryan's baby. What do you think about that?" Koshie said, rubbing her belly.

Yolanda thought about a conversation she had with Ryan about someone dropping off flowers and an unsigned card. She never figured out who it was.

Yolanda leaped for Koshie. Shay managed to stop her.

"Ryan would never sleep with someone like you, nonetheless, let you into our home," Yolanda said.

"I didn't say he was completely willing, but I had my way with him. Your white boy and the American dream, what about that? That's what you wanted, right? You didn't plan on Ryan fathering a child with someone else. Especially the likes of me, right?" Koshie sneered, then laughed. "I loved shattering that dream for you. You're welcome, bitch!"

"I'll kill you," Yolanda said.

"Try it," Koshie said.

"I was sent pictures of the party. They clearly show Yolanda getting into the driver's seat of my car. Then there are others of her driving away. Thanks to Jay, who had gathered many pictures of the party, I have the proof and will use it. I guess you've paid enough for now. Jayda paid it for you all. Thanks for the money, Jayda. It isn't nearly enough for the years I spent behind bars for a crime I didn't commit," Koshie said.

"This is all about money? I can't believe you did this to me!" Jayda yelled. "That money has my daddy's blood on it!"

"Poor Jayda," Koshie said sarcastically. "Yes, you owe me. I want ten thousand from the other two of you and anything else I ask, or I will turn you three in to the police," Koshie threatened.

"I don't have ten thousand dollars," Shay said.

"You'll get it, if you like your freedom," Koshie said. "I'm done sharing."

"Get the fuck out of my house. NOW!" Jayda yelled, standing to her feet.

"So, I gotta go? Yolanda, go home and make love to your husband, who doesn't know he has broken his wedding vows or will be a father again. Shay, go home and take care of your children. Maybe you will find another bag, and I will let you have it. You're getting old, and the clock is ticking. And, Jayda, good luck with Jamison. Who knows if he really loves you, or was he paid to love you? I guess you'll figure it out. Fuck you and wouldn't want to be you. I'll be back for my money," Koshie told them.

Jayda was already standing when Yolanda lunged towards Koshie. Yolanda grabbed the gun out of her hand as Koshie tried to step back from her. Jayda helped to free the weapon from her grasp. The gun fell to the floor, and Jayda picked it up. She pointed the weapon at Koshie, who was now fighting with Yolanda. She didn't have a clear shot because Yolanda was in the way. The two women struck each other with their fists and pulled at each other's hair. Shay, standing nearby, swiped Koshie's feet from under her, sending her to the ground. Yolanda jumped on top of her and began to choke her. She had her hands wrapped tightly around her neck. Koshie pulled at Yolanda's hands while thrashing around, struggling to break free.

"Let her go before you kill her!" Shay said.

Shay and Jayda ran over to Yolanda and pulled her off of Koshie. Koshie rolled to her side and coughed violently, holding her throat. The women watched as Koshie tried to breathe.

"Get the fuck up," Jayda said to Koshie.

Koshie struggled to her feet.

"You had sex with my husband?" Yolanda shouted.

"No, not really. Strangely, he likes to beat his dick while wearing a condom. All I had to do was retrieve that condom. And boom! Just like that, I was pregnant. Look at me," Koshie said, rubbing her belly again.

"Fuck you, hoe! That isn't my husband's baby!" Yolanda shouted.

"I don't have anything to prove to you. I got what I wanted, and that's something you will never have again—Ryan's child," Koshie said.

"Is she even pregnant?" Shay asked.

"Take a look for yourselves," Koshie said, lifting her shirt to show a small bulge.

The women looked at each other.

"You know, you should've killed me," Koshie said.

"I tried, bitch. If they didn't get me up off of you, you wouldn't be standing right now," Yolanda said.

"You came to my house to blackmail us? After everything you've done to us, you still want us to pay you?" Jayda asked.

"You bitches owe me. You didn't have to spend years in prison for a crime you didn't commit. You don't know what I've been through," Koshie said.

"You've been locked up before. You acted as if it was nothing to you. You bragged about it all the time," Shay said.

"That was juvie, not prison," Koshie said.

"Let me handle this. We are here because of me," Yolanda said, interrupting them. "I know there isn't a thing I can do to take back the pain that I have caused you. I know that. Even giving you money isn't going to erase the pain or give back your lost years. You are going to come back for more and more. Then what?" Yolanda asked.

"I'm sure I will figure out something," Koshie said.

"I'm so sorry. I felt bad about what I did to you. I was selfish. I didn't think about you or your family. I thought only of myself and the things I wanted to do with my life. At the time, you seemed to be my way out of the hell I got myself into. Your mother—"

"Don't you dare mention my mother!" Koshie screamed.

"I was there for your mother," Yolanda continued. "I was the one giving her the money she sent you every month. When she found out she was sick, I was there with her. I was with her when she died," Yolanda said.

"Wait a minute. You were still in contact with her mother?" Shay asked.

"She's lying. My mother would've told me," Koshie said.

"Your mother swore she wouldn't tell you because I asked her not to," Yolanda said. "I wanted to take back what I did to you, but I couldn't."

"You could've confessed anytime you wanted to. You didn't want to trade places with me," Koshie said.

"I thought it was going to be a simple DUI or something like that. I didn't know that man was going to die," Yolanda said.

"So, you threw me to the wolves," Koshie said.

"Yes, I did," Yolanda admitted.

"And that's why we're here right now. I want what you owe me. You three will pay me for the time I spent doing for the crime you committed. That is only fair. Jayda already made a payment to Alonzo. Who pays a stranger that kind of money? I'm sure Khalil told you not to pay. It's all about saving your ass," Koshie said.

"You sent Alonzo?" Jayda asked through gritted teeth.

"I sure did. Now I want the rest of my money."

"How do we know you won't go to the police?" Shay asked.

"Yeah. You could get the money and still turn us in," Jayda said.

"I could, or I could just live off of you for the rest of my life. I see how you all have made a good life for yourselves on my back. I want to live the same. I'm a convicted felon, so you do the math," Koshie said.

"Is that all you want?" Yolanda asked.

"Is that all I want?" Koshie asked. "I want a life. The life I deserve. I want it all."

"I agree to make sure you get your payment, but only if you get rid of the baby," Yolanda said.

Jayda and Shay gasped.

"There is no way she is going to have that baby if it belongs to Ryan. My daughter is gone, and we will never have another child. She's not going to get away with this," Yolanda said.

Koshie laughed.

"What the hell is so funny?" Yolanda asked.

"You really think you're calling the shots, don't you?" Koshie said. "Look at you two, just going along with whatever she says. Think for yourselves! Speak up for a change. She only cares about herself. What she did to me, she would've done to either of you. I think you know that too."

Shay and Jayda looked at each other.

"Don't listen to her. She's the one who came in here waving a gun at us," Yolanda said. "Lose the baby, get paid, and we never see you again. Do we have a deal?"

"How much are we talking?" Koshie asked. "I've been thinking about relocating. There's nothing else here for me."

"I have thirty thousand saved. You can have it all," Yolanda said.

"Thirty thousand isn't enough," Koshie replied.

"I'm not going to pay you any more than that. I just don't have it," Yolanda said.

"What are you two working with?" Koshie nodded towards Shay and Jayda.

"I'm not giving you any more money," Jayda said.

"I don't have any money," Shay told her.

"Fifty thousand, and I'll destroy the pictures," Koshie said.

"What about the baby?" Yolanda asked.

"What about my baby?" Koshie said.

Yolanda walked over to Jayda and took the gun from her hand. She pointed the gun at the side of Koshie's head.

"What are you doing?" Jayda asked. "Careful now, YoYo. She's not worth it."

"She's not going to have my husband's baby," Yolanda said with tears streaming down her face. "There's no way I can let her."

"Shoot me! You don't have the balls to do it, so get that gun off me," Koshie said.

"Say you agree or I'll do it," Yolanda said.

"Give me the gun," Shay said, moving behind Yolanda.

Yolanda lowered the gun to Koshie's stomach. Koshie became visibly concerned.

"What are you doing?" Koshie asked.

"Do you agree to my terms?" Yolanda asked.

Koshie laughed in her face. "You're not going to hurt Ryan's baby, are you?"

Click, click.

Koshie grabbed her stomach. "You were really going to shoot me!"

"You came in here with an unloaded gun?" Yolanda asked.

"Yes. I didn't want to hurt you," Koshie said. "You have a deal. I want my money in two weeks. That's when I'm leaving."

Koshie began walking towards the front door.

"How will I know when it's done?" Yolanda asked.

"That's all you're worried about?" Shay asked. "She has evidence that shows you are responsible for that man's death. We also lied for you."

"No, but I have to know that it's done," Yolanda said.

"I guess you'll have to trust me. I'll be back in two weeks. Have all of my money, and then we're squared," Koshie said.

Yolanda rushed behind Koshie and hit her in the back of the head with the gun. Koshie fell to the floor and struggled with Yolanda, who screamed obscenities as she relentlessly caved in her head.

"No!" Jayda screamed.

Jayda and Shay stood in shock at Yolanda's sudden attack on Koshie. Jayda then jumped into action at the sight of blood. She rushed Yolanda, knocking her off Koshie. They rolled a few times, struggling with each other. Jayda fought to hold on to Yolanda; she had mighty strength in her rage.

"Help me!" Jayda called out to Shay. She tried to see where Shay was, but she couldn't see her. "Shay, help!"

"Get the fuck off of her!" Shay shouted.

Yolanda immediately stopped struggling when she saw Shay. Jayda and Yolanda stood to their feet as Shay stood in front of them with Jayda's gun, which they all knew was locked and loaded.

"What the fuck are you doing, bitch?" Yolanda asked.

"Look at you!" Shay responded.

Yolanda touched her face, then looked down at her bloodied hands and the gun.

Koshie moaned, giving relief to thoughts of her being dead.

"Come on, sis. Put the gun down," Yolanda said, dropping the gun she had been holding to the floor.

"Sis? You have the gull to call me sis? You are not my sister. You're no one's sister," Shay said. "People are so quick to throw that word around, and most aren't worthy of using it. We were your sisters because of all this shit right here. We kept your secret, so we were bound by that. Real sisters wouldn't have taken others down for something they didn't do. I'm done covering for you," Shay said.

Jayda helped Koshie to her feet.

"Yes, we are done. Let the chips fall where they may," Jayda said.

"So, what, you're going to call the police on me and tell your version of what happened? You'll be held responsible as well. Are you dumb?"

"Look at this shit! You could've killed her," Jayda said.

"You two are just seeing what I've always known. Your fragile friend here is crazy as a bat out of hell! She's going to take you two down with her," Koshie said.

Yolanda laughed at Koshie's statement.

"I'm not done with you," Yolanda said coldly.

"We're done as soon as I get my money for doing your time. Until then, stay the fuck away from me or else," Koshie said as she wobbled towards the door.

"Are you okay to drive? She hit you pretty hard. You could have a concussion," Jayda said.

She attempted to examine Koshie's head, but Koshie slapped her hand away.

"Get the fuck off of me, bitch!" Koshie said.

"Fine. Just get the fuck out of my house!" Jayda responded.

Koshie left, leaving behind Jayda and Shay, who were still holding Yolanda at gunpoint.

"It ends here," Shay said. "We are going to pay her so this can all go away."

"Yeah, I'm going to pay her exactly what she deserves. The two of you can sit back and let that bitch fuck you out of your money, but I'm not. I didn't come this far for her to come back and make demands of me. I'm going to fix this once and for all. Thank me later, bitches," Yolanda said as she left the house.

Chapter 35

Jayda tossed and turned in her bed. She eyed the gun that rested on a pillow beside her. She still felt the cold chill in the air from the night's events. Her house had been invaded by evil, and she couldn't shake the eerie feeling.

Every creak and squeak made her bones shutter. She tried to think her way out of the predicament that she and her friends found themselves in.

The look in Yolanda's eyes scared her. For the very first time, she feared Yolanda. Yolanda had pointed a gun at a pregnant woman's stomach and pulled the trigger. Jayda never saw such coldness in anyone's eyes, not even Khalil's, and it scared her. She knew Yolanda wouldn't stop until she had what she wanted, and that was Koshie.

The things she found out about Yolanda further changed the way she saw her. She didn't know Yolanda was still in contact with Koshie's mother. What Yolanda admitted to doing was all a surprise to Jayda. They had agreed to fall back from Koshie and her family. Now to find out that Yolanda did the complete opposite made her question her loyalty to the pact that the three of them made. She wondered what else Yolanda hadn't told them. For a quick second, a chilling thought ran through her head.

Could Yolanda have murdered her child in cold blood?

She shook the horrifying thought out of her head. Just then, her phone rang.

"Hey. Are you home?" Jayda asked.

"Hey. Yes, I'm home. I've been thinking about what happened tonight, and I can't shake it. Did you know she was helping Koshie's mom and sending her money?" Shay asked.

"Hell no. We agreed to fall back. I did. Did you?" Jayda inquired.

"Of course, I did," Shay replied. "That's why that sounds so strange to me. She was there when Koshie's mother died. Doesn't that sound strange to you? She never told us that."

"Tonight was the first time I've heard any of this. I don't know, but something ain't right."

"Exactly! She scared me tonight," Shay told her. "She showed a different side of herself."

"Yes, she did," Jayda agreed.

"That bitch that we saw was not our girl. I don't know who that was."

"Stop it!" Jayda said.

"No, seriously. You're not concerned?"

Jayda sighed. "Yes, very concerned."

"We need to talk tomorrow—just us. I have something I need to tell you," Shay said.

"Let me know when and where. I'll be there. I just want to try and get some sleep and forget what happened here tonight," Jayda expressed.

After ending the call with Shay, she tried to fall asleep. She tossed and turned some more, trying to find a comfortable position. After finding no comfort, she came to the conclusion that she wasn't going to get any sleep, at least not there. She wanted to sleep anywhere other than her house, so she called Jamison.

When she arrived at Jamison's house, the sun was rising. She used the key that he had given her to let herself into the house. The smell of bacon was the first thing she noticed. That created a smile on her face. After setting her bag down and locking the door behind her, she walked into the kitchen to find Jamison preparing breakfast.

"Hey there," she said.

"Hey baby," he replied, turning over the bacon in the pan.

Jayda gazed at him and wondered what she ever did to deserve a man like him. Jamison walked to her and greeted her with a warm kiss.

"I was hoping to have breakfast ready before you arrived. I guess I underestimated how long it would take you to get over here," he said.

Jamison took a step back and looked at her.

"Are you alright?" he asked.

"Yeah," she answered.

"It doesn't look like it. A slumber party is supposed to last at least until the next morning. What happened?"

"Let's just say, when you think you know someone but then find out you really don't know as much as you think you know about them, it can be rather shocking. Some things came out that I never expected. So, it was best we ended the slumber party."

Jamison prepared their plates and sat down at the table. Jayda remained standing.

"Are you going to join me?" Jamison asked.

"Sure," Jayda said.

Jayda took a seat at the table.

"What happened now? I grant you attorney-client privileges," he said.

"No, I don't trust you that much, Jamison," she joked.

"Come on," he said.

"I'm asking for a friend. What if someone was being blackmailed? The information could have them in serious trouble. What should this friend do about it?" Jayda asked.

Jamison finished chewing his food and wiped his mouth with a napkin.

"This friend should get a lawyer. Oftentimes, these situations turn out horribly. People can get hurt. The blackmailer usually wants something in return for their silence. Sometimes it's something the victim can't provide. I would advise your friend to see a lawyer to protect themselves," Jamison explained.

He took another hard look at Jayda.

"Is Khalil threatening you again?" he asked.

"No, I haven't seen Khalil since he was in the hospital. I don't think he's going to bother anyone anytime soon," she said.

"Well, who is it?"

"It's not me. I was asking for a friend," she said.

"You know I have your back, Jayda. You can tell me anything," he said.

"I know. That's why I asked for my friend," she responded.

Jamison took another long look at her.

"I have to take your word for it. Tell Shay or Yolanda that they need to talk to someone about what's going on. It can only get worse."

"Who said it was one of them?"

"You didn't have to say. Now, eat your food," Jamison told her.

Jayda let out a chuckle and began eating.

"There's been something I've wanted to share with you," Jamison said.

"What's that?" Jayda asked.

"It's about Yolanda."

Jayda choked on her food. She took a sip of orange juice.

"Are you okay?" Jamison asked, standing to help her.

Jayda waved him off.

"I'm fine. I swallowed my food too fast. What about her?" she asked.

Jamison sat back down.

"Yolanda can be a piece of work. There are things about her that concern me. I can't go into too much detail, but did you know she has a mental illness? For the record, I'm not speaking from her case. I'm just sharing what I've come to know about her."

"How did you come up with that conclusion? Her being committed after her daughter died was the first time she has ever broken down like that. She has never been in a state like that. I would've been in that state, too, if I would've lost a child," Jayda defended.

"No, that's not the first time," Jamison said.

"What?" Jayda asked.

"I've already said too much, but you need to know who your friends are."

"I know who my friends are. What are you saying?"

"Is Yolanda blackmailing you?" Jamison questioned.

"No. Why are you speaking of her like this? She's my friend."

"I know that's your friend. I didn't want to bring this up. Yolanda has a mental disorder."

"No, she doesn't. I've been friends with her since middle school. I know her family. I would know."

"You may have never seen any signs because she has been treated for this for years."

"I didn't know that."

"And you didn't hear it from me."

"Of course not," Jayda replied.

"Just be careful. People like that are always on shaky ground," Jamison cautioned.

"It's just hard to believe. She's such a good person, but there have been some moments when I've questioned her judgement."

"I just don't want to see you hurt. I felt that was something you should know, especially with your friend's dilemma that you brought up."

"Thanks for letting me know. I wish I would've known this before."

"Why? It shouldn't change much. You are just aware of it now."

"No, it does change things. There's one thing I would've changed for sure."

Jamison reached across the table for Jayda's hand. He lifted her hand and kissed it.

"I'll clean things up and meet you in the bedroom," Jayda said.

"No, we can tackle this later," he told her.

"Are you trying to get me in your bed?" Jayda asked in a joking, yet seductive manner.

"Oh, is that what I'm doing?" Jamison replied while leading the way to his bedroom.

Chapter 36

Shay rubbed the back of her neck where the tension and pain sat. She knew stress was the result of her symptoms. She couldn't find sleep fast enough, so she did what she would normally do to help her sleep. Two glasses of wine were the way to go. She wasn't due to pick up her children from her mother's house until Sunday because she originally had plans with Yolanda and Jayda. After the sleepover, the plan was to get massages, attend a paint party, and conclude the weekend with dinner and drinks. The way the night ended; she wasn't sure if anyone was going to show up for their scheduled massages.

She really needed to have a private conversation with Jayda. A necessary conversation. After what she had just witnessed, she wasn't sure if their newly found friendships were going to last. One of them was different; one of them was violent. Yolanda exhibited a type of violence Shay had never seen from her before. It wasn't the Yolanda she had come to know. The person that placed a gun to a woman's womb was insane. Shay knew something Jayda didn't know, something she promised she would never tell. But, now, all bets were off. Some things needed to be said sooner rather than later.

The next morning, Shay called Jayda to confirm that she was going to join her for their scheduled massages. They decided to meet at Shay's house and ride together. Jayda confirmed she would be there. Shay then called Yolanda but didn't get an answer. So, she left her a voicemail and waited for her to return her call. She was somewhat relieved that Yolanda didn't answer. She had hoped Yolanda would stand them up and not come. It would give her and Jayda time to have a conversation. Shay decided to take a shower as she waited for a response from Yolanda.

After her shower, Shay proceeded to get dressed. As she rummaged through her closet in search of a top, she came across one of Rob's shirts. She stopped and ran her hands over the material. Then she lifted the shirt to her nose and inhaled his scent. She missed him. She found herself blocking him from her thoughts as she moved along but was forced to deal with the fact that she may have been the reason for his death. She didn't think about it like that until just then. She dropped the shirt to the floor and stepped back from the closet.

"Oh, my God! He's dead because of me!" she cried.

She heard the things that Koshie confessed but rebutted them by blocking Rob's death out of her mind. It had just hit her. She was the reason he was gone. She sat on her bed and allowed herself to do something she had been fighting. She allowed herself to cry and to feel. She was still traumatized by his robbery and death. It changed her, but it also numbed her. She had a good cry and then proceeded to get dressed.

"Hey, girl!" Jayda said, walking through the front door of the house.

"Hey! I'm back here!" Shay shouted from her bedroom.

She rolled her eyes when she heard the sound of Jayda's heels on the hardwood floors.

When Jayda appeared in the doorway, Shay asked, "Why do you have on heels?"

Jayda looked down at her feet. "What's wrong with heels? I felt like wearing heels today. What's the problem?"

"Nothing," Shay responded.

"I see the neighborhood hasn't changed any. You still have those dealers next door. They raped me with their eyes and assaulted me with those weak-ass catcalls," Jayda commented as she sat down next to Shay on the bed.

"New mattress?" Jayda asked, bouncing up and down on the bed.

"Yes. You would know if you came over more often."

"What's the matter with you?"

"What's the matter with you? You act like we didn't have a horror story play out in your house last night. I don't know how well you slept, but I slept awful."

"I went over to Jamison's. I didn't feel comfortable staying there after crazy Koshie broke into my house. You and Yolanda just left me hanging there."

"You didn't pillow talk, did you? I know you and Jamison are in love."

"Hell, no. But I did find out something."

"What?" Shay asked.

"He told me that Yolanda has a mental disorder."

Shay dropped her head.

"Did you know?" Jayda asked.

"I knew for a while now."

"What's a while?"

"One time, Mr. Clarkson told me that she had some mental problems. I didn't know exactly what kind of mental problems back then. He told me that he was worried about her and grateful for us being her friend. He said our friendships helped her."

"Why didn't you tell me that we were friends with a psycho? I don't mean to say it like that, but I feel like I don't really know her."

"Don't call her that."

"What else do you call that? Did you see what I saw last night?"

"After he told me that, I started paying attention to things," Shay continued. "She is so extreme at times, but she functions. For me, that was fine."

"Yeah, I can agree, but I didn't know she has real mental issues."

"If you think about it, all the signs were there."

There was an awkward pause in the conversation.

"Do you think…"

"Don't you dare ask me that," Shay interrupted. "Don't you do that."

There was another awkward pause.

"No, I know she wouldn't do anything like that. She loved her daughter. It was just an awful tragedy," Yolanda said.

Shay walked over to her mirror and gave herself a once over.

"I really need this massage. I need to relieve some stress," Shay said.

"Traffic was backed up on my way over here. Check the traffic updates to see what's going on," Jayda told her as she examined Shay's perfume collection on her dresser.

Shay checked her phone for traffic updates in the area.

"An accident is clearing up. We could wait another fifteen minutes before leaving."

"Cool. What do you have to eat?" Jayda asked, heading to the kitchen.

"There's a fresh fruit salad in the fridge," Shay said.

Jayda's phone rang.

"Why is Ryan calling me?" Jayda asked.

"I don't know, but don't answer it. I tried calling Yolanda earlier, and she didn't answer. He's probably looking for her," Shay said.

"Are you sure? He's going to keep calling, or he's going to call you next," Jayda said.

"So what? We have to talk to her first. Send him to voicemail," Shay said.

Jayda sent the call to voicemail. They anxiously waited to see if he would leave a message. A few seconds later, a voicemail notification appeared. Jayda listened to the voicemail via speakerphone.

Hey, this is Ryan. I've been trying to reach Yolanda. I guess you ladies are busy having fun. Please tell her to give me a call.

"Let's go. She might be meeting us there," Shay said.

"I'll try to reach her again," Jayda said.

Shay and Jayda headed to their appointments. On the way, Jayda called Yolanda repeatedly.

"Stop calling her. You know they can trace calls," Shay said.

"So?" Jayda responded.

"What if she needs an alibi?"

"What if she needs an alibi?" Jayda repeated. "I'm not covering for her again. You see where that has gotten us. That one lie has ruined all of our lives and driven at least one of us crazy," Jayda said.

When they pulled into the parking lot of the spa, they immediately noticed Yolanda's car. Shay swung her car into a parking space beside Yolanda's car. Shay and Jayda anxiously struggled while getting out of the vehicle. They couldn't wait to see Yolanda and find out where she had been.

"Come on," Shay said.

They exited the car.

"Be cool. Don't be so accusatory when you see her," Shay said.

"We are just going to play it cool," Jayda said.

They entered the spa quickly, stumbling over each other as they walked through the door. Jayda casually checked-in as Shay greeted Yolanda.

"Hey, girl. How was your night?" Shay asked, taking a seat beside Yolanda.

Yolanda was casually flipping through a magazine.

"I had a hard time sleeping after the night we had. How was your night?" Yolanda asked, placing the magazine back on the table.

"I had a hard time sleeping, too. We tried calling you. How come you didn't answer your phone?" Shay asked.

Jayda sat down beside Shay.

"Hi, Jayda," Yolanda said.

"Hey," Jayda replied, then added, "I'm so ready for this."

"Well, we have one more person we're waiting on. She should be here in a second," Yolanda said.

"Who?" Shay asked.

"Did you invite your sister? I'm trying to relax today, not fight with her ass," Jayda said.

"No. Koshie is joining us," Yolanda said.

"Koshie!" Jayda exclaimed.

"Oh, hell no! I know you're fucking with me," Shay said. "I know damn well you didn't invite crazy Koshie to our spot."

Shay stood to her feet. She looked to Yolanda for an answer.

"It's cool. We have an understanding. Now, sit down and stop causing a scene," Yolanda said through clenched teeth.

She pulled Shay back down in her seat.

"After I left last night, Koshie messaged me. I agreed to meet her, and we had a talk—a talk that made way for today. Trust me, I got us," Yolanda explained.

"There's no way I'm going to sit for this. I don't trust your ass at all. You keep pulling us into these crazy ass situations with you. I'm done with all of this. Do what you want to do. I'm out," Jayda said.

Jayda stood and headed to the door. Shay followed her. Both women were visibly upset as they walked out of the door.

"Hey! Don't you dare act holier than thou!" Yolanda shouted while running behind them. "You bitches are just as guilty as I am. We all ruined her life. At least I tried to make amends while the two of you went on with your lives as if nothing happened."

She caught up to them once they stopped and turned to face her.

"Are you serious? You were the driver. *You* killed that man," Shay stated.

"And you two bitches went along with it. I'm the only one who made sacrifices in this friendship, and now you want to judge me? I did what I did to save all of us. You and you," Yolanda said, taking her finger and pushing them in the forehead.

"You know what? I'm done with all of this shit. Leave me the hell out of your bogus-ass crime spree. You aren't a criminal. You will get caught, and you're not taking me down with you. Fuck no! Not for this shit!" Jayda said.

"Fuck you, Jayda!" Yolanda shouted.

"Fuck your crazy ass!" Jayda shot back.

Yolanda laughed. "Oh, I'm crazy now?"

"Calm down. We're out here looking real ratchet right now. We don't need this kind of attention," Shay told them.

"Whatever the hell this is, I'm done," Jayda said, walking away.

"Me too," Shay said.

Yolanda didn't respond. Tears rolled down her face as she flashed a picture-perfect smile to Shay and Jayda before shifting on her feet. They looked at each other and then back at Yolanda, who had started trembling. Shay found herself wanting to swoop in and save Yolanda from a breakdown, but she decided to let her have at it.

"Let's go, Shay," Jayda said, walking back to the car.

Shay followed.

"You think you can just leave me out here like this after everything I've done for you? If it weren't for me, the two of you would've been dog food without me! Fuck you! I don't need you! You're going to need me long before I need you. Weak ass bitches!" Yolanda shouted after them.

Jayda and Shay walked briskly back to the car as Yolanda continued to curse them. Jayda cried as her heart broke. Shay sniffled while fighting back her tears. After the two of them were in the car, Shay started the engine and pulled off, but not before looking back at Yolanda. She was apparently still in a rage.

"Just go," Jayda said.

<h1 style="text-align:center">Chapter 37</h1>

Jayda sat straight up in her bed as she watched the local news report about a woman found dead in a vehicle. She shook her head in disbelief as the name of the victim was revealed; Koshie Sutton. As bad as she wanted to call Shay, she knew it would be the wrong move. She imagined all of their phones were tapped. She concluded that the awesome threesome was no more. Yolanda was capable of murder, but Jayda couldn't believe she would actually commit murder. Although she witnessed Yolanda's attempt to shoot Koshie, Jayda felt it was in the heat of the moment.

It was time for Jayda to get ready for work. Her stomach was queasy; she was nervous about the entire thing. The police could question her about Koshie's death. That night, she had stayed with Jamison after Koshie broke into her house. Everything up until Koshie showed up was a given. After Koshie arrived, no one was to speak of that. It never happened. As long as everyone kept their stories straight, they were in the clear.

As Jayda dressed for work, there was a knock at the door. The knock was unusual, as most people rang the doorbell. Alarmed, she looked out her bedroom window to find a car that she didn't recognize parked in her driveway.

Oh, my God. What is this?

There was another knock.

She went to the door and asked, "Who is it?"

"Khalil. Open the door," Khalil said.

"What are you doing here? You're not supposed to be here," Jayda said through the door.

"I need to talk to you. I'm not here to cause you any problems. We need to talk," he said.

Jayda slowly opened the door.

"I'm not letting you in," she told him.

He put up his hands and took a step back.

"No problem. We can talk out here," he said.

Jayda stepped on the porch and folded her arms across her chest.

"I'm getting ready for work. What do you want?"

She noticed that Khalil didn't look like himself. He looked like he had been through hell.

"You look like shit," she said.

"I feel like shit, too. After the bitch tried to kill me, my body's been fucked up. I'll bounce back. How have you been?"

"I can't complain."

"Thank you for saving my life. You didn't have to do that after all I put you through."

"I was just doing my job."

"I hurt you, right? I have anger issues. I want to say that I'm sorry for how I treated you."

"Damn. That's a shame. I would believe you if I didn't hear this a thousand times before. I don't need your apologies! I'm pretty sure you will not be hurting any other women."

"That's all you have to say? I'm here to make peace with you," he said.

"Yeah, you told me that. Is that all you wanted?"

"I just came to make sure you were okay."

"I'm great. I have to go to work. Thanks for stopping by," she said sarcastically, then turned to go back into the house. "Just leave, and don't come back. I don't need you messing up what I have going on. I'm with a man who really loves me. I don't want you or any of your bullshit messing that up for me. After all that you've done to me, you owe me that."

Throwing his arms up in defeat, he responded, "You're right. I'll fall back."

"Thank you," Jayda said, surprised.

"If you ever need me, I got you. I owe you three times over. Again, I'm sorry, Jayda."

"Yes, you are sorry."

For the first time, Khalil's words were sincere. Jayda watched as he walked to his car and left. She didn't know whether his recent incarceration or coming close to death had changed him. All she knew was that he was different. That one interaction between the two of them healed a small part of her. At that moment, she decided to forgive him.

Chapter 38

Shay arrived at the diner wearing a straw hat and shades, attracting unwanted attention to herself. Although she ate there a few times a week for lunch, she felt the need to hide her identity. She was on a mission and didn't want to be found out. She walked to a corner booth in the back where she had instructed her guests to sit. On the way, Shay fumbled with her phone, dropping it on the floor. She looked around in embarrassment as she kneeled to pick it up. The seams of her tightly-fitted skirt gave way, sending a tearing sound into the air.

"Fuck!" Shay said.

She stood to her feet as a waitress came running over, removing her apron.

"It's okay. I got you covered," the waitress said, throwing her apron around Shay's waist.

"Thank you," Shay said.

Laughs and snickers erupted from the corner booth.

Shay quickly sat down, slamming her handbag and phone on the table.

"Not funny," Shay said.

"Oh, yes, that was funny. First, you come in here looking crazy, and then that big ass fought its way out of the skirt you trapped it in. Funny as hell if you ask me," Jayda said.

Shay narrowed her eyes.

"Alright now, ladies. What did you call me out here for? I know it wasn't to referee this fight," Mr. Clarkson said, pretending to break up a fight.

"I'm sorry, Mr. Clarkson," Jayda said.

"We asked you to come here because we need to talk to you about Yolanda," Shay said.

Mr. Clarkson's face flushed of its color.

"What about her?" he asked.

"Is Yolanda okay? Does she have a mental illness?" Jayda inquired.

"She has been acting different lately. She hasn't been herself," Shay added.

"Waitress, can I get some water please?" Mr. Clarkson said, unfastening the top button of his shirt. He began to sweat.

"Are you feeling okay?" Jayda asked.

"Yes. I just need some water. I didn't expect to be asked this question. You just caught me by surprise," he replied.

"Please, we need water over here!" Shay shouted.

The waitress, who helped her, rushed over with an empty glass and a pitcher filled with ice and water. She poured the water and handed the glass to Mr. Clarkson.

"Is there anything else I can do to help? He doesn't look good," the waitress said.

"He'll be fine. Thank you," Jayda said, dismissing her.

Mr. Clarkson turned up the glass and gulped the water.

Shay could feel his anxiety from across the table. Whatever it was, it couldn't be good. Jumping into nurse mode, Jayda began asking him questions and instructing him to breathe. After a few minutes, he was calm. Shay wanted to push him to talk but decided to allow him to speak when he was ready.

"Ladies, you know I love the two of you like my own, despite the things that transpired between us. I put those things behind me, and I ask for your forgiveness," he said.

"That is not why we are here," Shay snapped. "We're talking about your crazy ass daughter. How could we have been friends with her and never know something was wrong with her?"

"Shay, don't be disrespectful," Jayda said.

"She's right. She has every right to be upset. Yolanda is my baby girl. She was the most beautiful baby I've ever seen. From the first time I held her, I knew my job was to protect her, even if it meant to the detriment of myself. Yolanda showed early signs of violence and destruction as a toddler. We thought it was just her being a kid. Then things escalated as her personality began to show. My wife wanted to have her evaluated, but I refused. That created a wedge between us. I protected her. Eventually, things got so bad that we had to get her to a doctor. When she was in elementary school, she stabbed a little girl in the arm with a pencil. She felt that she was trying to take her friend away from her. The answer was counseling and medication. It worked, so we went with that. When she met you, Jayda, she got better. She started acting normal. She gained confidence, and we thought all she needed was a friend. We told her not to tell anyone about her medicine or her condition. It was our family's business," he explained.

"Wow! We're friends with a psycho. Do you know what she has done?" Shay asked.

"How could you hide something like that for so long?" Jayda inquired.

"You two changed her life. She got better, came off the medication, and learned to live like you and me."

"Do you really believe that?" Shay asked. "This bitch has fucked up my life, Jayda's life, and—"

"Stop!" Jayda shouted.

"What has she done?" he asked.

Shay laughed as she gathered her things.

"You'll find out soon enough," Shay said.

"I'm sorry for whatever she did to you. Is there anything I can do?" he asked.

"Yes. Commit your daughter, son of a bitch," Shay said as she walked away.

"Mr. Clarkson, you knew your daughter was dangerous, and all you cared about was her safety. Does Ryan know?" Jayda asked.

"Of course, he does. He found out when my granddaughter passed away. We had to tell him everything so she could get the help she needed. That's when they put her back on her medication," he said.

"She's back on medication now?" Jayda asked.

"Yes, as far as I know," he said.

"Thanks for meeting us. Please keep this meeting between us. I don't want Yolanda getting upset about us going behind her back talking to you," Jayda said, then rushed to catch up with Shay, who was outside the diner smoking a cigarette and pacing.

"Did you hear him? All these years, we were playing with fire, literally. Thank God we didn't piss her off that time at the lake. She could've drowned one of us. Oh, and what about all those times she served us at her house, preparing our food and pouring our drinks? She could've poisoned us. The bitch could've smothered me in my sleep all those times we had sleepovers!" Shay shouted.

"I know you're upset, but you need to calm down. We have to figure out a way to help her," Jayda said.

"Oh, no! I'm not helping her. I'm going to help myself and my children by protecting us from her. She is not okay. She killed somebody. What makes you think she wouldn't kill one of us?" Shay asked.

"Come on, Shay. If she wanted to hurt us, she would have, especially after finding out about her father and us," Jayda said.

"See, that's what I'm talking about. If you believe she really forgave you, then you must be the crazy one. She is different, Jayda. Or she has always been this way, and we are just removing the blinders," Shay said.

"I understand what you're saying, but she's our friend," Jayda said. "If she comes after us, of course, we will protect ourselves. But we need to try to help her," Jayda said.

Mr. Clarkson came out of the diner and didn't look their way. They watched him walk away in shame.

"I have a plan. I just need you to sit tight. Don't do anything until I talk to you. Can you do that for me?" Jayda asked.

Shay lit another cigarette.

"I have children to protect. Your friend is a murderer. I'm not going down for anything that Yolanda has done in the past or the present. We lied for her once, and I'm not doing it again. If you want to sacrifice yourself, go ahead. But leave me out of it!" Shay said.

"I'm looking out for all of us."

"Like you were looking out for us when Yolanda decided to blame Koshie for the accident? Yeah, good looking out," Shay said.

"*We* did that. That wasn't on me. You could've stopped what she was doing as well as I could. That was on *us*."

"Who is responsible for Koshie's death?"

Jayda didn't respond.

"Do whatever you think is going to save her or save us, but don't take too long. We will see her again," Shay said. Then, while tightly hugging Jayda, she added, "Please don't be too good of a friend to someone you never knew."

Chills ran up Shay's spine as she wrapped her arms around her friend. For no apparent reason, they both wept. An eerie feeling remained in the air between them. It felt more like a goodbye than see you later.

As Shay began the three-block walk back to her office, her cell phone rang. Her first reaction was to ignore it. Then she remembered she was waiting on a call from her real estate agent. The call was from a number she didn't recognize.

"Hello?" she answered.

"This is Detective Knight. Sorry for calling you at such short notice. We have some new information about the robbery and would like to speak to you about Koshie Sutton."

At the sound of Koshie's name, Shay stood as still as a statue in the crosswalk. Cars laid on their horns as the light turned green. For a few seconds, she couldn't think or hear. Someone pulled her by the arm, snapping her out of her trance.

Shay yanked away and jogged to the safety of the sidewalk. The good Samaritan tried to ask if she was okay, but she ignored him.

"Hello?"

"I'm here. Sorry about that. When would you like to talk?"

"Come down and see me today if you can."

"Sure. I have to make arrangements for my children first. I'll come right away."

"Thank you for your cooperation."

"Sure, no problem."

Chapter 39

Shay sat inside her car outside of the police department. She had called Jayda at least five times with no answer. Finally, she left her a message letting her know where she was. She gave herself five more minutes before she would go inside. She wanted this storm to be over, but it seemed to keep getting worse.

Okay, Shay, you got this.

She entered the police station and asked for Detective Knight. As she waited, Jayda finally called her.

"Hey," Shay whispered into the phone.

"What's going on?" Jayda asked.

"I don't know. He just asked me to come down here to answer some questions. I couldn't say no."

"Just stay cool, and don't offer any extra information. You got this, Shay."

"I hope so. I just want this to be over."

"It will be. If you run into trouble, just say you need your lawyer present. Call me, and I'll make sure Jamison comes down."

"Thanks, girl."

"Anything for you. Let me know when you're done. I'll be waiting."

"Okay, I will," Shay replied. "Have you heard from her?"

"Hell no," Jayda responded. "You?"

"No."

"She's not our problem anymore," Jayda told her.

"I guess not."

"No, she's not."

"I have to go. I'll call you later," Shay said.

Detective Knight was approaching her. It seemed to have been his day off because he was dressed in sweats. Her eyes went immediately to his visibly satisfying package.

"Ms. Bryant?" Detective Knight said.

"Yes," Shay said, snapping back to reality.

"Let's talk in my office."

Shay followed him to a small office. It wasn't an interrogation room like the ones she saw on television. That gave her some relief. She took a seat and looked around at all of the photographs of dogs.

"I see you love dogs," she commented.

"Yeah, I do. I have three right now. My family loves them, too," he said, pointing to a family photo of his wife, two small children, and three dogs.

Shay smiled and wiped away her dirty thoughts.

"Ms. Bryant, thank you for coming down. There's been a new development in the case, and I need to ask you a few more questions," he said, then paused to take a sip of his steamy coffee. "Pardon my manners. Would you like a cup?"

"No, thank you." Shay sat very still.

She knew what that new development was, and she had been thinking of the many ways she would handle this once it came out. She hadn't recognized Koshie at first. So many years had passed, but she couldn't be positive at the time.

"What can I help you with?" she asked.

Detective Knight reached into a folder and removed several photos, placing them on his desk.

"Do you recognize any of these women from the robbery?" he asked.

Shay looked down at the photos, studying each one for the sake of it.

"Take your time," he told her.

She moved in closer to the photos, noticing an unflattering picture of Koshie.

Detective Knight cleared his throat and handed her a marker.

"Circle the photo of the woman you saw the night of the robbery. They may or may not be in this lineup."

Shay took in a deep breath and contemplated circling her former friend's picture. It was clear she had been identified for the robbery or else her picture would not have been included.

"Circle anyone that you recognize from that night," he repeated.

"I think I know her. She looks like an old friend, but then she favors one of the girls who were at the hotel. I haven't seen her in years, so I can't be sure."

"If you think that is one of the women, please circle the picture."

Nervous, Shay began to bite her nail. She didn't want to make the wrong move and identify her because they would probably ask her why she didn't say something before. They would accuse her of withholding vital information for the case. They might even accuse her of being a suspect. In this case, she was innocent.

She placed a circle around Koshie's picture.

"I think she could've been one of them," she said.

"Thank you, Ms. Bryant." He sat back in his chair and began to rock.

"That woman's name is Koshie Sutton. She is deceased. We found her strangled to death in her vehicle. We have the other suspects in custody for the murder of Mr. Gibbs. She was also identified as a suspect. During our investigation of her murder, we found a connection between the two of you. Now, we just need to know if you were involved in the robbery and death of Mr. Gibbs. If you knew Koshie was one of the accomplices, you should've told us."

She strangled her to death.

"I didn't have anything to do with what happened that night. I haven't seen her in years! I told you the person looked familiar, but her face was partially covered. I didn't even know she was home from prison. If I knew who killed him, I would have told you. I could've been killed that night too. I am a victim here as well."

"Maybe, but his family is adamant about making sure we have all suspects."

"Does his family think I had something to do with it?"

"His family wants anyone involved held accountable, no matter the part they played. It's my job to do that."

"You have to tell them that I had nothing to do with what happened. It's a coincidence that I had history with Koshie. To be honest, I only knew her in high school. I don't really know her now."

"Were you one of the girls involved in the accident with her?" he asked.

"Yes," she answered hesitantly.

"You girls found yourselves in a world of trouble back then. Koshie was the driver?"

"Yes, she was the driver. She was the cause of the accident."

"And now, why would someone want to kill her?"

"I don't know. I haven't had contact with her since the accident."

Shay didn't like where the conversation was going. She was damn near being accused of something she had nothing to do with.

"I need to call my lawyer."

After a painful silence, Detective Knight smiled at Shay.

"I believe you. I have to explore all possibilities, including you as a suspect. I had to be sure. At this time, we will be closing Mr. Gibbs's case unless we receive new information."

"You didn't have to pressure me like that," Shay said, relieved.

"I was just doing my job. I had to be sure. If anything new comes up, we will be right back here."

"I'm glad you got the people responsible. He didn't deserve to die like that."

"Well, we almost got them all. Now, we have another murder to solve."

"Unfortunately, I won't be able to help you with that."

"We'll see about that," Detective Knight said.

Shay began to feel uncomfortable all over again.

"I really have to get to my children. I had to find someone to watch them so I could come down here to talk to you."

"Thanks again, Ms. Bryant."

"No problem. Thank you for solving Robert's case."

Detective Knight nodded.

Shay immediately left his office and headed home. On the way home, she filled Jayda in on the interview with Detective Knight. As Shay pulled up to her house, she noticed a familiar car. Strange cars on her street were a norm, but this car she knew.

"I know this bitch ain't at my house!" Shay said.

"Who?" Jayda asked.

"Yolanda's car is out here. She better not be in my house."

"Shay, be careful."

"Oh, I'll be careful," Shay said while reaching into her glove compartment and retrieving her gun.

"Do you need me to come over?"

"No. I got this. I'll call you back." Shay disconnected the call.

She walked to her house and opened the door. It was quiet.

"Mom?" she called out.

No answer.

"Mommy's home!"

Still no answer.

She closed the door behind her.

She headed towards the living room where everyone was watching a movie. Yolanda was sitting among her children, enthralled in the movie.

"What the hell are you doing here?" Shay asked.

"Shay!" her mother blurted out.

The children looked surprised.

"Mom, what did I tell you about letting uninvited guests into my home?" Shay asked.

"Honey, I didn't know there would be a problem. What's going on?" her mother asked as she stood and motioned for the kids to come to her.

"Shay, why are you acting like this? I was just waiting here with the kids," Yolanda said.

"Come out here so I can tell you why," Shay said.

Yolanda went to hug the children but was abruptly stopped by their grandmother.

A familiar slick smile spread across Yolanda's face. Shay gripped the gun tighter behind her back. Yolanda walked up and stood face to face with her. They stared at each other. Then Yolanda walked away.

"What's the matter, Shay? I just came by to see you," Yolanda said.

"After everything that's happened, why would I want to see you?" Shay asked.

"I wanted to make sure you were okay. I haven't heard from you."

"I'm fine."

"Well, I guess I'll be going then."

"Yeah, you do that. And don't you ever come back here uninvited," Shay told her. "That's a warning."

"What are you going to do?"

Shay moved the gun to her side. "This here is over. I don't trust you."

"Good."

Yolanda walked out the door. Shay quickly locked the door behind her and checked on her family. Her mother demanded an explanation for her behavior. All she could tell her was that they were no longer friends, and Yolanda was no longer welcomed in her home or around her children. It almost hurt her to treat someone she loved that way, but she had to protect herself and her family.

<h1 style="text-align:center">Chapter 40</h1>

The headboard banged hard against the wall as Ryan pounded into Yolanda. As she held herself up on her hands and knees, Ryan gripped her hips and pulled her into him. She felt that familiar throb, warning her that he couldn't hold on much longer. So, she pulled herself away from him and turned to kiss him. She then gently pushed him back onto the bed and straddled him, all without breaking their kiss.

Ryan held on for the ride as Yolanda rocked in a harmonic rhythm on top of him. Sweat dripped down her smooth skin. She threw her head back as she prayed to God for a miracle to happen. Maybe she could become pregnant, although her tubes were tied. She visualized that one determined sperm finding its way to her egg and fertilizing it. There was also the option of having her procedure reversed, but even then, it wasn't guaranteed that she would conceive again. Then there were other costly medical procedures they couldn't readily afford.

Ryan's strokes met her rhythm, then became faster and more deliberate. A smile spread across her face as she braced herself for his blessings. She felt his release. She laid down beside him and closed her eyes.

"God, please bless me with a child. Just do this for me this one time. I promise I'll be a better mother this time. I'll keep her safe," Yolanda prayed.

Ryan looked over at her in curiosity.

"Baby, what are you talking about?" he asked.

"I was praying that we would have another chance at being parents again."

"You can't have another child."

"Don't say that! You don't know. You're not God."

"No, I'm not God. But I know you had your tubes tied, which prevents you from getting pregnant again. Did I miss something?"

"Just because you can still have babies doesn't mean I can't, and it doesn't give you the right to tell me what I can't do. It's your fault that I'm in this mess."

"What are you talking about? You're tripping, YoYo."

"I'm childless, Ryan. I'm empty inside. I'll never let another woman carry your child if I can't."

"You'll never have to worry about that. I'm not going anywhere. Why are you talking like this?"

"I had to let you know that. If you think about leaving me to start another family, I'll kill you."

"Now you're going too damn far. Don't threaten me like that. We have been through a lot of heavy shit together, but we are not going to do this."

The seriousness in his voice made her think twice before she said something she would later regret.

"I'm sorry, Ryan. I don't know what came over me."

"Have you taken your medicine? Maybe we need to call the doctor."

Ryan got out of bed and put on his boxers. Yolanda also got out of the bed and stood beside him naked.

"Don't you dare use my illness against me. I know exactly what I'm talking about!"

"Okay. Just calm down," he said, moving backwards to put more space between them.

"Don't tell me to calm down! You made me do this."

She punched herself in the stomach twice. Ryan grabbed her arms to stop her from hitting herself again.

"Stop it! We made that decision together. You can't blame me for this. Look, I need you to take a deep breath and calm down," Ryan told her. "Are you crazy?"

He regretted those words as soon as they left his mouth.

"Don't you ever call me crazy!"

She slapped him across the face.

"That's enough. Get a hold of yourself," Ryan said, grabbing Yolanda by the shoulders.

Yolanda tried to gather herself, but her thoughts raced in her head. She grabbed her head with both hands, trying to slow her thoughts. Once she felt she had a grip, she looked up to find Ryan in tears. In front of her was a man she had never seen before. Pity and defeat painted his eyes.

"We were just making love, and then you go off the rails," Ryan said.

"I'm tired of pretending that we have this picture-perfect marriage. I've been hiding my feelings for years, numbing myself with pills so I can function normally. There's nothing normal about pushing down your feelings. This is what happens!" Yolanda said.

"Yolanda, you know that I love you. I've accepted you and loved you for you. All of you. Not once have I asked you to hide how you feel. I care about how you feel, but this isn't the way to express yourself. Things have been stressful, but this is just too much."

"Now you want to leave? Go ahead! Go!"

"It won't be that easy to get rid of me. We're going to get you the help you need. Maybe you need to go back to the hospital. It seemed to help last time. What do you think about that?"

"You just want to get rid of me. You can just leave."

"I want to help you because I love you. I won't give up on us."

When Ryan left the room, Yolanda began to cry. She thought about what just happened. She knew Ryan wouldn't leave her, even if he wanted to. He didn't deserve to be tied to her any longer. She did nothing but apply pressure and pain to him. He of all people accepted her for who she was—flaws and all. His love for her never wavered no matter what came their way, and he proved that when their daughter died. She had already destroyed her friendships and now her marriage.

She could hear the panic in Ryan's voice as she listened to him make phone calls on her behalf. She wanted to stop him, but she didn't have it in her to fight with him. She trusted that he would do what he felt was needed to help her.

She didn't want to be fixed anymore. She wanted peace. After all of the horrible things she had done, she knew peace would be far away. So far that she would have to go through great lengths to find it. Her soul was tormented by Koshie. She could only imagine the horror stories Koshie experienced while incarcerated at such a young age for a crime she didn't commit. In Yolanda's mind, that didn't give Koshie a right to violate her, Jayda, and Shay's lives. Her treachery was greatest of all. She made it too personal. For that, she had to die. That was how she rationalized her actions. She didn't want to kill her, but she had to. She forced her hand to defend herself and her friends.

She tried to fight off the memories of her stalking Koshie. She lured her. She promised to pay her the money. She convinced Koshie to let her sit in her truck so that no one sees them handing off money and get the wrong idea. Koshie hesitantly agreed, especially since she was on probation and didn't need to be approached by police. While in the truck, Yolanda stalled by apologizing for what she had done. Koshie didn't want to hear it. She pressed Yolanda for the money and to end their meeting. Yolanda slowly handed Koshie an envelope filled with cash. As she counted the money, Yolanda leaped over her and placed her hands around her neck. She squeezed hard as she placed a knee into her stomach. Koshie fought hard but couldn't get Yolanda off of her. In the end, Koshie and her unborn child were dead.

Forcing herself to her feet, she needed to cleanse herself and attempt to cleanse her soul. She walked slowly into the bathroom and ran a bath. When the tub was full, she stepped in and slowly submerged her body into the hot water. Images of Koshie flooded her mind. She lowered her head under the water and held her breath. She came back up for air, taking in deep, steamy breaths.

"I'm so sorry for what I am," she said. "Sorry for what I've done."

As she lathered her body, she splashed soap in her eyes, causing them to sting. She stood to reach for a towel. As she rubbed her eyes, she tried to open them, blinking several times. After the burning subsided, she looked around the bathroom to test her vision. In the corner, she thought she saw a reflection of Koshie—the same image that haunted her mind but seemed to be in her bathroom now.

"Get out! You aren't real!" she screamed frantically, banging her head against the tiled shower. "I killed you! You can't be here!"

Yolanda leaped out of the shower, falling to the floor. She then crawled to the door and ran out. Blood dripped from her head as she ran while screaming unintelligible words. She stood at the top of the stairs, shouting over the balcony. Ryan stood below trying to calm her. Blood had spilled down over her naked body.

"Baby, stay right there. Don't move. You're bleeding. I'm coming to help you," Ryan said.

He moved quickly towards the stairs, keeping his eyes on her. Suddenly, she stopped screaming. Ryan reached the first step, moving slowly as he watched her stumble closer to the balcony.

"Move back, please," Ryan said as he started up the stairs.

Yolanda looked at him right before she appeared to lose consciousness. Her body fell forward and over the balcony.

"Nooooo!" Ryan screamed, collapsing on the step as he watched Yolanda's limp body fall and land on the floor below.

He stumbled down towards her body. There was no sign of life in her. He kneeled beside her and lifted her towards him. Cradling her, he rocked her in his arms.

Chapter 41

Yolanda's death caught everyone who loved her by surprise. The loss of Yolanda rocked Ryan. Her funeral was just the way she wanted it. Yolanda wanted a celebration of life, and Ryan honored her wishes. The flowers were pink and white. She had purchased two plots beside her daughter when she planned her funeral because she wanted to be with her. Ryan decided to sell his home and start over with his parents by his side. No one expected him to keep the house where he lost both his daughter and wife.

Shay and Jayda mourned Yolanda. They also found relief in her death. The untimely death of Yolanda and Koshie ended the string of lies that bonded them together. It overshadowed what genuine love they had for each other. It overshadowed the countless good memories that they shared. They thought they knew one another but found that they didn't really know each other at all. This made them question the validity of their friendships.

What they believed real friends were, was not the definition. What forged such a deadly alliance was the misconception of friendship. Their friendships were driven by lies. A friend would have told Yolanda to stand in her truth, all the while supporting her in doing so. Friends were people who loved each other in their right and wrong, spoke the truth, and supported each other. Friendships weren't easy, agreeable, or painless. It was the complete opposite. Shay and Jayda had to redefine what their friendship was, or if it was one at all. After the funeral, they spoke and saw each other less and less until they didn't speak at all.

Jayda and Sophia sat behind the nurse's station, pretending not to listen to what was going on behind the curtain of bed number four. A woman was brought in with severe stomach pain by her son and daughter-in-law. She was screaming obscenities and accusing them of trying to kill her to take her house.

As Jayda checked the charts, she noticed a familiar name. Her stomach flipped. Shay Bryant was being seen in her emergency room. She hadn't seen or spoken to her since Yolanda's memorial service. She wasn't mad at her but being too close to her reminded her of the pain of losing Koshie and Yolanda. Although their deaths exonerated both she and Shay, it still didn't sit right with her.

Jayda pulled back the curtain to surprise Shay. Instead, she was surprised.

"Oh, my God! Where did that come from?" Jayda asked.

"Hey, girl! I was about to ask if you were here," Shay said.

"You're pregnant?"

"No! How insulting! You know better than to assume that just because a woman has a big stomach that she must be pregnant."

Jayda laughed and said, "Oh, bitch, you're very pregnant."

"Surprise! I was too when I found out. I guess I got what I wanted, but not the way I thought."

"Wow. Robert?"

"Yes, Robert. I'm having his baby."

"You look like you're going to pop. How far along are you?"

"I'm almost eight months."

"Does his family know?"

Shay took a deep breath and rolled her eyes.

"I wish I never told them," she whispered. "They are going to drive me crazy!"

"That's good that you have his family's support. You don't want to do this alone, especially with Robert gone. You're going to need them."

"I know. I just have to get used to all of this. I didn't experience this with the other two. Believe me, if his mother knew I was here, she would be right here asking the doctor a thousand questions. Don't you know she has gone to every doctor's appointment with me?"

Jayda began to feel embarrassed. Embarrassed that she didn't know Shay was pregnant.

Someone else was there for her the way that she should've been.

"Sorry. I didn't know you were pregnant. I would've been there for you," Shay said.

"No, I don't think so. We both needed this time apart. We needed time to figure things out for ourselves."

"Shay, I'm so happy for you. I wish Rob could've been here to see all of this."

"Me too. But I have his family and mine, so he'll be okay. Maybe he'll play football like his father and buy me a big house someday."

"It's a boy!"

"Yes, and he'll be named after his father."

"Maybe you will get that big house." Jayda smiled, wiping away tears.

"Come over here and give me a hug," Shay said.

Jayda ran over and hugged her tight.

"I missed you so much," Jayda said.

"I missed you too," Shay said.

"I miss YoYo too," Jayda admitted.

"I think about her every day. I miss her too."

"I'm sorry. I forgot to ask you why you're here."

"I twisted my ankle." Shay pointed to her swollen ankle.

"Heels?" Jayda asked.

"Of course," Shay replied.

"No! You can't wear heels when you are this big. It's dangerous for you and the baby."

"I know, I know."

"I have to get back to work. It was nice seeing you," Jayda said.

"I'm glad I twisted my ankle if that meant I was going to see you today."

"I'll talk to you soon."

"Promise. I love you, girl," Shay said.

Jayda blew her a kiss and replied, "Promise."

"Wait! How are you and Jamison?" Shay asked.

"We're doing great," Jayda said, holding up her ring finger.

"Oh, wow. He put a big-ass ring on it!"

"Yes, he did. I'm happy, Shay."

"We deserve it."

"Yes, we do."

Also by Snook

Karma's Kiss
Karma's Kiss 2
The Down Turn
Issues of the Heart (poetry)
The Day The Walls Cried

To learn more about Snook and her books, visit
www.snooknovels.com